# Booked
## for
# Death

# Also available by Victoria Gilbert

The Blue Ridge Library Mysteries
*Bound for Murder*
*Past Due for Murder*
*Shelved Under Murder*
*A Murder for the Books*

Mirror of Immortality Series
*Scepter of Fire*
*Crown of Ice*

# Booked for Death

## A BOOK LOVER'S B&B MYSTERY

## Victoria Gilbert

CROOKED
LANE

NEW YORK

Copyright © 2020 by Vicki Lemp Weavil

All rights reserved.

Published in the United States by Crooked Lane Books, an imprint of The Quick Brown Fox & Company LLC.

Crooked Lane Books and its logo are trademarks of The Quick Brown Fox & Company LLC.

Library of Congress Catalog-in-Publication data available upon request.

ISBN (hardcover): 978-1-64385-307-9
ISBN (ebook): 978-1-64385-328-4

Cover illustration by Ben Perini

Printed in the United States.

www.crookedlanebooks.com

Crooked Lane Books
34 West 27th St., 10th Floor
New York, NY 10001

First Edition: June 2020

10 9 8 7 6 5 4 3 2 1

Dedicated to all teachers,
everywhere—with sincere gratitude
for your devotion, hard work, and
the many sacrifices you make to
share and nurture knowledge.

"If you are planning for a year, sow rice;
if you are planning for a decade, plant
trees; if you are planning for a lifetime,
educate people."

—*Chinese proverb*

# Chapter One

A ship may bob, safe at harbor, but that doesn't mean it hasn't experienced the wide world—or won't again.

Shading my eyes with one hand, I surveyed the flotilla of yachts and sailboats and skiffs anchored at the Beaufort, North Carolina, docks. When people questioned my decision to become an innkeeper in this historic waterfront town, I always told them I was like those vessels—quiet and settled at the moment, but still ready to sail off on a new adventure whenever I chose.

The morning sun swam in a sky streaked with ribbons of pink and amber. Although I'd have preferred to linger, I needed to leave the boardwalk and hike the few blocks to my home. It was early morning—time for my workday to begin.

As the owner of Chapters, a local bed-and-breakfast, I wanted to be present before any guests came down for breakfast. It was one reason I always rose early. We served breakfast until ten, and if I didn't fit in my daily walk before our seven o'clock start, I tended to get distracted and skip it altogether.

I strode up the narrow sidewalks, batting aside some low-hanging tree branches without thinking. I'd made this trek often enough to know when to avoid a slap in the face. Reaching Ann Street, I turned left, passing a row of tree-shaded homes. As always, my pace slowed as I admired the beauty of my neighborhood, where simple but elegant eighteenth-century houses were interspersed with mid-nineteenth-century cottages and gingerbread-encrusted Victorians.

Chapters bed-and-breakfast was one of the oldest homes in Beaufort. With a single triangular gable and white clapboard siding, it featured covered porches on both the main and upper levels. The shield-shaped historic designation plaque near the delft-blue front door proclaimed that the house had been built in 1770. This was true, although one could quibble about the rambling addition that had been added at a later date. The addition was deep enough to be separated from the picket fence enclosing the English garden only by a flagstone patio, but it was also narrow enough to render it invisible from the front. Many of our guests were shocked when they drove around to the parking lot and realized the house's true size. In fact, if I'd collected a dollar for every time someone said, "It's so much bigger than it looks from the street," I'd have amassed a tidy sum.

As I circled around the house to reach the staff entrance to the kitchen, I noticed that the wax myrtles that lined the side of the house had reached a height that would soon shadow the kitchen windows. They'd need a good pruning in the fall. I mentally added this to my never-ending list of chores as I pushed open the back door and stepped into the bed-and-breakfast's large kitchen.

Alicia Simpson, Chapters' sixty-two-year-old housekeeper and cook, stood at our commercial gas range, dubiously eyeing the fish she held over a cast-iron frying pan. "Now, I ask you—who eats this for breakfast?"

Although drawn by the aroma of strong coffee mingled with the tangy scent of black tea, I halted my progress across the kitchen. "Come on, you've done this sort of thing before. I'm sure Great-Aunt Isabella hosted some literary events that focused on British authors." I stepped back to avoid the splatter of grease as Alicia dropped the fish into the pan. "Besides, this being a Josephine Tey celebration, we need to serve a full English breakfast at least once. The guests expect that sort of thing."

"But why this abomination?" Alicia, who was shorter than me by a good five inches, turned and lifted her arm to wave another kippered fish in my face.

"You've had smoked salmon on bagels before. It's not that different," I said, while Alicia turned away again, muttering about "dang fool notions."

I crossed to one of our long work counters and lifted a silver cloche off a white ceramic serving platter. Inhaling the smoky aroma of cooked sausage and bacon, I glanced over at a foil-covered plate. That was probably the fried tomatoes. "All that's left to do is the eggs?"

"And the toast. And finish frying up these dang fish," Alicia said, squaring her plump shoulders. Her dark hair, streaked with gray the color and texture of steel wool, was caught up in a hair-net studded with multicolored plastic gemstones.

I smiled. Alicia always claimed that even though she was just a housekeeper and cook, that didn't mean she had to abandon all sense of style.

*Although*, I thought, *Alicia Simpson is hardly just an anything.* After running the bed-and-breakfast for over three decades—the first thirty-five years for my great-aunt and the last one for me—I suspected she was just as much an attraction as Chapters' literary-themed guest rooms and extensive library.

I covered the bacon and sausage before leaning back against the soapstone counter to survey the kitchen. Bright and airy, with a twelve-foot-high beadboard ceiling, it was one of my favorite rooms in the house. My great-aunt had remodeled the original space when she'd converted her home into a bed-and-breakfast, adding commercial-grade appliances and other features that enhanced the kitchen's functionality. But she'd thankfully retained its traditional style. Plain white cabinets, many with mullioned glass fronts, were fitted with black iron hardware. Light spilling from the large windows set into the pearl-gray walls sparkled off the bright-white subway-tile backsplash and stainless-steel appliances and sinks. A pair of French doors led to a large pantry that housed metal shelving, a standing freezer, and our commercial-grade dishwasher.

"When is Damian supposed to arrive to start dinner?" I asked, mentally bemoaning the complexity of the War of the Roses–themed dinner party I'd planned to honor mystery author Josephine Tey's most famous story, *The Daughter of Time*. Of course, I'd adjusted the menu to accommodate modern tastes—no one wanted peacock or swan today—but we were serving boar roasted with baked apples as one of the entrées.

"Not soon enough, I wager." Alicia flipped the fish in the frying pan before turning to me. She swept her metal spatula through the air like a rapier. "He tends to overestimate his ability to multitask, if you ask me." She thrust the spatula in my direction. "And it doesn't help when you have him cooking such complicated nonsense. Boar, for goodness' sake. Who serves boar?"

"Richard the Third probably did, which is why it fits our theme for tonight." I bit my lower lip, considering the cost of the meat, which I'd had to order in from a specialty provider. Hopefully, our freelance chef, Damian Carr, hadn't been exaggerating when he'd claimed he could handle such a unique menu.

"Well, I just hope no one chokes on a bone from those pike," Alicia said.

"I bought them already filleted."

"Maybe, but that's a fish with more bones than a cat has whiskers, and the bones are just about that thin, too." Alicia deftly scooped the final kipper from the pan and flipped it onto a pile of fish already layered on a serving plate. "Knowing how fast he likes to work in the kitchen, I'm not trusting Damian to check those fillets as carefully as he should."

"I'll look them over before he cooks them. But we'd better focus on breakfast right now. I hear stirrings in the dining room, which means at least some of our guests have already come downstairs."

Alicia slapped the spatula against one palm. "Well, after the ruckus they made last night, that bunch from Virginia can wait."

I straightened and stepped away from the counter. "What ruckus? I didn't hear anything."

"No, you wouldn't have. It happened before you got back from that party for your friend Julie." Alicia shook her head. "I almost had to say something, especially since that other lady, Ms. Rowley—the one with the yacht—complained."

"The Delamonts were making too much noise?" I frowned. The family—bookdealer Lincoln Delamont, his wife Jennifer, and their sixteen-year-old daughter, Tara—were three of the six guests staying at Chapters for the week. "Was Tara playing her music too loud?"

"No, it was the parents. Fighting like hens scrapping over a last kernel of corn."

"Really? What about?"

Alicia shook her head. "Didn't hear much. Just a lot of yelling. And before I could drag myself up the stairs to tell them to pipe down, the whole thing apparently blew over. Anyway, they got quiet, so I just left it alone. Although"—she turned back to the range—"I did pick up a word or two. Something from the missus about cheating, which doesn't surprise me, given that fellow's flirtatious behavior."

"Oh?" I mulled this information, which fit with Lincoln Delamont's aggressively charming persona and well-groomed good looks.

*A little too well groomed for my taste*, I thought, experiencing a pang as a vision of my late husband's tousled hair and lazy smile flashed through my mind. "I guess not all is well with that marriage. Too bad, when they have a child . . ."

I closed my lips to silence my next words as that child bounded into the kitchen, the dining room door slamming behind her.

"Any coffee yet?" Tara Delamont asked, popping a pair of earbuds out of her ears.

She was all legs and arms and wide chestnut eyes. A girl just this side of beautiful. *A shore she will soon reach*, I thought, *when she grows into that tall, slender frame.*

"That's served along with breakfast," Alicia said, without turning away from the range.

"But I just want coffee." Tara's lower lip jutted out.

I'd dealt with enough teenagers to know arguing over this topic was a waste of time. "On the counter," I said. "Mugs are in the cabinet above the percolator."

Tara grimaced as she stared at the silver urn. "That's different." She glanced back at me over one narrow shoulder. "So what, you just use that tab or something?"

"Yes, it's just like a water cooler," I said, hoping she'd experienced one of those. "We do have a single-cup coffee machine, if you prefer using that."

"Nah, this is fine." Tara grabbed a white ceramic mug from the cabinet and filled it with coffee from the percolator. "It's pretty cool, actually."

"Everything old is new again," I said, and smiled as Tara flashed me a grin.

*A good kid. I hope she isn't going to be too hurt by her parents' problems.* The knowledge that this was unlikely sobered me. I'd spent eighteen years as a high school teacher. I knew the damage family issues could cause in the lives of young people.

"Thanks," Tara said as she left the kitchen, cradling her mug to her chest.

"Children these days." Alicia cracked eggs into a large metal bowl. "It's a wonder they don't all grow up stunted, the way they eat. Or don't," she added, furiously whisking the eggs.

"They seem to survive somehow," I replied, fluffing my short cap of hair. I knew better than to argue with Alicia on this subject. *As on many others*, I thought with a grin. "Anyway, I suppose I'd better greet the guests."

I tugged the hem of my cranberry blouse down over my black slacks. After experimenting with wardrobe choices when I'd first taken over Chapters, I'd found that adopting an elegant simplicity was my best option. A flowing silk or linen-blend blouse paired with plain cotton or wool trousers was always my best bet. I needed to look put-together, but not too fussy.

Walking into the dining room, I called out "Good morning" and reminded myself to smile. Knowing guests liked a cheery hostess, I'd trained myself to smile more frequently. It wasn't too difficult—I'd also learned to project a pleasant but tough attitude when I'd taught high school English. This was just a different mask.

"Hello," said a tall, lean woman in her mid-thirties. She was seated at one of the three round tables in the dining room, wearing a tight tank top that showed off her well-toned arms. Her lightly tanned skin still held a sheen of perspiration from what I suspected was an early-morning run.

The husky man seated beside her was at least twenty years older. His cropped white hair gleamed in vivid contrast to his weathered face. Todd Rowley looked like someone who'd spent too much time in the sun, which wasn't surprising, given his self-proclaimed love of sailing. "Good day, Ms. Reed," he said. "I hear we have a full English breakfast today."

"Yes, and it's just about ready. But please, call me Charlotte. I may be the proprietor of Chapters, but we don't stand on ceremony here."

"Good, so you can call me Todd," the man replied, with a broad smile.

"And Kelly," the woman chimed in, tossing her long braid of golden-brown hair behind her shoulders.

I studied the couple for a moment. Todd Rowley was a fifty-seven-year-old entrepreneur who owned a lovely yacht named the *Celestial*, currently docked at the Beaufort harbor. His much younger wife—his third, if what I'd heard was true—had once been a track star and had, according to her comments at the previous evening's cocktail party, almost made the U.S. Olympic team.

*Almost.* I examined Kelly's intelligent face. She had a natural beauty that most would envy, but I detected a well of sadness in those lovely hazel eyes. *As if her life was all about that "almost,"* I thought, with sympathy. It was a situation I understood. I'd almost led a different life as well—filled with love, and children, and . . . I shook my head. No, I couldn't dwell on such things.

"Had a good run this morning?" I asked brightly.

"Oh yes," Kelly Rowley replied. "Surprisingly, the streets were uncrowded. I heard there was a major fishing tournament going on over in Morehead City and was afraid Beaufort would be packed full of visitors this week."

"Oh, they're here. They just tend to head over to the Big Rock tournament early. You'll run into a lot more people later in the day, when they come back to their inn or hotel rooms," I said, as a tall, lanky man entered the room. "Hello, Scott."

"Hi." The man ran his hand through his silver-threaded auburn hair. "How's everyone this fine day?"

"Great," Kelly said, flashing him a bright smile. "It's Scott Kepler and you're an author, right? I hope I remember that correctly from last night. I'm afraid I might've had one too many glasses of wine."

"Nonsense," said her husband. "I'm the one who was a bit tipsy, as I recall."

"Yes, I'm Scott Kepler and a writer," the new arrival said, laugh lines crinkling his brown eyes. "And I don't recall either one of you being noticeably under the influence, so not to worry."

"You're not here for the Tey event, though," Todd said, looking Scott up and down. "At least that's what I thought you said."

"See, you remember." Scott tapped his temple with one finger. "No, I'm out in the carriage house. I rent that space from time to time to work on my book."

"Something about pirates, isn't it?" Kelly asked.

"Exactly. Soon to be a major best seller." Scott arranged his elastic features into a humorous expression. "And if you believe that, I've got a pristine stretch of beach to sell you."

Todd Rowley laughed. "Might take a pass on that. Sounds a bit dubious."

Scott grinned as he took a seat at the adjoining table. "Smart man."

"Good timing, Scott. Breakfast's almost ready," I said.

Alicia poked her head around the door. "A hand with the food if you don't mind, Charlotte?"

I helped Alicia serve the platters of food before retreating to the kitchen again to allow the guests to eat without someone hovering over them. When I returned to the dining room a little while later, I noticed that the three guests had apparently enjoyed the breakfast, judging by the empty plates. Although they'd studiously avoided the kippers, which would undoubtedly please Alicia.

As I cleared the dirty plates and platters, another couple strolled into the dining room.

"Good morning," said a short woman with a halo of curly dark hair framing her round face. "I hope we aren't too late."

"Oh no, we serve until ten," I replied. "I'll just tell Ms. Simpson to cook another batch of everything."

"Sounds good." The man following Jennifer Delamont into the dining room was of average height and build but exuded an air of confidence that made him appear taller.

*Larger than life*, I thought, with a wry smile. I managed a pleasant "Good morning" as Lincoln Delamont held out a chair for his wife. Lincoln's blond hair, slicked back from his broad forehead, along with his fine-boned features and large, deep-set blue eyes, lent him the air of a middle-aged F. Scott Fitzgerald. I thought this was probably a calculation rather than a coincidence.

Kelly shoved back her chair and stood up. "Todd, we should be getting along if we want to tour some local sites before tonight's party."

"Oh, right," Todd said, standing to join her. "I do want to check out the Maritime Museum and the Watercraft Center."

"And the shops," Kelly added, casting him a smile.

"Of course, and the shops." Todd slipped one hand through his wife's bent arm. "How could I forget the shops?"

"Let us know if you want a bag lunch to take along," I said. "That's part of your package deal. You can even put in an order and pick it up later if you wish."

"Hostess with the mostess," Lincoln said, giving me a wink.

I ignored him, irritated at his attempt to charm. "Just don't forget that the War of the Roses party is tonight. Costumes are optional but encouraged, and we've planned a lovely homage to the fifteenth century in the menu."

"Looking forward to it," Todd Rowley said, as he escorted his wife to the door. "Ready, dear?"

"Absolutely. The shops await," Kelly said with a smile, before they sailed out of the room.

Scott leaned back in his chair. "A costume party? Sounds like fun, but I have another engagement. Of course, to be honest, I'm not really a part of the Tey celebration, so I guess I can be forgiven for my absence."

"Yes, you're excused, but no one else." I kept my tone light. I never wanted to force my guests to participate in an activity. Their payment for the event, which ran from Saturday to Saturday after a Friday evening check-in, included the dinner party, but if they wished to skip it, that was their choice. "We do have some local people attending the party, so there are plenty of participants even if you can't come, Scott. Although you are welcome, of course."

"I, for one, wouldn't miss it for the world," Lincoln said. "I have the perfect costume, which I certainly don't want to waste."

"Let me guess," I said. "Richard the Third?"

"Oh no." A slow smile spread over Lincoln's face. "That's much too expected. No, I plan to represent his eventual adversary, Henry the Seventh."

"Siding with the opposition—the House of Tudor against the House of York?" Scott stood up and tossed his napkin onto the linen tablecloth.

Lincoln sat back in his chair. "The Tudors won."

"But even that line didn't last," Scott observed. "Still, your choice is unique, so good for you."

Jennifer tapped her chin with one finger. "According to Tey, Henry was the villain who killed the young princes."

Lincoln shrugged. "Who knows the truth of that story? Tey had her opinions, but nothing has ever been proven."

"At any rate, I hope you'll all have a good time tonight, virtually traveling back in time just as Tey's Detective Grant did," I said, as Alicia appeared with fresh eggs and other items and plopped them down in front of Lincoln and Jennifer.

"Full English breakfast," she said. "Enjoy."

Lincoln lifted his fork. "Thank you. Now, once more into the breach . . ."

I turned aside, swallowing a remark about the inappropriateness of his quote. Because, as far as I knew, no one was at war, or in any danger of death.

Of course, as later events soon proved, I was quite wrong in this assumption.

# Chapter Two

When breakfast cleanup was complete, I headed for my bedroom, which, unlike Alicia's suite and the guest rooms, was located on the ground floor. But as I strolled down the hall, I heard a melody wafting from the front parlor we also used as a music room. I paused outside the open door as someone launched into the opening bars of a current pop tune. This pianist was no rank amateur, but even their well-trained fingers were eclipsed by their voice.

It was a voice that captivated from the first note. Clear but lush, with deeper undertones, it held a special quality that made me press my hand to my heart.

I loved music enough to recognize the rarity of such an instrument. Ranging across registers, the voice never wavered. It also had a distinctive tone, as unique as it was beautiful.

When the song ended, I strode into the music room, determined to express my admiration for the singer. Imagining a mature performer, I was surprised to see Tara Delamont seated at the grand piano.

"Brava!" I said, clapping.

"Thank you." Tara pushed back the piano bench and stood up.

"No, really." I crossed over to the piano. "Your voice is amazing. And you're only sixteen, right?"

Tara tensed her narrow shoulders. "Yeah."

"You sound professional. Have you studied voice?"

"A little." Tara's brown eyes remained wary.

After teaching for many years, I knew that look. The girl probably thought I was patronizing her. "I could tell. Your breath control is on point, and you've already learned how to switch registers without any cracks."

Tara dropped her shoulders and offered me a real smile. "You know something about singing?"

I smiled in return. "Yes, but I'm just an amateur. Oh, I've sung in choirs and choruses all my life, but I certainly don't possess anything like your natural talent." I tipped my head and studied the girl. "Are you planning to study voice in college?"

Tara's smile faded. "I'd love to, but my parents . . ." She used both hands to shove her mane of curly dark hair behind her shoulders. "They don't see it as a real career."

"That's a shame. You have a remarkable instrument. It should be developed and heard."

Tara bounced on the balls of her feet like a track star preparing to sprint. "That's the thing—I *am* heard. My YouTube channel has over a hundred thousand followers, and I just started it a few months ago."

"That's impressive."

Tara lifted her chin and met my approving gaze. "And I've even been contacted by scouts for a couple of TV talent shows. I mean, I didn't do anything—they asked *me* to audition."

"Will you?" I asked, keeping my tone light.

"No." The word escaped the girl's lips like an explosion. "Not if my parents have anything to do with it. Which they do, 'cause right now I can't travel to auditions or sign any contracts on my own." Tara's dark eyes narrowed. "Maybe I could convince Mom, but my dad . . ." She shrugged. "He refuses to even consider something like that."

My lips twitched. "I don't think those TV shows are that bad, but I do wonder if it's really the best way to start a lasting career."

Tara spat out a word I had heard plenty of times from my students but tried to avoid using myself. "That's 'cause you're old. You don't get the way things are done today. It's like my dad telling me I have to study at a conservatory if I decide to pursue such a *perilous* career, as he calls it." Tara made a face. "And he even fights me on that idea, so what am I supposed to do? Go to college and learn a bunch of lame stuff that I don't care about just so I can work at some job I'll hate?"

I shrugged. "I doubt that's the best choice, but perhaps studying music at a good conservatory or university program would open the same doors for you as one of those reality shows. Or even give you better options."

Tara's lips curved downward. "Yeah, sure. Meanwhile, other girls will be getting the record deals and concert tours. While I age out of ever breaking into the business." She audibly sniffed. "You old people are all the same, thinking things have to be done the way they were back in the dark ages, when you were kids." She rolled her eyes as she stalked past. "Spare me the lectures, okay?"

"Sure thing," I said, as the girl strode out of the room.

I sighed. *What was I thinking, sharing my opinion with a young person I don't know?* It was force of habit, I supposed. I'd slipped into teacher mode without considering the fact that Tara, like her parents, was a guest at Chapters. *Your job is to be a hostess, not an instructor*, I reminded myself.

I waited a few minutes before I followed Tara out of the parlor. I was still determined to steal a few moments of quiet in my bedroom, but a noise made me pause. I peeked into the adjacent room, which was Chapters' extensive library. One of my guests was balanced on the sliding ladder that allowed access to the library's top shelves.

I stepped into the library, identifying the culprit as Lincoln Delamont even before he glanced over his shoulder. "Can I help you find something?"

"No thank you, Ms. Reed. I'm just examining the collection." Lincoln flashed me a roguish grin. "As you know, I'm a rare-book dealer. I simply can't resist a library like this."

"I wish you'd asked me first." I pointed at the pile of books scattered across the room's massive wooden desk. "Some of the items on the upper shelves are fragile. I prefer to pull those for our guests myself, specifically for that reason, as I'm sure you can understand."

I didn't mention that some of those volumes were also quite valuable. Lincoln would know that just by looking at them. But even if he was breaking one of the bed-and-breakfast's few rules, I reminded myself that my hostess status meant I had to stop short of accusing him of any wrongdoing.

When I inherited my great-aunt's extensive library along with her house, I'd shifted all of the fragile and rare books to the top shelves, leaving the sturdier, and generally more popular, books on the shelves that could be reached without deploying the rolling ladder. In my welcome speech I informed guests that they could freely use the library, but asked them to limit their selection of books to the lower shelves. If they wanted anything else, they had to run that by me, and if the book wasn't too fragile, I'd pull it for them. Not only did that prevent any unfortunate spills from the ladder, but it also allowed me to keep tabs on who was handling the more valuable volumes.

But Lincoln Delamont had obviously not heard my instructions, or had decided to deliberately flout them. I tapped my foot against the pine plank floor. "I'm sure you're fascinated by my great-aunt's collection, but I must ask you to get down. As I mentioned when you arrived last night, I prefer that guests not use that ladder." I twitched my lips into what I hoped was a pleasant smile. "Insurance liability being what it is, it just isn't safe, for you as well as for my pocketbook."

Lincoln climbed down to one of the bottom rungs before leaping to the floor. As he turned to face me, his sharp nose twitched like the pointed muzzle of a fox. "I assure you, Ms. Reed, I have more than a passing acquaintance with library ladders. Many of which are much less stable than this one."

"I'm sure, but those aren't located in my bed-and-breakfast." I strolled over to the desk and picked up a leather-bound volume. "You do have a good eye," I said, examining the title page. "A first edition *Romance of King Arthur* illustrated and signed by Arthur Rackham is quite rare, as I suppose you know. You wouldn't be searching for items to buy, would you?"

"Not exactly." Lincoln dusted off his hands. "But I am very interested in Isabella Harrington's library. Particularly in how she acquired it."

I placed the leather-bound volume back on the desk. "That's easy—she purchased the books. Sometimes individually, but also in large lots from estate sales or from those downsizing and selling entire collections. Why do you ask?"

Lincoln lowered his pale lashes over his blue eyes. "Having conducted a little research on your great-aunt, I'm curious how she was able to afford the initial investment. Didn't she start out as a maid in the early 1950s? It was at some grand estate on the James River in Virginia, but still, hardly a way to amass a fortune."

"True, but she apparently came into some money after that, before she bought this house." I frowned. "She never really explained how that came about."

"I bet she didn't." A smirk twisted Lincoln's thin lips.

"What's that supposed to mean?" I took a breath and reminded myself to temper my tone. Despite his annoying air of superiority, the bookdealer was a guest. "I'm sorry, I guess I don't understand your point, Mr. Delamont."

"Please, call me Lincoln." Tracing a spiral pattern in the rug with the tip of his expensive leather loafer, the bookdealer didn't meet my searching gaze. "I just find it interesting that a former maid was able to acquire so many valuable books. It takes a great deal of money to accumulate a library like this, you know. I assumed she must've inherited something from the family. As you did," he added, casting me a sly smile.

"I know nothing about that. My family on that side were farmers. I doubt she inherited a fortune from them." Annoyance had sharpened my tone, but I decided Lincoln Delamont was being provocative enough to warrant my displeasure. "I've always assumed she made some shrewd investments. And I know she occasionally sold some of her original acquisitions to buy other books."

"Yes, I recall seeing some of them on the market. A bit beyond my reach at the time, I'm afraid."

I studied his face, wondering why he looked so smug. "Anyway, since I did inherit her library as well as the house, it's my job to take care of both. Which is why I have an inflexible rule about guests not accessing the more fragile volumes. And staying off that ladder. How and why Isabella Harrington started her book collection is not really my concern."

"Perhaps it should be," Lincoln said. "I'd hate to see your reputation tarnished by a relative's past misdeeds."

I instinctively cast a glance toward the hall. Lincoln's voice was unusually loud and resonant, and I wanted to reassure myself that no other guests were loitering nearby. "Excuse me, is that a threat?"

Lincoln Delamont shrugged. "Just a warning. Based on my investigations, I've discovered something about your great-aunt's past that you, and indeed the rest of your family, might not know. A fact that, if disclosed, could be very bad publicity for your bed-and-breakfast. Very bad indeed. It might even force you to sell . . ."

"Books to you?" I snapped, no longer caring about his guest status.

"Oh, I'd love to pick up a few of those treasures"—Lincoln motioned toward the books on the desk—"but that wasn't what I was implying."

"Okay, so what exactly *are* you suggesting?"

"That you could lose Chapters if everything came to light. And I'd hate to see that." Lincoln's smile broadened. "I really would."

I examined the bookdealer for a moment as I collected my thoughts. It was obvious that he was attempting to blackmail me over some indiscretion from my great-aunt's past. Perhaps not for money, though. Although he hadn't come right out and asked me to sell him some valuable volumes from the library for next to nothing, I suspected he'd be demanding that soon enough.

I thrust back my shoulders and looked Lincoln in the eye. I had no plans to sell anything, despite whatever dirty secrets he'd dug up on my great-aunt. But before I rejected his little scheme outright, I decided to do some sleuthing of my own. If I could uncover whatever he considered so damaging, and proactively diffuse that bomb . . .

"You must've misunderstood. I'm sure there's nothing in my great-aunt's past that could possibly lead to such a disastrous consequence. Now, if you'll excuse me, I should get back to work. Please, leave the books you've pulled on the desk. I will reshelve them later." I left the room, but paused in the hall to call back at him, "And stay off that ladder. The last thing I want to deal with is a dead guest."

# Chapter Three

I abandoned my dream of a peaceful hour spent reading in my room and walked back into the kitchen to question Alicia. Maybe I could pry enough information out of her to dismiss Lincoln Delamont's hints of scandal.

"I just had the most unpleasant encounter."

"With that Delamont fellow?" Alicia asked, without glancing up from a short stack of lunch-request forms.

"Yes, how did you know?"

"Saw him head for the library right after breakfast. Figured he was going to check out the books, being a dealer and all." Alicia looked up at me, her dark-brown eyes narrowed. "He's a right royal pain, if you ask me."

"I have to agree with you on that point." I crossed to the counter where Alicia was working and rested my hip against the lower cabinet. "I was just wondering—you worked for my great-aunt from the beginning, didn't you? I mean, from the moment she converted this house into a bed-and-breakfast?"

Alicia tapped the pen she was holding against her palm. "Yes, she hired me in 1983, right before she opened the doors to guests." She fixed me with an intent stare. "Why are you asking?"

"Oh, Lincoln Delamont mentioned something . . ." I shook my head. "He seems to think there are some skeletons rattling around in Great-Aunt Isabella's past. Some stuff that could be damaging if the truth were to be exposed. You don't have any inkling as to what that might be, do you?"

Alicia dropped her gaze as well as the pen. "Nope. Can't think of a thing."

"I just thought . . . well, if there *was* something, maybe I could take care of the situation before Mr. Delamont decides to spread rumors." I tapped my fingernails against the charcoal-gray soapstone countertop, hoping to draw the housekeeper's attention, but Alicia kept her gaze focused on the lunch requests. "I appreciate your loyalty to my great-aunt, but it's really better if I know, whatever it might be. I mean, if there *are* any scandals in her past."

"There aren't. Leastwise, I don't know of any." As Alicia tugged on the hairnet again, the plastic gemstones flashed in the bright light falling from the tall kitchen windows.

I stared at the older woman's implacable profile. Alicia was always more than willing to tell me how Isabella had done things, especially in terms of managing the bed-and-breakfast, but getting any other information from her was like wringing water from a stone. "If it makes any difference, I already know Isabella had something of a wild past. At least if what my Grandma Ruth always said is true."

Alicia cast me a side-eyed glance. "Nice way to talk about her own sister. Anyway, I wouldn't know much about that. As I said, I didn't start working for Isabella until 1983. She must've been close to sixty at that point, and while she was always spry, even up until right before she died at ninety-two, she was never what I'd call wild. Energetic and charming, yes. But not wild."

I did a quick mental calculation. "Yes, she would've been fifty-seven in 1983." I tapped the countertop with my fingers. "Funny, I never thought about it before, but she started a business when most people would be about ready to retire."

"Necessity, I always figured," Alicia said, her focus back on her lunch requests. "Ran out of cash or something, so she decided to turn her home into a paying concern."

"Grandma's theory was that Isabella was just bored, but you could be right." I gazed around the impressive kitchen. "Even though, according to Grandma, the house was paid for, I suspect maintaining this place without any return on investment could drain a bank account pretty fast." I frowned, thinking of Lincoln Delamont's insinuations. "If you want to know the truth, my family never figured out how she was able to buy this place and live here for twenty-five years without any real income. Especially since she was supposedly a social butterfly who threw lavish parties."

"Don't look at me, I have no idea. Although I do remember the parties." Alicia shot me a quick glance. "Not that I ever attended any, of course. But my mom worked for a local catering company when I was teenager. Mama used to serve at some of Isabella's parties, and she'd come home and tell me and my sisters about the rich and famous people she saw here. Actors and politicians and wealthy businessmen and folks like that." Alicia shook her head. "In little old Beaufort, no less."

"Really?" I stood up straighter. "I knew she gave a lot of parties in the years before she turned the house into Chapters, but I had no idea she was entertaining celebrities. I wonder how she met them?"

"That's the question all of Beaufort was asking, back when I was young," Alicia said. "Isabella was beautiful and charming, but she must've had some connection who introduced her into such circles. I mean, this town has a long and respectable history, but it's not exactly cosmopolitan."

I considered this for a moment. "Maybe part of the attraction was getting away from the city? Enjoying a taste of small-town life near the sea?"

Alicia laid aside one lunch request. "Could be. I just know it always baffled us regular folk in town. While it was going on, but even more so when it all stopped. Just like that"—she snapped her fingers—"no more parties. Then Isabella up and converted her house into a bed-and-breakfast about a year later. Which is why I figured it was a money issue."

"That's certainly possible, I suppose." I traced a figure eight on the countertop. "But if there were numerous wealthy and famous people at these parties, maybe this secret scandal is related to one of them somehow."

"Could be, but again, I wouldn't know anything about that." Alicia picked up the paper she'd set aside and waved it at me. "Now excuse me, but I need to get to work on this request. Mr. and Mrs. Rowley wanted to pick up their lunches early."

"All right, don't let me keep you." I gave Alicia a brief nod good-bye before I headed for the hall. Preoccupied with thoughts of

Isabella's mysterious past, Lincoln Delamont's cryptic threats, and his daughter's angry comments, I almost collided with Todd and Kelly Rowley, who'd walked into the front hallway from the porch.

Plastering on a smile, I faced the couple. "I hope you've had a good time this morning?"

"Oh yes," Kelly replied. "The town really is quaint, and it's still quiet, at least right now."

"It'll get a lot busier later when all the Big Rock tournament participants and visitors return for dinner and drinks at the restaurants near the docks. Fortunately you won't have to fight the crowds this evening, since you're having dinner here."

Todd Rowley glanced at his wife. "We're excited about that, aren't we, sweetheart? Kelly had a beautiful costume made," he added, turning his gaze back on me.

"That's great," I said, thinking about everything I had to do before I could don my own costume, a hand-me-down from Isabella I'd found while rummaging around in the attic.

Jennifer Delamont clattered down the stairs, stopping short when she noticed me and the Rowleys. "Oh, hello. Have any of you seen my husband? I can't imagine where he's gotten to."

"He was in the library, Ms. Delamont." I noticed the lines creasing Jennifer Delamont's brow and softened my tone. "But that was a little while ago. I'm not sure if he's still there."

"He's not," Kelly said, with a toss of her long braid. "Todd and I were just out walking and saw him dashing off somewhere when we turned onto this block."

"Really? He didn't tell me he was going out . . ." Jennifer Delamont bit her lower lip as if to stop herself from saying anything more.

"He was in a hurry." Todd winked at Jennifer. "Maybe he wanted to sneak out and get you a gift before you realized he was gone?"

"I doubt that," Kelly said sharply. As Jennifer turned a myopic gaze on her, the younger woman twitched her lips into a smile. "I just mean, not everyone is as sentimental as you are, Todd." Kelly slipped her arm around her husband's waist before turning to me. "He spoils me. Always buying me little surprise gifts."

"You deserve it," Todd said, patting Kelly's hand.

"No, that wouldn't be it," Jennifer Delamont said, her shoulders slumping. "Well, thanks anyway. I guess I'll catch up with him later." She turned and headed back upstairs.

"Poor thing," Kelly said, when Jennifer had disappeared into the upper hallway. Catching my eye, she shrugged. "I heard them yelling at each other last night, after the cocktail party. I think you'd gone out by that time."

"Yes, it was my friend Julie's birthday." I turned away slightly. "Sorry, but I really should get moving. There's so much to do before this evening's festivities."

"Don't let us keep you," Todd said. "We're heading back out as soon as we grab our bagged lunches. I want to spend some decent time at the Maritime Museum before we need to change for the party."

"Well, have fun." I noticed that Kelly was staring up the staircase, as if her thoughts remained focused on Jennifer Delamont.

*She probably feels as bad for the woman as I do*, I thought. *Especially since, unlike Jennifer, she seems to have such a happy marriage.*

*As I did, once upon a time.*

# Chapter Four

Later that afternoon, I worked in the English garden that filled most of Chapters' backyard. Cutting a flower stem, I jerked back my hand as a thorn pierced my skin. The crimson roses fell, scattering across one of the white gravel paths that outlined the formal flower beds. I stepped back, twitching my finger away from the blood that pooled inside my suede gardening glove.

"War of the Roses, indeed," I muttered to myself as I yanked off the glove and waved it at my friend, Julie Rivera, who'd agreed to help me decorate Chapters for the costume party. "The things I do for my guests."

"It will be worth it. You'll see," Julie said.

I wasn't so sure, afraid I'd taken on too much with my War of the Roses dinner party. When I'd planned a week-long literary event as a celebration of Golden Age mystery author Josephine Tey, I'd thought it would be fun to include a costume party honoring Tey's famous story *The Daughter of Time*. A War of the Roses–themed event had seemed a natural nod to the book, which featured Tey's detective, Alan Grant, investigating the truth about Richard the Third and the princes in the Tower. But the complexity of offering a fifteenth-century-influenced dinner, along with the necessary decorating, had proven so stressful, I wished I'd never come up with the idea.

I peeled off the other glove and shoved both into the pocket of my jeans. Hanging my garden shears off the edge of my bucket, I stared at the containers overflowing with flowers. *Now we've really done enough*, I thought, considering the swaths of scarlet and white fabric Julie and I had already hung in the dining room to frame a reproduction of a medieval tapestry panel. With the addition of fabric chair covers and two faux-metal shields, I'd thought my decorating was complete. But Julie had noticed the blooming shrubs in the garden and suggested adding vases filled with red and white roses. Which I'd thought a great idea at the time. Until I encountered the vicious thorns studding the stems of the flowers, of course.

"I feel like a pincushion," I said, wrapping a tissue around my bleeding finger.

"*But he that dares not grasp the thorn should never crave the rose*," Julie said, her brown eyes sparkling with good humor.

"Good old Anne Bronte—she sure had that right," I said, not surprised that Julie could quote a classic but not-so-well-known author. A voracious reader, she owned Bookwaves, an independent bookstore on Front Street.

We'd actually met when I visited Bookwaves not long after I moved to Beaufort. Julie, upon discovering I was the new owner, had graciously offered to lead the local book club discussions held at Chapters once a month. "Until you get used to it," she'd said. Appreciating her kindness, I'd made a habit of visiting

Bookwaves to buy new books. Which had led to a close friendship. Even though Julie, at thirty-five, was seven years younger than me, we'd bonded over our mutual interest in books, music, good food, and intelligent conversation. And while I was a widow who had no current interest in dating, I enjoyed Julie's tales of her romantic adventures. I suppose it was a bit of living vicariously.

"I think we probably have enough." I motioned toward Julie's pail of white roses before leaning over to collect the scattered crimson blooms and drop them into my own bucket.

Julie shoved a pair of garden clippers into the pocket of the green canvas apron I'd lent her. "I won't argue with that," she said, stripping off a pair of borrowed gardening gloves.

"Here, let me grab that bucket so you can take those things back to the garden shed," I said, crossing to her.

We were about the same height, but Julie possessed the curvier figure—a fact she sometimes bemoaned. Although she enjoyed flirting, she didn't like to be appreciated simply for her dark-haired, dark-eyed, voluptuous good looks. She preferred men who admired her mind as well as her physical attributes.

*Who are harder to find than they should be*, I thought.

I forced an image of my late husband from my mind. Even though it had been three years, I still had a hard time believing Brent was gone forever.

*And I still have no interest in dating someone new*, I thought, as Scott Kepler walked around the corner of the holly hedge that separated the carriage house from the rest of the backyard. Julie had urged me to consider Scott as more than a friend, but I knew it was impossible for two reasons. First, because I was still in love with my late husband. And second, because although she hadn't noticed it yet, Scott was way more interested in Julie than in me.

I thought it was a perfect match. A booklover and an author: what could be better? Not to mention that Scott seemed like a kind and intelligent man. While he lived in Asheville, North Carolina, which was around six hours away, he visited Beaufort often to conduct research for his books.

"Hello, ladies," Scott said, giving me a nod before his gaze swung back to Julie.

"Hi there." Julie slipped off her apron, revealing her curve-hugging pink T-shirt and denim shorts.

Scott's expression brightened as he looked at her. "Helping Charlotte out with the party prep?"

"Yeah, she always has so much to do, getting ready for these things."

"I'm sure," Scott said, with a swift glance at me. "Anything I can do?"

"No, we're pretty much done," I said. "I just need to get these roses into some vases, and that will be it. For the decorating, anyway."

Julie flicked her dark-brown braid behind one shoulder. "Are you coming to the costume party, Scott?"

"Sadly, no. I have another engagement. Will you be there?"

"Wouldn't miss it," Julie said. "I actually have a costume I'm just dying to wear, although I'm afraid it may be a little warm for it this evening. But it's so flattering, I think I'm willing to suffer. It's velvet, and about the color of those roses," she added, pointing toward my bucket.

"I'm sure that will look quite lovely on you." Scott's eyes were bright, but his voice held a note of disappointment.

*I bet he wishes he were coming now*, I thought, before clearing my throat. "Well, I'd better get these flowers inside before they totally wilt."

Of course, since the buckets were filled with water, that wasn't likely, but neither Scott nor Julie seemed to notice my little deception. I grabbed both buckets and headed for the door that led into Chapters' kitchen, leaving Scott and Julie chatting in the garden.

I felt no shame in playing matchmaker, especially because I'd been worried about Julie lately. She'd told me in confidence that her latest boyfriend—a "mystery man" she refused to name—was married. "But separated and getting a divorce any minute now," she'd told me. "I'll introduce you to him as soon as that happens, I swear."

Biting my tongue, I'd avoided making any negative comments about this situation, even though it concerned me. I didn't want to see my friend caught up in some messy domestic drama.

Especially since there was Scott—long divorced and currently single, as he'd told me. *Hoping I'd share that information with Julie, I bet*, I thought, a little smile curving my lips.

As I was about to head into the kitchen, a series of sharp yips diverted my attention. I set the buckets on the steps that led up to the back stoop and turned to my neighbor's home—a three-story Victorian whose cream-colored siding was enlivened by turquoise-and-maroon-painted gingerbread trim.

The house's owner, Ellen Montgomery, was a seventy-five-year-old former location scout who'd spent years traveling for film and television companies before moving to Beaufort. Ellen was also the executor of Isabella Harrington's estate and manager of the trust Isabella had established to assist with the maintenance of the bed-and-breakfast.

Like the rest of my family, I'd been perplexed when this codicil to Isabella's will had been announced by the lawyers. I liked Ellen, but having to ask a virtual stranger for funds when the B and B's expenses outweighed profits was embarrassing.

*Another thorn*, I thought, cradling my pierced finger in my opposite palm as the volume of the yips increased.

"Hey there, Shandy." I crossed to the gate that led into Ellen's lush backyard. A small black-and-tan dog, with hair that veiled his black eyes, leapt up at the inside of the gate.

"Oh, be quiet, you." Ellen Montgomery picked up the Yorkshire terrier and held him against her breast before shoving back the battered straw hat shading her face. Sunlight glinted off her snow-white bob, which was streaked with deep-purple and cerulean-blue highlights. "And hello, Charlotte."

"Looks like you're doing a little gardening too." I ran my fingers through my own hair. *Emerald might look good in mine*, I thought, before shaking such a silly thought from my head. I was an innkeeper who hosted literary events. Given the wide variety of guests who visited Chapters, it was best if I kept my appearance, like my manner, gracious and unassuming. No matter how boring and confining that sometimes felt.

"Just trying to fight some of the weeds. Seems like they can take over if you let things go even a few days, especially at this time of year."

"Absolutely, and it's probably the best time to do it today, even though it's hot. Most of the tourists are over at Morehead City right now." I made a face. "I don't know about you, but I always hate it when I look up from weeding and find visitors staring at me over my back fence."

Ellen stroked the long fur on the Yorkie's back. "Yes, the streets will definitely get busier in the evening. But perhaps I should've left Shandy inside. I don't want him to bother your guests with all his yapping." She grinned. "I don't call him the 'holy terrier' for nothing."

"It's fine. Chapters' walls are thick enough to block out most outside noise, even a yippy dog." I leaned over the gate to pat Shandy's head, earning a sloppy lick across my hand in return.

Ellen fixed me with her intense, and somewhat disconcerting, gaze. "You have a full house for the week, I hope?"

"No, unfortunately we aren't completely booked."

"You should've rented out any extra rooms to the fishing folk. Lord knows they're always looking for places to stay in the area. I had someone knock on my door just the other day, hoping I'd rent a room during the tournament. Which I won't."

"I thought that would be disruptive to my other guests." I frowned. "I guess if I'd lived here longer, I would've known not to schedule this author celebration for the same week as the Big Rock tournament. But I had no idea how many visitors it brought to the area."

"It's one of the largest fishing events in the world, but cut yourself some slack, Charlotte—people who don't live here don't realize just how huge it is. You might want to remember it for next year, though. Isabella used to forgo her literary events and rent out to the fishing crowd for top dollar."

"Next year, sure." I mentally chided myself. I could've used the extra money. Although Chapters did pay for itself, I had little in the way of extra funds and was reluctant to ask Ellen for too much from the trust. "But I'd already planned this Tey event when I realized the conflict."

"Live and learn," Ellen said. "At least, as you told me yesterday, you have some local people paying to participate in the events even though they aren't staying with you, right?"

"Fortunately." I curled my injured finger in to touch my palm. I really could've used the lodging fees. Next year I'd know better.

Ellen shook her head. "You aren't as ruthless as Isabella. She had a firm rule that anyone who wanted to participate in the literary events had to stay at the house, at least for a night. Even if they were local."

"Really?" I fanned my flushed face with one hand. *What an idiot I am. Not even as savvy as Isabella, a woman fifty years my senior.* "I'll definitely know better next year. Now, if you'll excuse me, I need to get back to work. There's a lot to do before tonight's party."

"Of course," Ellen said. "Come on, Shandy. Let's grab ourselves some water and a snack, shall we?" She gave me a little wave before heading toward her back door, the Yorkie trotting at her heels.

I cast one glance toward the garden. After noting that Scott and Julie were still engaged in what looked like a lively conversation, I grabbed the flower buckets and carried them into the kitchen.

Alicia spared me one glance before turning her focus back to her vigorous scrubbing of the counters. "Call for you. I didn't pick up because I was elbow deep in cleaning. Anyway, they left a message."

I set the buckets in one side of our deep double sink. "Oh? Well, maybe I better check that before I do anything with these flowers. Just in case it's someone wanting a future reservation. You don't need to mess with the roses, by the way. I'll collect some vases and deal with them as soon as I check that phone message."

"Don't worry, I'm always happy to leave the floral arranging to someone else," Alicia said, as I headed into the pantry.

Since we needed to provide phones in our guest rooms, we still had a landline. I punched the playback button on the answering machine connected to the phone.

The caller announced herself as Claire Stevenson. My mother.

I shook my head. I should have figured. Mom always called the landline number rather than my cell phone, and left her full name. She'd told me that she'd been trained to do so when she'd called her aunt in the past, so that Alicia would know to leave the message for Isabella rather than answer it herself.

Mom's message was a request that I return her call, which I did after checking my watch. Mom had left Dad to care for their menagerie of rescue dogs and cats so she could visit my older sister, Sophie, and her family for a few weeks. Since Sophie lived in California, I always checked the time, aware of the three-hour time difference. I'd once accidentally phoned Sophie at eight, which was five in the morning her time. I wouldn't make that mistake again.

"Oh hi, Charlotte, thanks for getting back to me. I have some great news I couldn't wait to share." Mom's effervescent tone sparkled over the phone. I smiled. While both my sisters had inherited Mom's bubbly personality, I was more reserved, like my dad.

"Sophie is pregnant again?" I asked, since that was one of the few things that could inspire my mom to call me in the middle of the day.

"Heavens no, she's forty-five now, you know. And while it's certainly possible, I don't think either Sophie or Bill want more than the three they've already got." Mom's bright laugh rang in my ear. "I mean, little Jaden is such a handful, I think they said enough is enough a while ago."

"Yeah, he's something else. Wait, did you hear something from Mel?" I held my breath, hoping this was true. My younger sister, Melinda, a costume designer, lived in New York City. She had just turned forty a few months ago, a milestone the family had celebrated at my parents' home in Charlottesville, Virginia. Mel had married her longtime partner, Beatrice, two years before, in a ceremony made bittersweet for me by the combination of Mel's joy and Brent's absence.

"Yes!" my mom said in a triumphant tone. "The procedure worked. Bea is pregnant!"

"That's wonderful," I said, my chest tightening. Brent and I hadn't been able to have any children. We'd been discussing adoption right before he died.

I shook off my foolish pang of envy and told Mom I'd call Mel as soon as I could. There was no point in allowing my own sadness to cloud my sister's, or my mother's, happiness. Besides, Mel and Bea's baby just meant another niece or nephew for me to spoil.

Not that I got to see the ones I already had as much as I liked. I coughed to hide a bit of rawness in my voice and asked after Sophie, Bill, and the kids before telling Mom I had to go and deal with some more bed-and-breakfast chores.

"Sometimes I think all you do is work. I hope you manage to squeeze in a little fun and adventure now and then," my mom said, before telling me good-bye.

As I hung up the phone, I shook my head over the reply I'd given her.

"Of course I do," I'd said, even though it wasn't exactly true. Except for Julie and a few members of Chapters' book club, I scarcely talked to anyone other than Alicia, Damian, or our guests.

Grabbing some pewter vases off one of the pantry shelves, I had to admit that while running the bed-and-breakfast was challenging and interesting, it wasn't often what I'd call fun or exciting. *I really wouldn't mind a little adventure*, I thought as I arranged the roses.

Which, as it turned out, was one of those instances that proved the old adage *Be careful what you wish for.*

# Chapter Five

"The orange ginger cake was a hit." I entered the kitchen, balancing a teetering stack of dirty dishes. "Even Pete agreed that it was one medieval recipe that has stood the test of time."

"Probably because it was soaked in enough brandy to cover the unusual combination of spices." Damian Carr, the bed-and-breakfast's part-time chef, took the plates from my hands and deposited them in the sink before turning back to face me.

I met his intense gaze and tugged my sleeve up over my shoulder. The square neckline of the emerald velveteen gown was cut so wide that the sleeve cap tended to slip down my upper arm. "Could be. He wasn't too complimentary about the vegetables or the pike. But he did say that the boar was nice."

"Damned with faint praise, as always." Damian tucked a dangling dreadlock back up under his starched chef's hat. "I think Pete Nelson would complain about the food at a Michelin-starred restaurant. Just because he and his wife run a café, he thinks he's an expert on all things food related."

"Oh, I expect he just likes to rile you up. You know—professional jealousy." I tugged on the recalcitrant sleeve.

Despite a lack of interest in playacting, I'd decided when I'd taken over Chapters that, as hostess, I should participate in any costume parties. Damian had no such sense of obligation. Tall, lanky, and fifteen years my junior, the part-time chef refused to don anything other than a white chef's jacket over a black T-shirt and pants. In fact, Damian had emphatically stated during his interview that he wouldn't "play dress-up" during any special events. I'd acquiesced, knowing he was one of the few local freelance chefs who possessed the skill required to create specialty menus.

I examined the young chef's angular face, noting the bags under his dark eyes. Damian hadn't been able to land a full-time position at a prestigious restaurant yet, despite numerous interviews. Which meant he worked a patchwork of jobs, including acting as a personal chef for some of the yacht owners who regularly docked at Beaufort. Knowing his erratic schedule probably took a toll on his health, I tended to cut Damian some slack, even when his temper got the better of him.

"Hello, dear," called out a loud voice.

I turned to face one of the dinner guests, an older woman wearing a peach-and-gold brocade gown that made her look like an overstuffed bolster.

But that first impression was instantly dispelled by the twinkle in the woman's bright-blue eyes. Seventy-six-year-old Bernadette Sandberg was a longtime member of Chapters' book club. She lived locally and often participated in the bed-and-breakfast's special literary events, as did her sister, seventy-three-year-old Ophelia.

"I must say, you've outdone yourself. Fee and I are having a grand time, even after fighting these ridiculous things." Bernadette patted the taut linen stretched between the wires of the head covering that completely obscured her gray hair. The headdress, which she'd commissioned, along with her gown, from a local costume designer, replicated the saillike head coverings worn during the late fifteenth century.

"Yes, simply delightful." Ophelia, who was as tall and thin as Bernadette was short and stout, popped up behind her sister. Her headdress, pointed at the top like an upside-down ice cream cone, was draped with a sparkle-dusted sheer veil. Unlike Bernadette, Ophelia had made her own costume, apparently without relying heavily on historic sources. The lilac satin of her gown was not something I'd ever seen in paintings from the period.

*More like a Saturday morning cartoon depiction of a princess*, I thought, covering my mouth to hide a smile.

It was charming, nonetheless, as were the two ladies, who claimed to have never missed a special event at Chapters since the bed-and-breakfast opened in 1983. And before that, as they'd informed me on numerous occasions, they'd often visited Isabella when the house was still her private home.

"And Damian—bravo. Everything was perfectly delicious, even that strange concoction of dried fruit and potted cheese." Bernadette flicked Ophelia's trailing veil away from her shoulder. "Fee, dear, please back off. That bubblegum atrocity of yours is going to poke my eye out."

Ophelia snorted in a distinctly unprincesslike way. "Hardly. You're far too short for that, Bernie." The pointed end of her headdress wobbled as she tossed her head for emphasis.

Damian, watching this scene with a smile, held up his hands. "Thank you for the kind words, ladies. I know medieval-inspired food is not exactly the rage right now."

"But perfect for celebrating *The Daughter of Time*," Bernadette said. "Takes one right back to Richard the Third's era, just like Inspector Grant studying all those books after he saw that sympathetic portrait of Richard."

"I'm afraid your reference is lost on me," Damian said. "I haven't read the book."

As Ophelia bobbed her head, her headdress slid over toward her left ear, exposing her short hair. Dyed a brilliant cardinal red, it provided a startling contrast with her rosy-pink headgear. "You ought to. It's a classic. Anyway, you should be proud of yourself, chef. Not many could pull off a meal like that."

"Fee, you're losing your hat," Bernadette observed, before waving her fingers at Damian and me. "We must go. Everyone has headed outside, and I expect a literary discussion is in the offing." She beamed. "My favorite thing, as you know."

"Yes, mine too." I cast both sisters a warm smile. "Go ahead. I'll join the group as soon as I can."

The older women bustled off, their hard-soled shoes ringing against the pine plank floors.

"Go, join your guests," Damian said, waving a tea towel. "Alicia will finish tidying the dining room any minute. She can help me clean up in here."

"Thanks. I guess I'd better see what they're all up to." I gave Damian a wink. "And keep an eye on the open bar, even if it is just wine and beer."

"Good idea." Damian turned back to the sink. "Pete was hitting the sauce pretty hard at dinner, along with that Delamont guy. You might need to supervise those two."

Stepping out the back door, I had to admit that my guests' colorful costumes created a fabulous tableau. Of course, up close most of the costumes gave off a high-school-drama-club vibe, but the flickering tongues of light cast by the lawn torches lent their outfits an uncanny air of verisimilitude. Standing at the edge of the flagstone patio, I could imagine gazing across the stone plaza of a fifteenth-century English castle, observing festivities at court. The illusion was broken only when I glanced up at the lights twinkling above my head. They weren't stars—only tiny white Christmas lights threaded through the slats of the pergola.

I lifted my heavy skirts and headed for the outdoor bar at one edge of the patio. Fortunately, this party was beer and wine only, although I'd also included some bottled mead. I'd informed the guests that this was in keeping with the party's theme, but of course it was also a cost-saving measure—one I couldn't get away with when I hosted events based on twentieth-century authors and books.

I nodded at Todd and Kelly Rowley, who'd obviously spared no expense on their costumes. Todd was dressed like a medieval scholar, complete with robes that wouldn't have looked out of place at a ceremony at one of England's finer universities. Kelly wore a lovely gown that appeared to be a reproduction of one of the few images of Anne Neville, wife of Richard the Third. Her rose-pink gown was trimmed with fake fur mimicking the ermine depicted in the illustration, and she wore a cloak of deep rose, also edged in the fake fur. I'd discovered the same illustration in the Rous Roll—an illustrated chronicle created by fifteenth-century historian and priest John Rous—and was impressed by Kelly's devotion to period accuracy. From my own research, I'd learned that Anne Neville had probably commissioned the chronicle, making her Rous Roll portrait the one most likely to reflect an accurate image of Richard the Third's queen.

When I reached the bar, I was greeted by Pete Nelson. A local man in his mid-fifties, he'd embraced his rotund figure and dressed as a medieval monk. Lifting a tankard of ale, he saluted me.

"Great party, as always. Although some of those dishes . . ."

"I know," I said. "You already told me you weren't too thrilled with a few things."

"The pike still had bones," said Pete's wife, Sandra, a petite middle-aged woman swallowed up by the sapphire-blue velvet folds of her Renaissance-inspired gown. Sandra had eschewed the tall headdresses worn by the Sandberg sisters for a black velveteen beret-style hat decorated with drooping white feathers.

"As it would have back in the time of Richard the Third," I replied. I should have known, as Damian had alluded to earlier, that the Nelsons would have an opinion on the food. They ran a café called the Dancing Dolphin. Open for breakfast and lunch and featuring farm-to-table cuisine, it was popular with both locals and tourists. "We gave you verisimilitude, Sandy."

"I could've done with a little less of that," Sandy said. "But it's fun, nevertheless."

"As I mentioned, I did like the boar," Pete said, before downing another swig of ale. "But I need to talk to that chef of yours about his heavy hand with spices. I almost choked over those vegetables."

I adjusted my own headdress, which was a simple starched linen coif. "Please don't blame Damian for that. He was following the recipes I gave him."

"A chef should taste his food and adjust," Pete said.

"I'm sure Damian sampled all his dishes." I glanced over the café owner's shoulder and noticed Tara Delamont following Jennifer into the back garden. By the teen's furious gesticulations, I suspected the mother and daughter were embroiled in some sort of argument. "Excuse me," I said, clutching several folds of my velvet skirt with one hand. "I need to check on something."

I raised the hem of my gown above my sturdy walking shoes and hurried over to the white picket fence that enclosed the garden. It looked like trouble was brewing between Tara and her mother, and I wanted to stem any argument that might spill over onto the rest of the party. Staying behind the fence, I slid in close to a large lilac bush and peered into the shadowy garden. Yes, I was eavesdropping, but if I could head off a major incident that might ruin my carefully orchestrated event, I didn't care.

"You never listen to me," Tara wailed, plucking at the glass baubles decorating the neckline of her amber velvet gown. Tara had proudly informed everyone at dinner that she'd made her own costume, which had impressed me. The teen's gown was elegant and historically appropriate, although the fake gems she'd hot-glued to the black satin trim were too gaudy to appear real. In keeping with her age, Tara had left her hair uncovered, but she'd skillfully woven her dark locks into tiny braids looped back in a style I recognized from a few da Vinci portraits.

"That's not true." Jennifer fiddled with the edge of the white linen scarf she'd tied around her head to form a simple coif. She'd allowed some of her dark curly hair to peek out from beneath the scarf, which actually flattered her round face. Unfortunately, her dark-gray wool gown and its corded belt made her plump figure appear as dumpy as a sack of flour.

*She's obviously dressed as a servant or peasant woman.* Pondering this choice, I couldn't help but wonder if Jennifer Delamont was sending a pointed message of some kind. Perhaps to spite her husband, who looked every inch the medieval king. His costume, based on a portrait of Henry the Seventh, the Tudor king who'd defeated Richard the Third at the Battle of Bosworth Field, was a resplendent ensemble of black velvet trimmed with amber brocade.

"Oh right, because constantly telling me Dad won't approve is listening?" Tara tapped her ballet-slippered foot against a garden path paver. "You're destroying my life and you just don't care."

"No one is ruining your life," Jennifer replied, more gently than I thought I could've managed in the situation. "You can still study voice, and perform professionally someday, but those TV shows are out."

"But you watch them!" Tara placed her balled fists on her slender hips.

"Yes, and if it was up to me, maybe . . ." Jennifer shook her head. "But that's a moot point. Your father will never approve."

"Dad is such a jerk." Tara spun around so fast that her heavy skirts swung like a bell. "I wish he were dead!"

I shrank back deeper into the shadows as Tara stormed out of the garden. Jennifer Delamont sighed deeply before following her daughter.

After they'd passed me, I strolled over to the other edge of the yard. When I reached the row of hollies that created a natural fence between the patio and the carriage house, the sound of voices halted my progress.

Perhaps Scott was entertaining a guest. I stepped back, not wishing to intrude. But when I recognized the voices, I sucked in a breath. Lincoln Delamont was engaged in an animated conversation with Julie. Assuming they were talking about books, I considered joining their discussion until I heard words that stopped me in my tracks.

"And apparently you're married, not separated." Julie's normally pleasant tone was edged with anger.

"I never claimed that I was separated." Lincoln's voice was slick as oil on wet pavement.

"Liar. You did too. On the phone as well as by text. I wouldn't have attended this party otherwise, and you know it. I thought we were going to meet here for a fun evening, and what do I find? Why, just your wife, who's obviously not divorcing you anytime soon. Not to mention your teenage daughter, who you somehow neglected to mention at all." The fury in Julie's voice was as obvious as the total lack of concern in Lincoln Delamont's.

I backed away, shocked by this discovery. Even though I was aware that Lincoln had visited Beaufort on many other occasions—when he'd registered, he'd admitted being familiar with the area from previous book-buying trips—I'd never heard Julie mention him.

*So Lincoln is her mystery man? That's certainly not what I ever imagined.* I took a deep breath and marched back across the patio, ignoring a question from one of the Sandberg sisters.

"Sorry, need to check something in the kitchen," I called over my shoulder.

What I really needed was a moment to collect my thoughts. Unfortunately, as soon as I stepped into the kitchen, I realized I'd be thwarted in that goal. Pete Nelson and Damian were embroiled in an argument—one that had reduced them both to shouting and forced Alicia to demand that they take their issues outside.

"Enough!" I strode to the center of the kitchen, stepping between the two men. Peter swore and stomped out of the room, while Damian ripped off his chef's hat and turned and kicked the ice maker with such force that the machine rattled and fell silent.

"Now look what you've done," Alicia said. "Broken that thing just when we need more ice."

Damian spat out a string of expletives that would've done a merchant sailor proud. "I'm done," he said, rolling up his knives in a canvas pouch. "The meal is over, so you no longer need me. Have fun dealing with this bunch for the rest of the evening." He tied off the pouch with a vicious knot before grabbing his hat and storming past me. "Dock my pay if you want."

"I will," I said, although I knew I probably wouldn't do any such thing.

Alicia, fiddling with the controls on the ice maker, glanced over at me. "Dead as a doornail. What do we do now? That crew outside is going through ice like tourists lost in the Sahara."

I sighed and whipped the coif off my head, exposing my not-ready-for-the-fifteenth-century hair. "I'll run out and pick up a bag or two at the local food mart. You stay here and man the barricades."

"All right." Alicia looked me up and down. "But that getup might cause a bit of confusion with the slushy-and-malt-liquor crowd."

"They'll have to deal. Back in thirty minutes or less," I added as I grabbed my purse from the storeroom. "Check on the bar and replace any empty wine bottles, okay?"

"Sure, sure." Alicia waved me off. "I've handled worse. Remember the Roaring Twenties weekend and that bunch that tried to outdo Fitzgerald's boozing? If I could deal with that, I'm pretty sure I can manage this crowd."

I cast her a grin and headed out the door.

Twenty-five minutes and several curious stares and comments later, I pulled my car up in front of the carriage house. I often parked there, as it was an out-of-the-way spot that kept the main lot free for the guests. Popping open my trunk, I grabbed two bags of ice and headed for Chapters' back door.

"Here, can you deal with these? I have to go back out for a couple more," I said as I entered the kitchen. When Alicia took the bags, I noticed deep lines crinkling the corners of her dark eyes. "Anything wrong?"

"No, just missing a knife. I think Damian must've taken it when he stormed out of here. Mixed it up with his own, I guess."

I turned to head back outside for the other bags of ice. "Well, we can ask him about that easily enough."

"Sure, but then there's the key."

"What key?" I paused, holding the back door ajar.

"To the carriage house. The extra one I keep in the drawer here with all the other duplicates." Alicia pointed toward an open cabinet drawer, which held an insert that organized keys. "I can't imagine who would've taken that. Mr. Kepler has his own."

I frowned, but the thought of ice melting in my trunk made me shrug off this anomaly. "I'll ask around in a minute. Let me grab the rest of the ice first."

Looking up when I reached my car, I recognized the tall, lanky figure standing in the open doorway of the carriage house. It was Scott.

I waved. "Oh hi. Mind helping? It'll only take a minute."

When he stepped forward into the light spilling from a nearby streetlight, I noticed that his skin seemed stretched too tightly over the angular bones of his face. He was pale, too, which threw his freckles into sharp relief and created a vivid contrast with his auburn hair. "Sorry, I . . . but I think you'd better forget that," he said, his voice eerily devoid of emotion.

"What do you mean?"

"It's Lincoln Delamont." Scott blinked rapidly, and his hands, which were hanging loosely at his sides, twitched like beached fish. "He's inside."

"Doing what?"

"Nothing, I'm afraid." Scott pressed one shaking hand to his temple. "He's been stabbed. There's blood everywhere, and I think"—his lips trembled so violently he had to take an audible breath before speaking again—"I'm afraid he's quite dead."

# Chapter Six

I stared at Scott, my mouth working while no sound emerged from my lips. "I have ice in the trunk," I finally said, as if that ordinary statement could erase what had happened.

Scott shook his head. "I should stay here. I've already called 911, so someone will be here soon."

"Sure, okay." I drew in a shuddery breath. "You stay, and don't let anyone else get too close. I'll take these bags inside."

Scott's stare was unfocused, as if he was seeing something other than the scene in front of him. "I was out at another engagement. Just got back. Door was open when I got here."

I thought about Alicia's missing key. "Of course." I grabbed the two remaining bags of ice, slamming down the trunk lid with my other hand. "I can come back if you want."

Scott leaned against the wood siding of the carriage house. "No, I'm fine. You go on inside."

Clutching the ice bags in one hand and several folds of my gown in the other, I ran to the back door, the damp plastic soaking one side of my raised skirts.

Alicia took the dripping bags from my hands as soon as I entered the kitchen. "What in the world? Looks like you just saw a ghost."

A bubble of nervous laughter burst from my trembling lips. "Not exactly," I said when I got my voice under control. "But prepare yourself for a visit from the police."

Alicia tossed the bags of ice in the sink. "Why, in heaven's name?"

"It's Lincoln Delamont."

"Is he fighting with his wife again?" As Alicia turned away to dry her hands on a tea towel, I realized she had removed the full apron she typically wore over her plain black work dress. "I saw him making eyes at your friend Julie over dinner. Wouldn't be surprised if Mrs. Delamont noticed that too."

"Uh, no. He's not doing anything," I said, echoing Scott. "He's dead."

Alicia kept her back turned, her hands twisting the towel into a fabric rope. "Heart attack?"

"No, stabbed." My gaze flitted to the wooden knife holder on a nearby counter. The empty slot for one of the larger kitchen knives gaped like a wound.

Alicia's gaze followed. "You aren't thinking our knife was used . . ." She looked back at me, lines furrowing her brow. "Do we have to tell the police about that?"

"I think so," I said, yanking my drooping sleeve back up over my shoulder. "Don't you?"

Alicia looked away again. "It might get Damian in trouble, that's all."

I narrowed my eyes. That was odd. Alicia was not Damian Carr's biggest fan. There was no reason for her to protect him, unless . . .

*Unless she's actually protecting herself.* Alicia had been devoted to Isabella Harrington. She might've decided to silence Lincoln Delamont before he could besmirch the good name of her former boss and friend.

*Then there's all the guests . . .* I had no way of knowing where they'd all been while I was off getting ice. I shivered—any one of them, including Scott, could've stabbed Lincoln Delamont while I was gone. Not to mention Damian, who'd stormed off earlier but lived in a converted garage apartment nearby.

*Close enough to walk back again*, I thought. *And then there's still Alicia. Who knows where that key is kept and could've easily snatched a knife from the kitchen.* I stared at the housekeeper's broad back. *She might've mentioned the missing knife and key simply to establish an alibi.*

I shook my head, reminding myself that this wasn't one of my favorite mystery novels. I wasn't Miss Marple, or Inspector Gamache, or even Nancy Drew. I couldn't try to solve this mystery—I needed to clear my head and calmly inform my guests that there was an emergency that required them to come inside.

"Alicia," I said, fighting the urge to laugh hysterically as my brain conjured scenes from *Clue* or *The Mousetrap*. "Could you please wait in the parlor? I'll get the others and join you in a few minutes."

Alicia cast me a sharp glance. "All right, although I've got a lot of cleanup to do. But if you think it's necessary . . ."

"I do." I waited until Alicia exited the room before heading out the back door to collect the others.

*Including Lincoln's wife and daughter.* I stiffened my spine as I marched onto the patio, determined to deal with the situation without breaking into tears.

I could do it. I'd handled worse news before.

\* \* \*

I managed to herd the guests into the parlor, despite their protests and several demands that they be allowed to change out of their costumes. Ignoring my request to remain as they were, Pete Nelson had already whipped off his monk's robe, revealing a plain T-shirt and shorts. After briefly explaining to the entire group that there had been a suspicious death in the carriage house, I told Pete to be prepared to hand over the costume to the authorities, while assuring Kelly Rowley, who'd obviously shed her cloak, that anything left on the patio would be collected in due time.

At least I was spared the onerous duty of informing Jennifer and Tara about Lincoln's death. Even in the small town of Beaufort, the authorities sent enough officers to swarm the backyard and the house, as well as two detectives, who immediately separated the staff and guests so they could interview each person individually. I didn't even see Jennifer or Tara, who'd apparently been whisked away as soon as the police arrived.

After an ambulance had taken away Lincoln's body, I slumped down into one of the library's worn leather armchairs. I could barely remember what I'd told the investigator, a tall, regal, woman whose name was Detective Johnson. I just hoped I'd included all the pertinent facts.

*The knife from the kitchen, the missing key, Damian Carr's angry exit, the argument between Tara and her mother, Scott standing so close to the murder scene, and that snippet of conversation between Lincoln and Julie . . .* I massaged the throbbing pain above my right eye with one finger. Had I told the detective all of that? I couldn't remember. All I knew was that I hadn't mentioned one other suspicious fact—Lincoln's earlier hints that he had collected some dirt on Isabella Harrington.

I knew I probably should've said something, but somehow the idea that the investigation might expose my great-aunt's secrets had silenced me. I needed to know more before opening that Pandora's box.

I leaned into the chair's high back and stared up at the web of fine cracks in the plaster ceiling. Detective Johnson had informed me that the guests would need to stay in town for at least a week. With the Big Rock tournament filling up all the local lodging, I knew they'd probably need to stay on at Chapters, even though that would undoubtedly be uncomfortable for Jennifer and Tara Delamont.

*Not like it's going to be a fun week for anyone*, I thought. A fog of suspicion would undoubtedly envelop the entire party. Detective Johnson had promised to post a few officers near the carriage house and the house, so help would only be a quick call or a shout away, but still . . . I massaged my temples. If one of my guests had killed Lincoln, I'd be sharing my home with a murderer.

I jumped to my feet when Detective Johnson strode back into the room. "Our interviews are done. We'll leave you and your guests in peace for now. Of course, we'll continue our work out back. There'll be a perimeter established around the carriage house, staffed with an officer, for at least a few days."

I locked my knees to stiffen my wobbly legs. "I guess the locals can head home?"

The detective examined me. "Yes, but I'm afraid you do have to host the other guests for the remainder of the week. I made some calls, and there's no place for them to go."

"It's fine. They've already paid, so at least it won't cost them anything extra."

Detective Johnson tapped her computer tablet with a stylus. "You will lose two guests. The Rowleys are going to stay on their yacht. Not surprising, given the circumstances. Of course, they've been warned not to leave the area until we finish our questioning."

"And Mr. Kepler?"

"He said he wants to stay, but of course not in the carriage house. I suppose you can put him up in one of your rooms?"

"That won't be a problem."

"Good. One of my officers will collect Mr. Kepler's personal items from the carriage house. We need to ensure that the scene isn't disturbed."

*And give your officers time to search the area.* I nodded instead of voicing this thought.

Detective Johnson tipped her head. "Is there something else you wish to share with me, Ms. Reed?"

I swallowed the ball of bile lodged in my throat. "No."

"I just thought you seemed to have something else on your mind when we talked. But if you say there's nothing . . ." The detective slipped her tablet into an inside pocket of her tailored jacket.

"I can't think of anything right now," I said, fighting my urge to blurt out Lincoln Delamont's hints about a scandal in my great-aunt's past. "But I promise, if I remember anything else, I'll be sure to let you know."

"Excellent. Now, if you'll excuse me, I'm going to head back out to the scene. I suggest locking up after Mr. Kepler comes in, but don't worry—my officers will keep watch tonight. If anything suspicious occurs later, anything at all, just remember that help will be standing right outside your back door."

I bobbed my head. "Thanks, that's comforting. But I'm not really worried." I was surprised to admit that this was true. Although Alicia was still on my suspect list, along with everyone else at the party, I didn't feel personally threatened. If Alicia had murdered Lincoln Delamont, it would've been done to silence him before he could reveal salacious information about Isabella, not because she was some crazed serial killer.

*Same with the others*, I realized. Whoever had killed Lincoln had obviously wanted him dead for a very specific reason. The murderer probably had no inclination to kill anyone else. I gnawed on the inside of my cheek. *Hopefully.*

"Good. If it makes you feel better, I can say that at this point we have no evidence to suggest that anyone at the party is a prime suspect," Detective Johnson said. "Although of course we will continue to investigate every angle, including the possibility that it could've been a random attack, or an unknown individual with a vendetta against Mr. Delamont who had tracked him here."

"I've also wondered if it could've been an outsider." I forgave myself for the lie because, while I hadn't actually considered that angle, it was definitely another logical option. "I can't imagine anyone who was at Chapters tonight wanting to kill . . ."

"Liar!" Tara Delamont stormed into the room, followed closely by her distraught mother, who, except for the scarf covering her hair, was now wearing her street clothes. I assumed the police had allowed her to change once they'd questioned her.

But Tara was still in costume. One of her thin braids had slipped free of her carefully arranged hairdo, and she tossed it behind her shoulder before rubbing the back of one hand over her mascara-stained cheek. "She's the one you should lock up."

While Detective Johnson looked on with interest, Tara stabbed her forefinger at me. "I bet she killed him, and I know exactly why."

# Chapter Seven

To her credit, Detective Johnson didn't even blink.

"Please, Miss Delamont," she said, "this is neither the time nor place for such accusations. I believe you've already expressed this opinion in your interview. We will follow up on that information as well as everything else we've heard."

Tara flung out her hands in a dramatic gesture. "It's not just an opinion. My father had some dirt on her great-aunt. Something about the old lady stealing books and other stuff when she worked at a rich family's house. That's why Ms. Reed killed him—she didn't want that story to come out and ruin her business."

"What are you talking about?" Jennifer Delamont yanked the kerchief from her head and used it to fan herself. "I never heard any such thing."

"Of course you didn't." Tara's full lips curled into a pout. "It's not like Dad told you. Or me, actually." She tossed her head, dislodging another one of her braids. "I found out Dad had some incriminating info on Ms. Reed's great-aunt."

"How did you discover any such thing?" Jennifer asked, her gaze focused on her daughter. Her jaw, which had been clenched, relaxed, and I put two and two together. Apparently, Lincoln's wife had been expecting a different revelation. She was obviously aware of her husband's dalliance with Julie and was relieved Tara hadn't uncovered anything about that particular secret.

"I saw it in Dad's appointment book. Yeah, I snooped, but he'd left it in your suitcase for anyone to see. I found it when we were in my room getting ready for the party, and you sent me to look for some more pins for my hair. Remember? You told me to check the suitcase in your room, so I did. And there was Dad's book, with a piece of paper sticking out of it, so . . ."

Jennifer pursed her lips. "You read it? That wasn't right, Tara, no matter what."

"I just wanted to see what letter or memo was so important that he'd keep it stuffed in his appointment book." Tara focused on the tips of her slippers poking out from under her long skirt instead of meeting her mother's gaze.

*Poor thing*, I thought, realizing that Tara had been dealing with suspicions of her father's infidelity. *She probably felt torn apart and figured it was better to know, one way or the other. I bet she hoped that piece of paper was a love letter or something. Just to have the proof.*

"And this paper included something about my great-aunt?" I asked, keeping my tone as gentle as possible.

Tara lifted her head and shot me a fierce glare. "Yeah. He'd scribbled notes, like a memo to himself or something. It was info on someone called Isabella Harrington. That caught my attention because I remembered from Ms. Reed's welcome talk that Ms. Harrington used to own this house. Anyway, Dad mentioned something about her stealing rare books and other stuff from her former employers, and using the money she got from her crime to buy this house and set up a fancy library."

"That's ridiculous," I said, my voice sharpening in spite of myself. "My great-aunt was no thief."

"Oh yeah? Dad seemed pretty convinced." Tara met my gaze without faltering. "I bet that's why you stabbed him. You had to shut him up before he revealed your family's dirty secret."

I took a deep breath before I could trust myself to speak. "Nonsense. I wouldn't kill anyone over an old scandal."

"I think we'd better halt this conversation right now." Detective Johnson cast a sharp glance at Tara. "You've already expressed this opinion to my partner, Miss Delamont, so there's no need to say anything more. If there is any truth in it, we'll find out soon enough. For now, I suggest you resist the urge to broadcast your suspicions. You don't want to muddy our investigation with unsubstantiated rumors."

"But it's the truth," Tara whined, before her mother grabbed her arm and pulled her out of the room.

"So sorry for that. I regret that you'll have to live with those two for the next week." Detective Johnson buttoned up her jacket before gazing speculatively at me. "Of course, we have to investigate her claim, but I do apologize for the unsubstantiated accusation."

"Investigate me all you want. I have nothing to hide," I said, my mind racing with thoughts of Lincoln's earlier insinuations of blackmail. I should've mentioned that up front, during my interview. If I brought it up now, it might look like I was trying to cover up my guilt.

*Which doesn't exist*, I reminded myself. *So why worry?*

But I was concerned—for Alicia, if no one else. I'd confided in the housekeeper about Lincoln's threat to expose a scandal from Isabella's past. What if my careless confidence had spurred the older woman into silencing the bookdealer?

"We'll clear out now," Detective Johnson said. "From the house, I mean. Naturally, we'll continue to gather evidence from the crime scene and will need to speak with you, your staff, and your guests again."

"Of course. Whenever you want," I replied, my mind preoccupied with thoughts of Alicia stabbing Lincoln Delamont. *But then again*, I thought, as the detective left the room, *maybe Tara's just pointing fingers to lift the shadow of suspicion off herself. She did tell her mother she wished her father was dead.*

I shook my head, hoping to clear the haze that filled my mind. No, Tara might've been angry over his refusal to allow her to pursue her dreams of stardom, but surely that wasn't enough to drive a young girl to kill. Besides, there were any number of people who might've wanted the bookdealer dead, including his wife. Jennifer could've become enraged when she realized her husband's lover was one of the party guests. And then there was Julie, who'd been involved in a relationship with Lincoln—a relationship she'd thought quite different from what it actually was. Julie, who'd spent plenty of time in Chapters' kitchen, could've easily grabbed a knife, found that key, and convinced Lincoln to meet her in the carriage house . . .

I exhaled and sank back down into the armchair. Every option for a culprit was worse than the last. A wife, a daughter, a coworker, or my friend—all of them had had a reason to hate Lincoln Delamont, as well as the opportunity to kill him.

The tap of shoes against the wooden floor made me sit up. "Scott, hello. I suppose you want to know which room to use?"

"If you don't mind." Scott set down a suitcase and adjusted the strap of the briefcase hanging over his shoulder. "The police helped me collect a few things from the carriage house. Just the essentials and my laptop, but it will do for now. If you can show me to a spare room, I'll get out of your way."

"I thought the Children's Room," I said, rising to my feet. "No one was using it, so it's clean. Just follow me."

Upstairs, I ushered him into the large bedroom, which had one wall lined with bookshelves, like every other room in the bed-and-breakfast. But the decor in this room was decidedly more fanciful than in the other suites. Antique toys served as bookends for the books, which included brightly colored paperbacks as well as leather-bound volumes of children's classics shelved alongside hardbound picture books. Reproductions of famous illustrations by Beatrix Potter, Arthur Rackham, and Maurice Sendak decorated the pale-yellow walls, while the bed was a canopied affair that wouldn't have looked out of place in a setting described by Frances Hodgson Burnett.

I fluffed the bed pillows as Scott dropped his suitcase in front of a wardrobe whose size and style suggested that it might lead to Narnia. "I hope you'll be comfortable. I know everything looks like an antique, but the mattress is actually quite new."

"I'm sure it will be fine." Scott surveyed the bookcases. "Plenty to read. That's always a plus."

I leaned against one of the bedposts. "No shortage of that in this house. Although I'm afraid this room is all children's books."

"No problem. I see a lot of classics I wouldn't mind reading again." Scott ran his fingers over a section of the old books, stopping at a volume bound in sage-green leather embossed with gold accents. "*Treasure Island*. Just the thing."

"That's right—you're writing about pirates, aren't you?"

Scott cast me an amused glance. "The historical ones, of course. Not the fanciful type. Although the real ones were as colorful in their own way as old Long John Silver."

"I suppose you've already investigated the famous cemetery in town."

"The Old Burying Ground? Yes, I did that early on. Fascinating how much history is captured in those gravestones."

"But sad too. That poor little girl buried in the rum cask . . ." As exhaustion swept over me like an ocean wave, I tightened my grip on the bedpost. "It's sweet how people still keep decorating her grave, though."

"If only she'd made it back here alive, think who her descendants could've been." Scott's smile turned bittersweet. "It's funny how things turn out sometimes. I guess no one really knows how long they have on this earth."

"You're thinking of Lincoln Delamont." I shook my head. "I'm sure he didn't see his death coming."

"Probably not, but"—Scott rubbed his forehead with one hand—"maybe it wasn't as much of a shock as you think."

Releasing my hold on the bedpost, I crossed to a nearby wooden rocking chair. "What do you mean?" I asked as I sank down onto the hard seat.

"Just that Delamont may have had any number of enemies, judging by his business practices." Scott strode across the room, grabbing a bright-blue-painted chair and setting it down so he could face me. "He was a bit of a crook, if you ask me."

"Oh? I didn't know you were acquainted with him before this weekend."

"I wasn't. But my father had some dealings with him. Unfortunately, as it turned out." Scott rapped his knuckles against the wooden armrest on his chair before adding, "You wouldn't have connected the dots, because my dad wrote under a pseudonym. You may have heard of him—Nathan Caine?"

I studied Scott's face, which had lost its usual cheeriness. "The novelist?"

"Yes, the famous Nathan Caine." Scott's smile was wide but his lips had thinned, giving his expression a pained look. "Bestselling thriller writer, as I'm sure you're aware."

"Nathan Caine was your dad? Really?" I tried, and failed, to keep the awe out of my tone. Of course I'd heard of Nathan Caine. Everyone had. He was one of the handful of authors known by everyone, even people who'd never picked up a book. His thrillers had been adapted into numerous films and television shows.

"Really and truly. Which is one of the reasons I chose to write nonfiction. Even though he used a pen name, his real name was common knowledge among editors and publishers." Scott offered me a lopsided smile. "I didn't want to compete, you see."

"I understand. But what did your father have to do with Lincoln Delamont?"

"Dad liked to collect rare books now and then. He had the money, so why not?" Scott shrugged. "Anyway, he had some items he wanted to sell a few years back. Pretty rare stuff, so he thought he could get a good price for them. Unfortunately, based on some bad advice he got from a friend, he used Delamont as a broker. The books were sold, all right, but Dad soon found out he'd received far too little for them. Much less than they were worth."

"And you think Lincoln Delamont cheated him." Influenced by Scott's expression, I didn't frame this as a question.

"Yes, and so did Dad, once he talked to other people who were knowledgeable about rare books." Scott slumped in his chair, lowering his head so that I couldn't see his eyes. "Dad didn't take it well. He was very proud of his savvy and intelligence and never wanted to appear the fool. When Lincoln Delamont was able to dupe him, it hit him hard. I think it may have even contributed to his death." Scott sat up with a jerk of his shoulders, as if shaking off a chill. "Dad died of a heart attack, which was probably due to decades of smoking, even though he'd quit a few years before his death. I don't suppose I should attribute that to Lincoln Delamont's shady behavior, but I still think Dad's anger over Delamont's graft didn't help matters."

I slid my fingers along the smooth surface of my chair arm. "It does shine a light on Lincoln's personality. From everything I've heard, it seems like he wasn't the most honest individual."

"No, I'm pretty sure he wasn't." Scott stood up. "But this has been a terrible day for you, and here I am, bending your ear with my own problems. Sorry about that."

I rose to face him. "Don't worry about it. I know you must be exhausted as well. Being the one to find the body and all."

As I turned to go, I couldn't help but ponder Scott's words. If he truly thought Lincoln's actions had contributed to his dad's death, that was more than just proof of the bookdealer's thievery.

It also gave Scott a motive.

*As much of a motive as Alicia, or Julie, or Jennifer.* I tossed off a swift "Good night" and fled the room.

Halting my headlong flight halfway down the stairs, I gripped the handrail and considered my situation with a clearer head. Yes, several possible killers could be sleeping beneath my roof, but if anyone now staying at Chapters had murdered Lincoln, their motives had nothing to do with me. As long as I didn't pose a threat by voicing my suspicions, I should remain safe.

I descended the remaining stairs and locked up the house. *It's strange*, I thought, as I headed into my private suite. *Before today, I would never have imagined staying so close to anyone I suspected of murder. But now look at me—acting like everything is normal; not concerned that I could be sleeping in the same house as a killer.*

But just to be sure, I locked my bedroom door and slid a heavy antique trunk up against it. Better safe than dead.

# Chapter Eight

The next morning I decided that a walk was the best way to clear my head.

After donning a T-shirt and shorts, I headed out the back door. I explained my plan to the officer standing near the door and glanced across the backyard at the officer posted at the carriage house. "Just going for a walk," I called out when he stepped forward to intercept me.

He waved me off without asking any questions. *Which hopefully means the police aren't taking Tara Delamont's accusations too seriously.*

But I needed more information, if only to ease my own mind. Circling around to the front of the house, I waited on the sidewalk in front of Ellen Montgomery's stately home. I'd timed my excursion to coincide with Ellen's schedule for walking Shandy, even though I wasn't certain Ellen would have information on any criminal behavior in Isabella's past.

Ellen appeared on her wraparound front porch, wearing one of her typical colorful ensembles—a silky turquoise tunic over a pair of wide-legged purple, turquoise, and seafoam-green paisley pants. Apparently lost in thought, she reached the sidewalk before looking up. It was the dog, yipping and bouncing on the end of his leash, who first noticed me.

"Hey there, fella," I said, leaning down to pat Shandy's head. When I met Ellen's inquisitive gaze, I offered her a wan smile. "I want to apologize for all the ruckus last night. I guess you've heard what happened?"

"Yes, it was all over the local news." Ellen looked me up and down. "How're you doing? I know it must've been traumatic for you."

"I'm okay. It was a shock, of course, but the police were very efficient and polite, all things considered." Realizing I was twisting my hands together, I dropped them to my sides. "The only problem is that all the area hotels and inns are full, and the guests can't leave town yet, so some of them have to stay on at Chapters. Which is fine, I guess, except . . ."

"You're a little afraid one of them might be a murderer?" Ellen used her free hand to adjust her straw hat, which was tied under her chin with scarlet ribbons. "Come, walk with me. I imagine you could use a bit of fresh air this morning."

"Thanks." I fell into step beside Ellen as the older woman let out Shandy's leash, allowing the small dog to trot in front of us. "I did want to get out of the house, and it's nice to have company."

Ellen cast me a sidelong glance. "Happy to oblige, but why do I have this feeling you also want to ask me something?"

"Because you are just too darn perceptive," I said, as we strolled past Turner Street. Off to my right, I noticed an unusual amount of activity around the cafés and shops that lined the road leading to Front Street and the waterfront. The town's visitors were up earlier than usual—probably grabbing breakfast before heading over to Morehead for the fishing tournament. "I wanted to ask you something about Great-Aunt Isabella. It sounds silly, but there's apparently some suspicion clouding her past, at least according to the late Mr. Delamont and his daughter."

Ellen paused at the gate that led into a cemetery. The Old Burying Ground, which predated the adjacent Ann Street United Methodist Church by 145 years, was enclosed by a black wrought-iron fence set into a white concrete base. Established in 1709, the graveyard was listed on the National Register of Historic Places and was one of Beaufort's most unique attractions. It included graves from the eighteenth century, many covered with curved brick vaults. When I'd first explored the site, I'd been told that flooding and wild animals would've been a problem in the early years, hence the aboveground vaults. The cemetery was now owned by the town.

"I don't want to take the dog inside." Ellen motioned toward the gate. "Feels disrespectful, honestly."

"Agreed." I gazed into the graveyard, which was shaded by the twisted limbs of old trees and shrubs. "On the other hand, it seems fitting to ask my question here, since I'm searching for answers from the past."

"Something about Isabella?" Ellen reined in Shandy, who was fighting the leash. "No, we can't go in, you rascal."

"Yes. Now, maybe you don't know the answer . . ."

"I probably don't. Isabella could talk a blue streak, but she rarely spoke about her past. But I'll help you if I can." Ellen glanced off to our right. "However, if you don't mind, I'd prefer to sit down first. Let's head down Craven. There are plenty of benches in that little park between Front Street and the docks."

I nodded and followed Ellen and Shandy down the street, passing another church on one side and a bar, which sat back on an alley, to the right. If it had been later in the day, I would've suggested stopping. I'd always enjoyed grabbing a beer or glass of wine at the small bar on summer evenings when I wasn't hosting events at Chapters. The brick interior and outside patio were equally charming and offered a quiet retreat from the bustling crowds of tourists who filled the area closer to the waterfront.

Crossing Front Street, Ellen headed to a tree-shaded patio area off the main boardwalk. She scooped up Shandy and sat down on one of the backless wooden benches. "All right," she said. "Ask away. You look like you're dying to do so."

I grimaced as I took a seat next to Ellen. "Please don't mention dying."

"Sorry." Ellen stretched out her legs as Shandy spun around before snuggling in her lap. "I assume you're trying to figure out something related to Isabella's past?"

"Yes, mainly about the period in the fifties when she worked as a maid. I realize you didn't know her until much later, but I thought maybe she'd mentioned that time once or twice."

Ellen pursed her lips and looked over at the boat slips before replying. "I'm afraid I'm not going to be very helpful. She did tell me she'd worked at some fancy estate back in the early fifties, but that was all she said. She was always tight-lipped about her youth." Ellen absently stroked Shandy's back as she stared beyond the boardwalk.

Following her gaze, I focused on the forest of masts that filled the harbor. "That's the thing—she never talked about that time in her life with my family either. All we knew was that she went to work there when she was in her mid-twenties. I think that must've been around 1950, since she was born in 1926." I looked down at my hands, which were clutched in my lap. "Not sure why she took that job, to be honest. She actually had a college degree, so that always puzzled me."

Ellen, fiddling with Shandy's harness, didn't meet my questioning gaze. "It doesn't surprise me. From what I've heard from older relatives, women had difficulty finding professional positions in those days, especially since it was not long after the men came home from the war."

"I guess that makes sense. According to my mom, Isabella only worked at the estate for a few years. Then she disappeared for a year or two before showing up here in Beaufort and buying the house that later became Chapters."

"Really? Your family must've been very concerned."

"Yes, they were. Especially since she never contacted them between the time she left the estate and her eventual move to Beaufort. I remember Grandma fussing about that years later, at one of our family reunions."

Shandy wriggled with pleasure as Ellen absently scratched a spot behind the little dog's ear. "Things were a bit crazy in the fifties for a lot of people, but the economy was booming. Maybe Isabella found a way to make some quick cash." Ellen side-eyed me. "A way the family wouldn't have approved of, perhaps?"

"Yes, but that's the thing—how did she manage it? She was working as a maid, left that job, and then *poof!*—two years later she had enough money to buy Chapters and begin building her fabulous library." I scratched a mosquito bite on my bare forearm. "You know, I never really thought about it before, but when Lincoln Delamont suggested something was amiss with that story, it made me reconsider Isabella's past."

"Ah, the plot thickens." Ellen tapped her foot against the pavers. "Did Delamont insinuate that Isabella was involved in some sort of illegal activity?"

"Yes. He implied that she stole some rare books and other valuables from her employers, then sold the items to fund her new life in Beaufort." I pressed my thumb against the bite, which I'd scratched to bleeding. "I thought he was just threatening to expose an old scandal so I'd sell him some valuable books at a discount. Then last night his daughter, who read some notes he'd kept about his investigation into Isabella's past, accused me of killing him to keep the story quiet."

"I see." Ellen pushed back her hat, allowing it to hang from the ribbons tied around her neck. "I wouldn't worry. Personally, I doubt there's any truth in Delamont's tale. Yes, Isabella was very evasive about how she made enough money to buy her house and live there for so long before having to convert it to an income property. But I have another theory." Ellen cast me an amused glance. "I always suspected there was a man involved. A sugar daddy, I guess you'd say. Someone who couldn't marry her but wanted to keep her in style."

"Really?" Considering this suggestion, I realized it wasn't out of the realm of possibility. Despite possessing beauty, intelligence, and charm, Isabella Harrington had never married. In fact, she'd never even mentioned any "gentlemen friends" to my family. If she'd had a secret lover—perhaps a wealthy man who wouldn't, or couldn't, leave his wife—that might explain a lot of things. Not just her single status, but also her ability to live at Chapters for years without any obvious means of support. "Supposing that were true, do you think she turned Chapters into a bed-and-breakfast in the early eighties because her benefactor died or something? I mean, she didn't seem to need the money before then."

Ellen stared out over the harbor. "I can't say. Despite our many conversations, Isabella never breathed a word about such a thing. She claimed she went into the lodging business simply because she was bored."

"Which means Lincoln Delamont could've been lying, just as I thought."

"Probably, although"—Ellen set a restless Shandy down and rose to her feet—"it's hard to say for certain. Isabella, for all her outward chattiness, was quite secretive in many ways. I suppose it's possible she engaged in some shady business to set herself up in style. She did have a rather offhand relationship with the law."

"In what way?" I stood and trailed Ellen and Shandy onto the wooden boardwalk that flanked the docks.

"Oh, she fudged her taxes, for one thing." Ellen pulled her hat back up onto her head as Shandy danced on the end of the leash, anxious to keep moving. "I was always afraid the IRS would come calling, but as far as I know, they never did." Ellen glanced at me. "From my handling of the trust, I believe that mess was all sorted out before you inherited Chapters."

"The lawyers did tell me they had to pay some significant back taxes out of the estate." Processing the idea that perhaps my great-aunt had been a thief as well as a tax evader, I frowned. "But if what Lincoln Delamont said was true, why was she never suspected of stealing from her former employers during her life-time? Surely if things went missing, it would've been noticed when she left."

"Maybe that's why she disappeared? Or—perhaps she had an accomplice?" Ellen's tone was as light as the wispy clouds drifting through the pale-blue sky. "I understand there were several sons in that family, and a few of them were the right age to appreciate a young woman with Isabella's charms. Maybe one of them helped her take a few valuables and covered up any losses."

"You mean, one of them could've also become her lifelong benefactor." I grimaced as another thought occurred to me. "Or her blackmailer."

"I doubt that." Ellen leaned against the wooden railing sepa-rating the boardwalk from the water below. "Isabella wasn't the kind of person to put up with that sort of thing for long. No, I think if that was the scenario, it would've been a love match, and they would've been in on the theft together."

I gazed out over the water. The emerald shoreline of nearby Carrot Island, a refuge for wild horses and other native animals, glittered in the early-morning sunlight. "That's the romantic way to look at it, but I'm not convinced. Now that I think about it, I remember my late grandmother saying that Isabella seemed much happier in her later years, even though establishing and running Chapters required so much time and effort."

"Did she?" Ellen's gaze remained fixed on the horizon. "Of course, I didn't know Isabella until the eighties, so I couldn't say if that was true or not. But I'm glad to hear it."

"What if she made a devil's bargain and was only freed by the death of her secret lover?" I winced as I pondered this possibility. "She lost her benefactor but gained her freedom."

"Yes, freedom." Ellen rolled her shoulders as if casting off some burden. "That would've been important to Isabella, I think. She was definitely no shrinking violet or clinging vine."

"That's true. Not that I got to interact with her that much. She only visited us occasionally. We never came to Beaufort because she claimed her home was her business and she couldn't put up non-paying guests. But I remember how fiercely independent she was."

"Yes." Ellen seemed lost in thought. "Anyway, this is all speculation. We have no proof."

"And, maybe, neither did Lincoln Delamont, although he appeared confident about his information." I brushed a wind-blown lock of hair from my eyes. "But my guess is that he didn't really want to expose the truth, whatever it was. He just hoped he could use the rumors he'd collected to compel me to sell him some of Isabella's rare books at bargain-basement prices."

"That seems likely." Ellen moved away from the railing as Shandy pulled against his leash. "Honestly, Charlotte, I wouldn't waste any more time worrying about what Isabella might or might not have done." She yanked the brim of her hat down a little lower on her forehead. "We should keep walking. Shandy has no patience for just standing around."

"You really think Lincoln was bluffing?" I followed Ellen and the Yorkie to the end of the boardwalk.

"Don't you?" Ellen paused to check for traffic before crossing to the corner of Front Street and Turner. "Considering he wasn't the most honest of individuals . . ."

"That's true," I said, thinking of Scott's comments from the evening before. *But*—I stared speculatively at Ellen's back as I trailed the older woman and her dog—*I wonder how Ellen knew about that aspect of Lincoln Delamont's character.*

"Well then, who's to say he knew anything salacious about Isabella? As a dealer in rare books, he'd probably heard a great deal about her and her private library over the years. Maybe enough to concoct a story he planned to use to take advantage of you."

"That makes sense." I increased my stride to keep up with Ellen's fast pace. "More sense than my great-aunt being a thief, anyway. It's just too bad his daughter had to stumble over his lies."

"Before he was murdered, you mean?" Ellen cast me a wry smile. "No, I'm not suspecting you of stabbing him, although I can understand a desire to do so."

"That's just it, though," I said, as we trotted down Ann Street. "There are any number of people who actually had a reason to kill him."

"Oh?" Ellen paused at the gate to her front yard. "You've identified some suspects?"

I glanced at the back bumper of a police car parked beside the bed-and-breakfast. "Perhaps we shouldn't talk about that out in the open."

"Join me on my porch then. We'll be out of view of the officers there." Ellen unlatched her front gate and motioned for me to walk ahead of her. "You must share. I wouldn't mind a go at some amateur sleuthing. Things have been dull as tombs around here recently."

I stepped into Ellen's small front yard. "I don't know. I haven't worked it all out, so I might be casting aspersions without any basis in fact."

"Then you definitely need me as a sounding board. Who better? I'm certainly not a suspect, unlike anyone who was at Chapters last night." Ellen latched the gate behind her before unhooking Shandy's leash from his harness.

The dog bounded away, running in circles around the shrubs dotting the yard while Ellen and I climbed the short flight of steps that led up to the covered front porch.

"Okay, I'll share my thoughts. But only if you agree to tell me if my ideas are complete nonsense." I settled onto a white porch swing. "It would be nice to hear another opinion."

Ellen sat down in a turquoise Adirondack chair. "Just like in the classic novels. I can be your Captain Hastings or Watson."

I pushed off from the wooden floor of the porch with one sneakered foot, setting the swing in motion. "Sorry, but I don't think I qualify as a Poirot or Holmes. You'd fit that profile better."

"Nonsense. I'm just an eccentric old lady," Ellen said with a smile. "Now—lay out the facts for me, or at least as much as you understand."

I took a deep breath before outlining my observations of everyone I considered a suspect, including Alicia, Tara, Jennifer, and Scott. I didn't tell Alicia the details about Lincoln swindling Scott's father, though, and I didn't mention Julie, not wanting to share information, even with Ellen, about her involvement with Lincoln. I knew the story would undoubtedly come out, but I wasn't going to be the one to shine a spotlight of suspicion on my friend.

"I can't imagine Mr. Kepler stabbing anyone, can you? Although I suppose we must leave him on the list," Ellen said, when I'd finished my spiel. "And you left out Damian Carr. He had access to the key and the knife, and from what I hear, he does have a temper."

I crossed my ankles and lifted my feet, allowing the swing to move freely. "True, but I haven't figured out his motive. Although I suppose I don't really know everyone that Lincoln interacted with in the Beaufort area over the last few years."

"This wasn't his first trip here, from what I understand."

"No, when he made the reservation, Lincoln told me he'd visited here many times before." I eyed Ellen, wondering how she knew so much about a random visitor's activity.

"There you go. He could have made enemies you don't know about. Like Damian, or any of the locals at your party."

I couldn't repress a chuckle. "Surely not the Sandberg sisters."

"Are you certain? I daresay Bernadette could wield a knife with the best of them, and sometimes it's the most unlikely people who commit crimes. At least that's been my experience." Ellen leaned back in her chair and stared up at the slowly spinning ceiling fan. "From books and true crime shows, I mean."

"I suppose anything is possible, even if not probable." I halted the motion of the swing before glancing at my watch. "But look at the time—I'd better go and help Alicia with breakfast or I'll never hear the end of it."

"As long as she doesn't have a knife, I think you'll be okay," Ellen said, as I leapt off the swing and headed for the porch steps.

I cast her a raised-eyebrow look over my shoulder. "Very droll, but I think I'll be safe in my own kitchen."

"One of the deadliest rooms in the house. Statistically, I mean," Ellen replied, as I bounded down the steps and into the yard.

I shot her a smile before using one foot as a barricade to keep Shandy inside the fence while I slipped out the front gate. "Anyway, thanks for listening," I called out from the sidewalk.

"Always glad to play sidekick, detective," Ellen replied with a cheery wave.

Striding toward the kitchen door, I considered Ellen's offer. I knew I should keep my nose out of this case. And I definitely had no business dragging my elderly neighbor into it. Neither one of us was a trained investigator, or even an experienced amateur sleuth.

*But we're smart women*, I thought, as I shoved open Chapters' back door. *And like some of the famous classic mystery heroines, we're also older and easy to overlook. The kind of women a lot of people might underestimate.*

Maybe just the kind of sleuths the situation required.

# Chapter Nine

A clanging of pots and pans assailed my ears as I stepped into the kitchen.

"What's up?" I asked, closing the door behind me.

"Interfering cops, that's what." Alicia slammed a frying pan down onto the gas stove.

*Thank goodness the burners are heavy metal*, I thought, before forcing a smile. "Have they been in the house again this morning?"

"Yes, asking all sorts of stupid questions."

I strolled over to the counter where the percolator bubbled and hummed. "What about, or can't you say?"

"Some coat and hat they found out near the carriage house. Stuffed into a plastic bag that was shoved inside that gardening bin under the windows. Guess they thought the killer used it as a disguise or something. 'Course, as I told them, I know nothing about it."

I poured coffee into one of the white ceramic mugs Alicia had set out on the counter. "Neither do I, which is what I'll tell them when they ask."

"I'm sure they will. They seemed pretty darned interested in figuring out who hid that stuff there."

"Makes sense, I guess." Realizing I was stirring the creamer in my coffee furiously enough to whip butter, I removed the spoon and placed it on the tray set up to collect dirty utensils. "If the killer used those items to cover their clothes . . ."

Alicia shook her head. "No blood on them, from what I heard. Or overheard, I should say." She cracked an egg into the pan with one hand before glancing over her shoulder at me. "I may have listened in on a couple of the younger officers. Chatty lot, I must say."

"Which means they probably weren't worn during the murder." I pondered this as I sipped my coffee. "Maybe the killer was going to use them for a getaway but decided against it. Or realized they could slip away without any disguise."

"Could be. Or it might just have been a guest from another event. Someone could've stored those items there for some kind of surprise, then forgot all about them." Alicia waved her spatula through the air like a baton. "It was an old trench coat and fedora, from what I heard."

"Overheard," I said, my lips quirking upward.

"Well, if you want to get technical . . ." Alicia tugged her hairnet over some loose curls spilling down the back of her neck. "Anyway, the coat and hat looked like items from the thirties or forties, according to those cops. Like something a guest might've worn to the party we held for the Dashiell Hammett weekend."

I took a long swallow of my coffee as I watched Alicia expertly flip the eggs. The older woman seemed determined to find a reason the garments would've been hidden in that garden bin—a reason unrelated to the previous night's party and murder. Which raised my curiosity as well as the hair on my arms.

"I suppose that's possible," I said, deciding that alerting Alicia to my suspicions was not a smart move. "They took the coat and hat away for analysis, I suppose."

"Yep. Sending them to the lab, they said." Alicia lifted the perfectly cooked over-easy eggs with the spatula and slid them onto a plate. "Could you carry this into the dining room? Mr. Kepler's in there all by his lonesome. I thought I'd make something to order." She turned and held out the plate. "There's also some toasted English muffins and bacon in the warming oven."

"Sure." Taking the plate from Alicia, I looked her squarely in the eyes. "The carriage house key never showed up?"

"Nope. Nor that knife. Got asked about them again too." Alicia wiped her hands on her apron. "Vanished into thin air as far as I'm concerned, I told them."

"I'm sure the police will eventually sort it out." I kept my tone light. Staring into the housekeeper's dark eyes, I tried to imagine her as a murderer. It seemed improbable.

*But definitely not impossible*, I thought, as I collected the muffins and bacon from the warming oven. *Not if it meant protecting Isabella Harrington's reputation and the solvency of Chapters.*

I carried the full plate into the dining room, where Scott sat at one of the tables, reading the morning paper.

"Ah," he said, folding the newspaper and setting it aside. "Smells delicious."

"Ms. Simpson went all out for you this morning." I set the plate in front of him. "Eggs cooked to order, no less."

"Thanks." When Scott looked up, I noticed the dark circles under his eyes.

"No problem. The others haven't come down for breakfast and I think Alicia was eager to cook for someone."

"Well, I can certainly understand Jennifer and Tara Delamont not being interested in food." Scott picked up the pepper grinder. "They're the only other guests here, right?"

"Yes. The Rowleys are staying on their yacht. Although, surprisingly, I had a message from them about tonight's scheduled book discussion."

Scott, grinding pepper over his eggs, didn't look up. "You're going ahead with that?"

"I thought maybe I should. It's not the guests' fault everything has gotten so messed up. I thought I'd try to keep to the schedule as much as possible." I gnawed the inside of my cheek for a moment. "The Rowleys and the local people have all agreed to come back, so we'll have around six participants tonight. Of course, you're welcome to join in if you wish."

Scott set down the grinder. "I never paid for any events."

"I know, but I'm pretty sure that neither Jennifer nor Tara Delamont will feel like joining us. You could take their place. We planned the refreshments for the number of guests, and we'll be missing two." I grimaced at the thought of Lincoln lying in some morgue. "No, three. So you're welcome to join us."

"I'll think about that. I have read a bit of Tey. A while ago, but maybe I can remember enough to add one pithy comment to the discussion."

"Frankly, I think your presence would be a welcome addition. It might balance out the dynamic between the lodgers and the locals."

"Thanks, but you didn't have to add the disclaimer." Scott cast me a crooked grin. "I like to think I'm a welcome addition at any event."

I stared down at my hands, which were clasped tightly at my waist. "Of course. I didn't mean to imply otherwise."

"Don't worry. I was just teasing you." As Scott speared his eggs with his fork, the yolks pooled around the ruffled edges of the whites.

*Like a halo.* I shook my head at this fanciful thought. "I suppose I should get back to the kitchen. I do hope your day turns out much better than yesterday."

"Not too hard to achieve," Scott said, glancing up from his plate. "If anyone asks—like the police—I'll be visiting a friend at the Maritime Museum today. He has some information that might prove useful for my book."

"Okay." I flashed him my practiced hostess smile before leaving the room.

Entering the kitchen, I was surprised to find Damian slouched against one of the counters.

"What are you doing here so bright and early?"

"I got called in by the cops. They wanted to ask me about some stupid coat and hat, and"—Damian shot a fierce glance at Alicia—"a missing kitchen knife."

"And key," Alicia muttered, without turning away from the sink.

"Right, those clothes they found out in the garden bin near the carriage house." I kept my tone light, having no interest in enflaming the animosity brewing between Alicia and the young chef.

"Just as I did last night, I told them I left Chapters before that fellow was murdered," Damian said. "Lots of people saw me storm off after that argument with Pete Nelson. Pretty sure that's when Lincoln Delamont was still alive and kicking, so I don't know why I'd be considered a suspect."

*Because you could easily have grabbed both that key and the knife, and you live close enough to sneak back without any difficulty.* I bit my lower lip to prevent me from voicing those facts out loud.

Alicia turned around. "Don't be silly. They have to check into you, same as the rest of us. Everyone who was here last night is a suspect."

"Including me," I said. "I'm sure I'll be grilled again as well. It's what the authorities have to do in these situations."

"It still ticks me off." Damian crossed his arms over his chest. "Why would I want to kill some stranger? It's not like I knew the guy. You all had more interactions with him than I did. I only caught glimpses of him at dinner last night."

As I examined Damian, I noticed the tension tightening his shoulders and jaw. "You never encountered him in Beaufort before? When he registered, Lincoln told me he'd made several previous visits. I thought, since you've temped in several restaurants in the area—"

"What? That I stabbed him because he sent a dish back one too many times?" As the words exploded from Damian's lips, Alicia shot a questioning glance at me.

"Of course not. But I thought maybe you'd seen him some-where, since you've worked so many different places." I spoke in the soothing tone I'd perfected in dealing with hormonal teenag-ers. "If so, even if it's something you only remember upon reflec-tion, I think it would be better to tell the police that up front, rather than have them find out later."

I didn't add that I was suggesting this because I myself hadn't mentioned Lincoln's hints of blackmail. I'd have to deal with any fallout over my own omissions. I didn't want Damian to face the same problem.

"I didn't know the guy, okay?" Damian strode across the room and stared at the broken ice machine. "Sorry about this. Like I said, dock my pay to cover the repair."

"Trust me, I will. The next time you chef for us." I met Damian's gaze and held it. "Yes, I will hire you again. Your talent overrules some of your bad behavior." I raised one finger as he opened his mouth to reply. "Some. But don't break anything of mine again or I might change my mind."

"I promise to watch my temper in the future." Damian cast Alicia a sharp glance as she snorted at this comment.

"Good. Because I want to work with you, but I can't afford to replace kitchen appliances on a regular basis."

"Cheaper to replace chefs." Alicia turned away and made a great show of rattling the pan lids she'd pulled from the overhead rack.

The noise covered the sound of someone entering the kitchen from the hall.

"Sorry, I just wanted some coffee," Tara said without looking at me.

"Of course. Please help yourself." I moved away from the counter and motioned toward the percolator and mugs. "I think I'll just go check on a few things."

As she walked away, I noticed how pale and drawn she looked. *Haunted*, I thought. *Which isn't surprising, considering her father's untimely passing.* I frowned as I pondered Jennifer Delamont as a prime suspect in Lincoln's murder. If that turned out to be true, it would be tragic, not just for Jennifer—and Lincoln, of course—but also for their daughter.

After stepping out into the hall, I pressed my fingertips against my temples for a moment. I might suspect everyone at Chapters, but I couldn't allow those thoughts to cloud my mind. Yes, it was possible that Jennifer had stabbed her philandering husband, but it was also possible that the killer was someone else. *Someone like Scott*, I thought, glancing over at the open door to the dining room. *Someone Lincoln cheated or swindled.*

I sighed. Apparently, Lincoln had been the type of person a lot of people might have wanted dead. Which wasn't going to make discovering his killer a walk on the beach.

# Chapter Ten

"Can I help?"

I peered through the laddered back of the chair I was holding. Todd Rowley stood in the hall, the front door standing open behind him. "Yes, thanks. If you could close the door and then grab a couple of the chairs from the dining room, that would be great. I'm afraid there isn't enough seating in the library for this evening's book discussion."

"Kelly will be along in few minutes. She forgot her notes for tonight and went back to the yacht for them." Todd shut the front door before lifting a chair with each hand. "I'm surprised you expect a good crowd after last night. Honestly, one reason Kelly and I decided to join in was because we were afraid no one would show up."

My hands still gripping the chair, I blew a lock of hair away from my eyes. "It is a bit surprising, but everyone except Jennifer and Tara agreed to attend. I guess they wanted something to take their minds off yesterday's tragedy."

"Or to check out the other guests, looking for any telltale signs that one of them is the murderer." Todd strode past me, the chairs swinging in his grip. "Library, you said?"

"Yes, thanks. Just drop them anywhere. I'll arrange the seating later," I said, following him.

"I hope you don't mind that we decided to move back to the yacht." Todd set down the chairs and turned to face me. "It's nothing against you or your hospitality."

I set down my own chair before replying. "Don't worry, I totally understand. Honestly, I think if I could stay somewhere else for a few days, I would."

"It must have been quite a shock." Todd's gaze was as sympathetic as his tone.

"Yes, murders don't occur here every day." I offered him a wan smile.

"Ironic to have it happen during an event honoring a murder-mystery author." Todd looked over my shoulder. "Oh hello, sweetheart. Find your notes?"

I turned toward the door, where Kelly Rowley stood, clutching a notebook to her chest.

"Yes, just where I left them. Hello, Charlotte. I hope you aren't feeling too bad today. Yesterday was so horrible."

Kelly's honey-blonde hair was hanging loose, making her thin face look more angular than usual. I examined the younger woman, noticing her extreme pallor and chapped lips. *Of course,* I reasoned, *that's only natural. Not everyone has dealt with a shocking death before.* "I hope you recovered your cloak in all the confusion. Your costume was so lovely. I'd hate to think you a lost part of it."

Kelly blinked rapidly. "My cloak? Oh yes, I got it. Thanks." She used both hands to sweep her hair behind her shoulders. "Anyway, as Todd may have told you, he and I decided to participate in any events you host this week." Kelly moved to her husband's side. "I mean, we really doubt that Mr. Delamont was killed by one of the staff or a guest. It could've just as easily been someone from the outside."

Todd slipped his arm around his wife's shoulders. "Yes, we talked about it, and the truth is, Delamont was at the carriage house, which is hidden from view if you're in the main house or even on the patio. Anyone could've snuck into that section of the backyard without the rest of us noticing." He tightened his arm around Kelly. "That's partially why we were determined to be here tonight—to show that we don't suspect any of the staff or guests."

"Thanks for that. But I worry that a few others won't be quite so understanding." I tipped my head and looked over the entrepreneur and his wife. "I suppose you've heard Tara Delamont's claim that I'm the killer?"

Todd waved his free hand as if shooing away a bothersome insect. "Yes, but we dismissed it as the ravings of a young girl who'd just received a terrible shock. I'm sure she'll apologize once the investigation clears you."

"I don't even care about that. As you say, she was probably in shock." I scooted one of the chairs across the floor and placed it at the edge of the Oriental rug that covered the center of the room. "I just hope the authorities discover what actually happened, sooner rather than later."

"I'm sure they will," Todd said.

Kelly turned aside, staring at one of the bookshelves. "I don't know. Lots of murder cases go unsolved, you know. It's not like in books."

"Yes, life is never quite so neat and tidy." I dusted off my hands. "Thanks again for the help, but I won't keep you. I'm arranging the seating now just to have it done, but the discussion won't start for"—I glanced at my wristwatch—"another hour and a half."

The Rowleys offered further assistance with setting up the room, but I waved them off. "No, you've done enough. You are guests, after all. Please—feel free to stop by the kitchen if you'd like a drink of any kind. Alicia is putting together refreshments for later, but I'm sure she'd be happy to open a bottle of wine or whatever else you might like. If you just want to relax, the front-porch rockers are available, or you can use the parlor."

After Todd and Kelly left, I took a moment to lean against the desk, taking a deep breath to shake off a surge of panic. Every time I spoke to any the guests, my mind questioned their innocence, and although it seemed unlikely that either of the Rowleys could've been involved, I still couldn't strike them off my suspect list. Which made talking about the murder with them unnerving.

The hardest person to contemplate as a killer was Julie, of course. I really couldn't wrap my mind around the idea of my friend harming anyone, but I was worried that the authorities would view her motive as more compelling than most. Which just made me more determined to discover the actual murderer, sooner rather than later. Or, barring that, I hoped to at least clear Julie's name before her relationship with Lincoln became public knowledge.

When I'd arranged the chairs in a wide circle, I checked my watch again. With an hour to spare before the book discussion, I decided to retreat to my room. I wanted some time alone before facing my guests again.

Sitting on the edge of my bed, I absently picked up the framed picture of Isabella I'd placed on the nightstand. It was a black-and-white photo, showing a young Isabella arm in arm with her older sister, my Grandma Ruth.

"What exactly did you get up to?" I examined Isabella's face, with its classic features, arresting eyes, and well-shaped brows. She'd been a lovely young woman. Not as tall as her lanky sister but more voluptuous, she'd been blessed with masses of wavy brown hair and deep-set dark eyes. In the photo, her hair was swept back from her broad forehead by a pale velvet headband, giving her the look of an older Alice Liddell. "So, Isabella, what rabbit hole or mirror did you fall into after you left that estate? And what treasure did you find, or steal, there?"

Of course, I received no reply. I placed the photo back on the nightstand with a sigh. Having known my great-aunt only when she was older, I'd never given much thought to Isabella's younger years. I drummed my fingers against the nightstand. Perhaps because they'd never been a topic of conversation at family gatherings. Any discussions involving Isabella had focused solely on her life in Beaufort.

*Almost as if she didn't exist before then*, I thought, rising and crossing to my dresser. I picked up a silver-plated hairbrush that had once belonged to Isabella and ran its soft bristles through my own hair. *Or maybe the older members of my family did know about some scandal in her past and were careful to avoid conversations that touched on that subject.*

Knowing my Grandma Ruth's outlook on life, I could imagine her refusing to entertain any notion that her sister might've had a lover, especially if the man had been married. While Grandma was tolerant enough not to cut Isabella out of her life over such a thing, she wouldn't have publicly acknowledged the possibility. Definitely not to anyone else in the family, much less strangers.

*Which doesn't mean it didn't happen.* I tapped the back of the brush against my palm and considered the alternative, which was much less pleasant. If Isabella had actually been a con artist or thief . . .

*No*, I decided, *I definitely prefer the sugar-daddy option.* I laid down the brush and resolved to search the attic again. Digging through some of the papers and photographs stored there might reveal the truth.

But not today. As I peered into the mirror hanging above the dresser, I realized I looked almost as pinched and drained as Kelly Rowley.

Dashing into my attached bathroom, I slapped on another coat of lipstick and a swipe of blush before heading out to join Alicia in the kitchen.

*If I have to face a murderer*, I thought grimly, *I'd better look less like death.*

\* \* \*

Todd and Kelly were waiting in the library when I carried in the first tray of hors d'oeuvres. They were both clutching empty wineglasses, so I hurried back to the kitchen to grab some chardonnay.

"Is this okay, or do you prefer the red?" I asked when I returned with a bottle.

"No, white is fine," Todd said, and Kelly nodded her agreement. "Better for this warm weather."

I refilled their glasses before making several trips to the kitchen to collect more snacks and additional bottles of wine, along with the requisite glasses and a few nonalcoholic drink options.

The Sandberg sisters were the next to arrive. They bustled into the library like pigeons flocking toward a pile of bread crumbs, greeting the Rowleys in tones that held friendliness and suspicion in equal measure. They were followed by Pete and Sandy Nelson, who both clutched white paper bags.

"Thought you might appreciate some extra food." Pete held up the bag. "I've got lettuce wraps, and Sandy's toting some homemade veggie chips."

"Thanks, but you didn't have to do that." In their matching Dancing Dolphin logo T-shirts and khaki shorts, the café owners looked both ordinary and innocent. I couldn't imagine either one of them plunging a knife into Lincoln Delamont, but . . . someone had.

"Just leftovers from the lunch rush," Sandy said. "You want these in the kitchen?"

"Yes, thanks. Ask Alicia to find a serving platter for you."

"No problem." Sandy grabbed the other bag from Pete's hand and headed into the hall.

"How about our real murder mystery? It's the wildest thing I've been involved in, I must say." Ophelia Sandberg sank down into one of the room's leather armchairs, fanning her face with a sheaf of handwritten notes.

"Not me." Bernadette slumped into the library's other armchair. "I was a nurse in 'Nam. Nothing was, or ever will be, crazier than that. Or more tragic," she added, staring down at her broad, blunt-nailed hands.

Pete sat in one the hard-backed dining room chairs. "I guess after that, nothing shocks you anymore." He patted the chair next to him as Sandy reentered the room. "Sit here, dear."

"Yes, very little surprises me." Bernadette looked up. "Hello, Julie. Ready to discuss murder?"

I turned toward the hall, where Julie had paused, one hand braced against the door frame. "Hi, Jules. Glad you could join us."

"I thought I'd better, or you guys would probably label me as the killer." Despite her bright smile, tension edged Julie's voice. She stepped into the room but stopped short beside the desk, which had been converted into a serving table by the addition of a white linen tablecloth.

I noticed that Julie had also chosen to wear more blush and lipstick than normal, and that her long black hair was twisted into a messy ponytail. This was unusual. Julie was typically very particular about her appearance.

*Of course, if she's only recently stabbed her lying lover to death . . .* I shook my head as my friend poured herself a full glass of wine. No, that wasn't any way to think. The haunted expression in Julie's chestnut-brown eyes could just as easily be due to the one-two punch of discovering that her boyfriend was still quite married right before he was also suddenly found quite dead.

"Excuse me while I see if Alicia needs any help in the kitchen." I motioned toward the desk. "Please, help yourselves to the hors d'oeuvres and drinks. And go ahead and start the discussion if you want. I won't be long."

As I left the room, I reached out and patted Julie's rigid arm. "Glad you're here."

Her dark eyes flashed. "Thought I'd better be. I know how people would talk otherwise."

I opened my mouth to say something about no one thinking Julie was a murderer, but clamped my lips shut instead. I might not believe she was guilty, but I knew others could be eyeing her as the culprit. *All the more reason for me to keep looking for evidence that will point the finger elsewhere*, I thought.

In the kitchen, I conferred with Alicia about any additional food for the event before stepping out the back door. A little fresh air sounded like the perfect antidote for the headache throbbing behind my eyes.

A police officer was no longer stationed at the back door. But there was still one officer monitoring the area around the carriage house. I strolled over to the perimeter established by yellow caution tape. "Everything quiet out here?" I asked the woman.

"No sign of trouble so far." The officer shifted from one leg to the other.

It had to be uncomfortable to wear a full uniform, including a gun holster, in the June heat. "Can I get you some water?" I asked, allowing my gaze to sweep over the carriage house. Police activity had torn up the grass around the building, but at least the azaleas that flanked the front door had remained undamaged.

"Why sure, water would be great," the officer replied, pushing her hat back so she could wipe her damp forehead with her hand. "Pretty hot out here tonight."

"Yes, it is. I'll grab you a bottle, or at least have one brought out to you." As I considered whether I could spare the time to carry out the water myself or would need to ask Alicia's help, my attention was captured by a flash of purple in one of the azalea bushes. It wasn't a blossom, as those were already faded and, anyway, they had been pale pink. This looked like sunlight bouncing off a small, faceted object . . .

"Hold it. There's something caught up there, next to the door." I pointed toward the azaleas.

The officer turned to examine the shrub. "Yes, there is. Wonder how the investigators missed that." She pulled a pair of evidence gloves from an inside pocket of her jacket and slipped them on.

"It was dark out, even with the patio floodlights. They probably couldn't see that little thing buried in all that thick foliage."

"Likely so." The officer reached into the azalea and plucked out the object. Gripping it between her thumb and forefinger, she held it up to the light. "Looks like some sort of costume jewelry."

A swear word escaped my lips.

The officer, shaking out the small evidence bag she'd taken from her pocket, narrowed her eyes. "You recognize it?"

"Yes." I audibly swallowed before speaking again. "That looks like one of the fake gems I noticed last night at the party. It was glued to a costume."

"Worn by?" The officer dropped the bit of purple plastic into the evidence bag before focusing her intense gaze on my face.

"The victim's daughter," I said reluctantly. "Tara Delamont."

# Chapter Eleven

When I returned to the library, a lively discussion was already under way.

"I still don't think it would be possible," Bernadette said.

"What's that?" I asked, taking a seat next to Kelly Rowley.

"Bernie doesn't buy the premise of Tey's story *Brat Farrar*," Ophelia said.

I settled back in my chair. "Which part?"

"The idea that one person could successfully impersonate another," Bernadette replied, her face brightening as she gazed over my shoulder. "Oh hello, Mr. Kepler. Glad you could join us. It will be nice to have an author's input in the discussion."

"Not a fiction author, though. And please, call me Scott." He crossed the room to stand next to me. "Mind if I sit here?" he asked, motioning toward the adjacent empty chair.

"Of course not," I said absently, my thoughts occupied with my concern over the discovery of that piece of Tara's costume. *Surely the girl didn't kill her own father . . .* I took a deep breath to calm my nerves as I scooted my chair over slightly to allow Scott to sit down. "Now, what were you saying, Bernadette?" I asked, leaning forward. "Something about *Brat Farrar*? I do love that book. One of my favorites from Tey."

Bernadette pursed her lips. "Oh, nothing against the story or the writing. It's just that I don't think anyone could impersonate a missing family member so well that they couldn't be detected."

"Really?" Pete clasped his hands over the slight bulge of his belly. "Knowing how foolish people can be, I can accept that particular plot point without much effort. I mean, just think of some of our patrons." He shared a knowing look with Sandy.

"And it's not an unusual convention in mystery stories," Todd said. "Patricia Highsmith does something similar in *The Talented Mr. Ripley*."

Bernadette dug her heels into the pile of the rug. "But the protagonist in that book doesn't actually encounter family members. Not under his assumed identity anyway. I just think family would know their own."

Pete leaned back in his chair. "Never underestimate the gullibility of the average joe."

Bernadette cut Pete a sidelong glance. "You're saying you think most people would be fooled by someone impersonating a supposedly long-dead family member?"

"If years had passed, yes. Especially if the person was a child when they disappeared. People can change dramatically as they age." Pete glanced at Sandy, who was studying her manicure as if the chipped polish on her nails held some secret clue. "And not just their appearance."

"That is true," Ophelia replied. "Believe it or not, I used to be dreadfully shy."

"But that's just growing and maturing," Todd said. "Other characteristics, like vocal or physical mannerisms, don't change much. At least I don't think so."

Scott shifted in his chair. "Tey did ensure that Brat was schooled by someone who knew the family well. He didn't just show up and try to pass himself off to the family without possessing all the pertinent information."

"Yes, she handled that well. Otherwise, I think the story would've seemed preposterous." Sandy looked up and met Scott's gaze. "The way Tey handled it, I could suspend my disbelief."

Bernadette narrowed her eyes. "I still say it wouldn't work. The family should've questioned Brat more, in my opinion. That would've seemed more realistic to me."

Kelly Rowley, who'd kept her head bowed over her tightly clasped hands ever since I entered the room, murmured, "You'd be surprised what people will accept as the truth, if they really want to believe it."

I turned to her. "You mean the family accepted Brat's story primarily because they wanted it to be true?"

Kelly lifted her head, shoving her hair behind her ears. "Of course. Wouldn't you, if your beloved nephew or brother had come back from the dead? You'd desperately want to believe, so you'd overlook the red flags and convince yourself that the impostor was telling the truth."

Scott, leaning forward, templed his fingers before addressing Kelly. "Good point, Ms. Rowley. It adds an interesting psychological dynamic to the story, don't you think?"

"Please call me Kelly, and yes, I suppose it does."

I noticed the deep lines bracketing Kelly's mouth. She was distressed, but then, so were all the others, despite their attempts to appear calm. A surreptitious glance around the room revealed that Sandy was twisting the hem of her T-shirt between her fingers, Pete was repeatedly tapping his foot against the rug, and Bernadette had rolled her notes into a baton she gripped like a weapon. Meanwhile, Ophelia gnawed on her pinkie nail every few seconds. As for Julie—she cradled her now-empty wineglass between her hands so tightly that I feared it would crack.

*She sure sucked that down fast*, I thought, as Julie leapt to her feet and stalked over to the draped desk to pour another glass. *But of course they're all tense, like me. Sitting in a room with a possible murderer will do that to a person.*

*And the killer is probably doubly afraid, fearing detection.* I glanced over at Todd Rowley, who appeared calm. But only if I ignored the whiteness of his knuckles as he gripped his chair arms.

"You mean if Brat had been trying to fool people who weren't emotionally invested in his story being true, it would've been a lot harder?" Sandy asked, before unclenching her fingers and smoothing out the bottom of her T-shirt.

"Well, sure." Scott sat back and stretched out his long legs. "As Kelly observed, the family wanted to believe, so they were more receptive to lies."

As I side-eyed him, I registered the rigidity of his normally mobile face. *Even he might be a murderer.* I hated the thought, especially since I still had hopes that his interest in Julie might offer her a better boyfriend option than Lincoln Delamont, married or not.

Or perhaps, like the family in *Brat Farrar*, I was just seeing what I wanted to see. Desperately hoping to prove that Julie was not the killer, I was probably looking at all the other guests with more suspicion than necessary. I absently ran my fingers through my hair, spiking it before smoothing it down again when I realized what I was doing. "Lies and deception are at the core of most mystery novels, aren't they? Interesting how they get handled by different authors. Tey seems to want to make Brat likable, despite his deception. In her case, I think it works, don't you?"

"Oh, definitely," Ophelia jutted out her chin.

I suppressed a nervous giggle. With her long neck and slightly beaky nose, she looked like an ostrich.

"Maybe that says something more about the readers than the characters. I mean, most people root for Ripley in the Highsmith books, and he's a sociopath. Or psychopath." Pete shrugged. "I always get those mixed up."

"But a clever one," Scott observed dryly. "I think that's part of the attraction to that type of character—someone can be despicable, but if they're clever enough, and implement intricate plans that entertain us, we forgive them, and maybe even cheer them on."

Todd unclenched his hands and glanced around the room. "Confess it, we all feel that way. I think it's our strange attraction to morally gray characters. Perhaps because they are more psychologically compelling than someone who is simply good or evil?"

I nodded. "Ruth Rendell was a master at creating that sort of character. Flawed, yet fascinating."

"Didn't she also write under a pen name?" Sandy asked. "I think we read one of her novels for book club a while back, but it was under a different name."

"Barbara Vine," Todd said, with a glance at his wife. "One of Kelly's favorites, isn't she, dear?"

"Yes." Kelly stared down at her hands, which were clasped in her lap. "She had such an incredible ability to get inside the head of even the most damaged characters and make you care about them, even while you deplore their actions."

"Oh, for goodness' sake." Wine sloshed over the rim of Julie's glass as she stalked across the room. She plopped down in a chair and took a long swallow before continuing. "Someone's been murdered—someone we all knew, even if only for a day—and here we sit, discussing literature like a bunch of overeager undergrads."

"It's better than sitting at home with our own thoughts," Sandy said, with a quick glance at her husband. "I told Pete we had to come. The breakfast and lunch rush kept me so busy I didn't have to think earlier today, but as soon as that was over . . ." She took a deep breath. "Well, I just got so antsy, I told Pete we had to attend this discussion."

Julie flung the hand clutching her wineglass toward Pete and Sandy. "And to prove neither of you was the killer? I know that's why most of you are here. Putting on a good show." She yanked her hand back.

*Thank goodness it's the white*, I thought, as droplets of wine flew from Julie's glass.

"That would be the smart thing to do, even if you were guilty." Scott raised his eyebrows as he looked across at Julie. "But protesting too much could also be a clever tactic."

"As would appearing totally cool and firing off snarky comments," Julie spat, jumping back to her feet.

*So much for my matchmaking*, I thought.

"Excuse me, but I think this was a mistake." Julie strode across the room, plunking down her wineglass on the desk before fleeing into the hall.

I carefully set my own glass on the floor next to my chair and stood. "Not to worry. I'll go and see if she's okay. You all just carry on with the discussion. And please, enjoy some of this," I added, motioning toward the snacks before I exited the room.

A slam confirmed my suspicion that Julie had dashed out onto the front porch. I followed, mentally rehearsing what I might say to my friend. Even though I didn't want Julie to think I suspected her of killing Lincoln, I did want to learn more about their relationship.

But as the front door closed behind me, Julie wheeled around and jabbed a forefinger at me. "You think I was mixed up in this, don't you?"

A breeze ruffled my hair, carrying with it the scent of water and a sharp longing to escape to the beach. "I heard you talking with Lincoln by the carriage house." I cleared my throat. "I wasn't trying to spy. I just stumbled upon you two, but when I realized you were having an affair . . ."

"We weren't!" Julie's chest rose and fell rapidly. "Yes, we were considering it. That's what this weekend was about," she added, in a quieter tone.

"But then he showed up with his wife and daughter in tow."

"Yeah." Julie turned aside. Gripping the porch railing with both hands, she stared at the craftsman bungalow across the street. "And yes, as you've undoubtedly guessed, he was my mystery man. We met when Lincoln visited Bookwaves a couple of times. It was just friendly at first—a few shared lunches and strolls on the boardwalk and that sort of thing. But then we started chatting online, and well"—Julie tossed her head, making her long ponytail bounce—"things got more involved."

"I assume he led you to believe he'd soon be free to date you openly?"

Julie expelled a gusty sigh. "Yes, he told me he was getting a divorce, that he'd already moved out of the house he shared with his wife."

"And he never mentioned his daughter." I moved close to Julie and placed a hand on her shoulder. "I'm sorry. It seems he wasn't very honest."

"He was a good liar, I'll give him that. He had me completely fooled." Julie turned her head to look at me. "But I didn't kill him."

"I know you didn't. The problem is, you do have a motive. Which means we need to be careful. Don't lie to the police or anything, but I'd make sure they know the whole story. And be clear about the fact that you didn't plan to encounter Lincoln's family. That will remove any suspicion that any of your actions could've been premeditated. I mean, I'm sure you wouldn't even have attended the costume party if you'd known Lincoln wasn't going to be alone."

Julie looked away. "Naturally, I was shocked when I saw Lincoln had included his family in what was supposed to be our romantic getaway. I couldn't understand why he would do that, even if he *had* lied about being legally separated. And yes, it made me angry. It was like he was rubbing his deception in my face."

"Okay, you were angry. But what actually went through your mind? Did you think maybe he wanted to break up with you?"

"Perhaps. Or maybe he hoped I'd just accept the situation." Julie turned to face me. "Like I'd agree to be his secret mistress forever, or something."

I shook my head. "I know better. You'd never stand for that."

"You better believe it." Julie crossed her arms over her breast. "I wasn't about to continue to sneak around. Not this girl."

"And that's what you were telling him when I overheard the two of you?"

"Basically. And, in case you missed that part, I broke it off with him too." She scrunched her nose. "I informed him that I had no intention of ever speaking with him again, either online or in person."

"Well, I hope you told the authorities that. I mean, if you broke it off, why would you feel compelled to kill him?" I looked my friend up and down. "Anyway, it's important that you were the one to end the relationship. Make sure the police know that."

Julie bowed her head, hiding a clear view of her face. "Sorry to inflict this soap opera on you. I know I was stupid. So very stupid."

As I heard Julie's voice crack on that last word, another scenario flitted through my mind. Maybe Lincoln hadn't taken Julie's dismissal well. Maybe he'd tried to force himself on her. Maybe Julie had struck him in self-defense . . .

*But she would've had to have grabbed that knife and the key ahead of time. Which makes it premeditated. No, that can't be right. Maybe Lincoln took the key, as well as the knife, planning to lure her into the carriage house and threaten her. Although that seems out of character for him, from what little I observed.* I shook my head. I couldn't sort all this out on my own.

*I need my Sherlock*, I thought, with a swift glance toward Ellen's house. "Why don't you run on home? I can make your excuses to the others." I motioned toward the door. "Did you bring a purse or anything? I can grab your stuff if you want to wait out here."

"No, I just carried my phone and my keys in my pocket. And thankfully I walked here, so no worries about me driving after drinking." A single tear skittered down Julie's cheek, streaking her blush. "Sorry, it's just so much to take in, all at once . . ."

I gave her a quick hug. "I totally understand. It has to be rough, discovering Lincoln's true nature and then experiencing the shock of his death. Don't be too hard on yourself."

Julie's lips trembled. "I know you mean well, but I can't . . ." She dashed more tears from her eyes with the back of one hand. "You don't know everything, and I can't tell you. Not now."

I stepped forward and patted her arm. "It's okay. Go home. Relax. It will all get sorted, sooner or later."

Julie pulled away so roughly that my hand flew up in the air. Turning on her heel, she made for the steps. "I know," she called back over her shoulder. "That's what worries me."

# Chapter Twelve

The book discussion fizzled soon after I returned to the library, disintegrating into a few half-hearted comments and desultory replies. Faced with one another's obvious lack of interest, the guests soon made excuses to depart, leaving me with far too much leftover food and a headache that wouldn't subside until I finally fell asleep hours later.

The next day, I called Ellen as soon as I felt it reasonable to phone someone on a Monday morning.

"I'd love to chat," she said, "but I'm volunteering at the fort today. Maybe you could drive over and meet me during my lunch break? We could walk on the beach and talk."

The fort was Fort Macon, a North Carolina state park located at the tip of Atlantic Beach. Offering views of the Atlantic Ocean, Bogue Sound, and Beaufort Inlet, it was a historic site and popular tourist destination. I'd visited there a few times, taking in the displays depicting the fort's history, from its start as a military defense post built in the early 1800s and its part in the Civil War to its use for coastal defense during World War II. Ellen, a history buff, volunteered a few days a month, working as a greeter at the information desk in the park's visitor center and, as a member of the Friends of Fort Macon, assisting with special events.

"I could do that, but I suspect the parking lot will be jammed," I said. "You know how it gets during the summer, especially with people trying to access the public beach near the fort."

"True, but usually enough people are coming and going to make an opening. I tell you what—if you have a problem finding a spot, call me. I can move my car behind another volunteer's vehicle long enough to free a place for your car. Especially since you'll only be there for an hour."

"I'll give it try. Noon okay?"

"See you then," Ellen said, and wished me a good morning before hanging up.

I pocketed my cell phone and considered what I could accomplish before I had to head over to Atlantic Beach. With only Scott and the seldom-seen Tara and Jennifer Delamont lodging at Chapters that week, Alicia and I had made quick work of breakfast. I had no events planned for the day, and so, despite the heat, I decided it was the perfect time to start my search of Isabella's papers and photos.

But before I could put my plan into action, my cell phone rang. Seeing it was Julie, I thought I'd better answer rather than let it go to voice mail.

I barely had a chance to say hello before Julie launched into the real reason for her call. "I just wanted to assure you that I didn't hate Lincoln despite everything."

"You mean despite the fact that he lied to you about being separated and getting a divorce and all that? Oh, and the fact that he had a daughter that he didn't tell you about." I clucked

my tongue. "I can actually see getting pretty angry over something like that."

"Of course I was angry. You saw that last night. But you
should know by now that I'm not one to pine over men. I mean,
when it's over, it's over, as far as I'm concerned."

"How did Lincoln take you breaking it off with him?"

"Not well, although he stayed calm and tried to charm me
into changing my mind. He didn't lose his temper. Not like . . ."
Julie fell silent before finishing this thought.

"Not like what?" I sat up straighter on my bed. "Had he lost
his temper with you before?"

There was a stretch of silence before she responded. "Yes,
once or twice. I mean, he never hit me or anything."

"But he'd scared you a little?" I stared at the opposite wall,
where I'd hung one of my wedding photos. Brent looked back at
me, his smile as gentle as always. We'd had arguments, of course,
but they'd always been fair fights, never ones that escalated to
the point where I felt threatened in any way.

"There was this one time when I got a little nervous, I guess.
He was visiting me at Bookwaves. No one else was in the shop.
He tried to kiss me, but I was worried that a customer could walk
in at any minute, so I pushed him away."

"I'm guessing he didn't like that."

"No. He grabbed my arm when I stepped back—"

"He grabbed you?" I tried, and failed, to keep disapproval
from coloring my voice.

"Yes, but it's not like he left a bruise or anything. Only, he
did hold me pretty tight. Which made me feel . . . uneasy, I
guess."

"You continued to see him after that?"

"Look, Miss Manners, it wasn't as bad as you're imagining. And at the time I just thought . . . well, I believed it showed he was passionate about me, you know."

I *hmph*ed before replying. "You've been reading too many of those bodice rippers you stock. You should have dumped him as soon as he pulled that little stunt."

Julie sighed deeply. "I know. But I'd just broken up with Henry right before I met Lincoln. You remember Henry—the monosyllabic guy who always seemed more interested in watching sports than in making love to me."

"You wanted to dive into a more passionate relationship with someone a bit mysterious? I can understand that. I may have done something similar once or twice in the past. Before Brent, of course."

"I suppose I was veering too far in the other direction. But anyway, I've always played it so safe in my love life. I just wanted to experience something a little more exciting. Which unfortunately translated into me deliberately ignoring the red flags I noticed when dealing with Lincoln."

"Live and learn," I said.

"I suppose." Julie didn't speak again for a few seconds. "I just wanted you to know, in case the investigation turned up some stuff that might make you wonder if Lincoln was . . . abusive."

It was my turn to fall silent for a moment. "Was he?"

"Not to me. Not really. But I did get this phone call from another girl he'd dated on the sly a while back."

"Someone from Beaufort?"

"Yes. I'd rather not mention names, if you don't mind. No use dragging her into this."

"Okay, but if she experienced his abusive side . . ."

"She said there had been some instances, but I don't know . . ." Julie cleared her throat. "I didn't believe her at first, of course. I just thought she was a jealous ex trying to stir up trouble."

"How in the world did she know you two were dating?" I asked, wondering if Julie had been less than careful in her dealings with Lincoln. If they'd been seen around town, it might've stirred jealous feelings in more than one woman, if my suspicions about Lincoln's playboy tendencies were correct.

*And that could mean more suspects*, I thought. *Someone besides Julie could be a jealous "other woman."*

"She said she saw us in the . . ." Julie cleared her throat again. "In a restaurant in town. Which was stupid of me, I know. We should've met outside Beaufort. We usually did, but there was one day when I was just too tired to drive anywhere."

"You don't have to share her name with me, but maybe you should tell the police," I said. "If she knew Lincoln, she might also know people who had it in for him."

"You mean besides her, or me?" Julie's tone was edged with bitterness. "I don't know, I think this sort of thing just looks bad for both of us. Since we are both women Lincoln mistreated and all that."

"Maybe, but it also might point the finger of suspicion away from you, especially if he had a pattern of abusing women."

"That's the thing—I don't know that he did. Like I said, he never really took it that far with me. And as for the woman who contacted me—well, I only have her word about what happened between them."

"But why would she call you? Do you think she might've wanted money to stay silent about your relationship? Although, come to think of it, that's a bit of a stretch. It's not like you're rich."

"No, but Lincoln is. Was." Julie inhaled an audible breath.

"Maybe she thought he'd pay up but didn't want to approach him directly. She might've wanted to use you as an intermediary because she was scared of him . . ."

"I can't imagine this person trying to shake down anyone," Julie said.

"But how well do you really know her? Isn't it possible that in an attempt to blackmail Lincoln, this woman could've asked him to meet her at the carriage house that night? Perhaps he did, meaning to pay her, but it all went horribly wrong. Maybe he even threatened her and she had to defend herself."

"I suppose. Although why would she have had that knife? I mean, I can understand stealing the key to sneak into the carriage house to meet Lincoln, but the knife part doesn't really add up."

Julie sounded strangely reluctant to pursue this line of inquiry, which made me wonder just who the woman might be. I respected Julie's discretion if this involved a friend, or even one of her bookstore regulars, but felt compelled to urge her to take action to protect herself. "Consider this—maybe it was Lincoln who swiped the knife and the key. He might have planned to get into the carriage house to talk to someone, like this other woman, in private. And if he wanted to warn someone to remain silent about his misdeeds, he could've taken the knife as a weapon. Or even as protection, if he was concerned that whoever he was meeting could become dangerous. At any rate, you should tell the police about this, if you haven't already. This woman could be another viable suspect."

"I'll mention it, even though I don't think that's possible because she doesn't live in this area anymore. But I guess I should say something, just in case. Especially since Lincoln did tell me he had to be wary of people trying to take advantage of him to get at his money."

"Where did it come from? His money, I mean. Surely not just from his business."

"No, he inherited a good chunk of cash from his family. Or so he said."

"I guess that explains how he was able to get into the rare-book business when he was young," I said. "When he was booking the week, he mentioned he'd been in that career since his mid-twenties, which I found odd. Unless he had family money, of course."

"Yeah, he had a trust fund or something. I didn't really ask too much about it. Didn't want to look like a gold digger."

I snorted. "As if. I've never known you to care that much about money."

"Proven by the fact that I run an independent bookstore," Julie said, her tone brighter than it had been throughout the rest of the call. "Okay, I guess I'd better go. Even though we aren't open on Mondays, I need to do some office and inventory work in the store. I'm sure you've got plenty to do as well. I just wanted to call and make sure you knew the true story. Before you hear anything else, I mean."

*The true story?* I stared at the phone for a minute. From what Julie had just told me, I assumed she wanted me to know that Lincoln Delamont might or might not have been abusive with women, in case those stories crawled out of the woodwork during the investigation. But apparently he'd not really acted like that around Julie, and she wanted to make sure I knew that, because . . . ? *Because if he'd threatened or hurt her, it might give her too strong a motive to kill him? Even if only in self-defense?*

"All right. Thanks for calling, Julie." I thought of reiterating my request that she share the information she'd just told me with the police, but instead chose to simply say, "Good-bye."

I tapped my phone against my palm. I certainly wouldn't say anything to the authorities. Not yet. Not until Julie had time to come clean on her own. Otherwise, it might make her situation even worse. While I did believe in justice, I was sure Julie was innocent.

Because, if by some shocking twist, Julie *had* killed Lincoln, I was convinced it would have to have been an act of self-defense. If that was the case, I was sure she would ultimately confess. But maybe she wasn't ready to come forward with that sordid story yet—one I knew might, rightly or wrongly, affect the way others viewed her. Including the local patrons who frequented her bookstore.

No, I wasn't going to rush out and give the police second-hand information. I'd wait a few days, or even a week, to see what happened first. I'd give Julie that chance.

It was the least I could do for a friend.

# Chapter Thirteen

I glanced at my watch. Pleased to see there was still time to do a little digging in the attic after my morning phone calls, I grabbed my key ring and headed upstairs, pausing to unlock the door that led to the top level of the house.

I'd learned to keep the door locked after finding a few guests rummaging around in the attic during the first literary event I'd held at Chapters. I wasn't worried about items being stolen—many of the books in the library were much more valuable than anything in the attic—but I feared a lawsuit if someone got hurt tripping over the clutter.

The heat rose as I climbed the narrow wooden stairs. I was glad I'd opted for open-backed sandals along with a pair of light-weight shorts and a gauzy cotton top, rather than my typical hostess outfit. The unfinished attic was no place for nice clothes.

I flicked the light switch at the top of the stairs, turning on the three bare bulbs that dangled from the rafters. The attic ran the entire width of the older portion of the house. It included windows on either side, which helped to relieve the gloom of its aged-wood interior. But nothing could quite chase the shadows from the far corners or dispel the haze created by two centuries of dust.

Wrinkling my nose at the musty smell rising from stacks of old *National Geographic* magazines and a motley assortment of leather-clad trunks, I picked my way through teetering piles of boxes to reach one of the side windows. After previously digging through the attic to find Great-Aunt Isabella's stash of costumes, I'd moved all the boxes containing her personal effects to an area lit by one of the windows, hoping to eventually catalog them properly.

Not in the summer, though. That had never been the plan. I pulled a wad of tissues from the pocket of my shorts and wiped the sweat from my upper lip and forehead. Lacking air conditioning, the attic was at least twenty degrees hotter than the rest of the house. Opening one or both windows would've helped, but I knew from prior attempts that the frames were too old and warped to allow the sashes to move.

I decided to collect some material and sort through it downstairs. It wasn't safe to stay in the attic too long when it was hot enough to immediately plaster my hair to my head and neck. I picked up one of the boxes that held Isabella's photos and papers. Rising unsteadily to my feet, I headed downstairs. I could return for another box once I had sorted through the first batch.

Back in my bedroom, I kicked off my sandals before pulling the papers and photos from the box and arranging them in piles on my white chenille bedspread. I tried to sort roughly by decade. The loose documents and notebooks were dated, which helped me place them in their proper pile, and while most of the photographs didn't include inscriptions, I could make approximations based on hairstyles and clothing.

I picked up a photo taken at one of our family reunions. There I was, looking gawky and owl-eyed in the glasses I'd had to wear until I was old enough to handle contacts. Behind me, my mom and dad stared resolutely at the camera, their smiles frozen in the fixed expression common to posed photos. My grandparents flanked them, also looking stiff and uncomfortable. But off to one side, Isabella appeared poised to fly off into the woods, her attention captured by something unseen by the others.

*She looks like some wild or supernatural creature, trapped with these stodgy mortals*, I thought. A long-forgotten memory flashed through my mind—Isabella flitting from table to table at a party while Grandma Ruth admonished her to "sit still for once, for heaven's sake, Bella."

I tapped the edge of the photo against my palm. As a child, I'd been fascinated by my great-aunt. Her vivacious beauty, undimmed even in her later years, had seemed far too exotic for our rather unexceptional family. *Like a butterfly among the moths*, I thought, as I laid down the photo and picked up another.

This was an older picture. Slightly out of focus, it looked like a random shot of Isabella working in the garden at Chapters. And there, in the background, near a much shorter holly hedge, stood a tall, well-built man.

I squinted, hoping to make out who it was. Perhaps her father, my great-grandfather? No, this man looked to be closer to Isabella's age. It also wasn't her brother-in-law. As a young man, my grandfather's hair had been almost black, and this man's hair was light enough to read as blond in the black-and-white photo.

Rummaging through the drawer in my nightstand, I pulled out a magnifying glass. But even enlarging the photo didn't answer the question of who had accompanied Isabella in the garden that day. The man, handsome in a rough-hewn, strong-jawed way, was a stranger to me.

I flipped the photo over but found no inscription. Dropping the magnifying glass onto the bed, I held up the picture and noticed the smudge of fingerprints marring its glossy finish. I'd been careful not to touch the surface of the photo, but it looked like someone had handled it often, and carelessly, in the past.

"Now who are you?" I asked aloud. "Just some random visitor, or Isabella's very own mystery man?" I placed the photo on my nightstand, near the picture of my great-aunt and grandmother. It felt like a clue to Isabella's possible mysterious benefactor, or more tragically, her blackmailer. I decided to keep it separate from the other items until I could examine it further.

The rest of the materials were ordinary enough—more photos from our family reunions, as well as pictures of parties at Chapters and other Beaufort events, and a few postcards and letters sent to her from members of my family. There were also copies of legal documents I thought I'd look through later, although a cursory examination revealed nothing of interest.

My first dig into Isabella's past appeared to be a dud, at least in terms of proving, or disproving, Lincoln Delamont's claims. So far there was nothing that explained how Isabella had acquired the funds to buy Chapters. In fact, all the legal documents seemed to date from after her acquisition of the property. Once again, it was as if her life before that date had fallen into a deep well.

I sighed and fluffed my now-dry hair. What had I expected? A signed confession from my great-aunt, detailing daring acts of thievery and other crimes? I snorted at my own naivete. If

Isabella *had* stolen valuable items and sold them on the black market to fund her acquisition of Chapters and build her library, she certainly wouldn't have documented that behavior.

As I slid the separated stacks of papers and photographs into an empty cardboard expanding file I'd found in the library, a small gray journal slipped out of one of the larger notebooks. I picked it up, my fingertips dimpling the soft suede cover. It was not one of the typical spiral-bound notebooks that Isabella had favored for recording random notes and recipes. It looked like something meant for more permanent, and perhaps more important, information.

The cover and spine lacked lettering or embossing of any kind, but there was a date scrawled on the inside cover—*1952*. A quick calculation told me Isabella would've been twenty-six that year.

*One of the years she was out of touch with the family*, I thought, remembering my mom's comments about Isabella being at least "old enough to take care of herself" when she'd gone missing. I flipped to the first page in the journal, and slumped back against my pillows, baffled again.

The journal was filled with writing—in a hand I recognized from other documents written by Isabella—but the tightly packed script was total gibberish.

Flipping through the pages, I noticed changes in the ink used to write the curious arrangements of letters and numbers. It seemed that the journal had not been filled all at once but rather, as indicated by the fading and discoloration of the earlier entries, over a significant period of time.

I grabbed the photo of the mysterious man and slipped it between the pages before sliding the journal into the small purse I intended to carry when I drove over to Fort Macon.

Ellen Montgomery might know nothing about either the photo or the journal, but I didn't care. I desperately wanted to share them with someone I felt I could trust.

Taking a deep breath, I stood and slung the purse strap over my shoulder as I slid my feet into my sandals. A glance at the clock told me it was time to drive to Atlantic Beach and meet Ellen at Fort Macon.

I smiled grimly as I padded over to the dresser and yanked a comb through my hair. Yes, it was definitely time to see Ellen—not just to chat about the murder of Lincoln Delamont but also to share these mysterious items from my great-aunt's past.

*Because*, I thought, as I left my room and headed outside to my car, *Lincoln Delamont might have been wrong on certain points, but he could've been right about one thing—my great-aunt might indeed have had secrets the family would not want exposed.*

I climbed into my car, glad that the shade from the holly and a nearby magnolia tree had kept it relatively cool. As I placed my purse on the passenger seat, my fingers traced the edge of the journal where it pressed against the inside of the soft leather.

That ridiculous book, filled with nonsense.

*No*, I thought, fumbling with the key as I slid it into the ignition. *You know better. You saw the patterns. You've already realized it might not be gibberish after all. That it could be a code.*

Perhaps Isabella Harrington had not been a thief.

Maybe she'd been a spy.

# Chapter Fourteen

Morehead City was only a short hop over the new bridge that crossed the Newport River. I'd left for my meeting with Ellen a little early, expecting to face bumper-to-bumper traffic. But fortunately, most of the tournament visitors' cars were parked closer to the Morehead waterfront, and I realized that once they'd found a spot, they weren't about to move. So even though things were a little more congested than normal, I was able to reach the bridge that spanned Bogue Sound in decent time.

I always felt a little thrill crossing the sound, which, like the Newport River, was part of the Intracoastal Waterway. Something about the clarity of the sky above the cluster of buildings that crowded the Atlantic Beach side of the bridge hinted at the greater vista to come. Beyond a narrow band of land lay the sea, which had lost none of its mystery and majesty despite human attempts to civilize its shores.

At the light, I took a left onto Fort Macon Boulevard, as Route 58 was called at this juncture. The road, which ran from the state park all the way down the island to the town of Emerald

Isle, was called different names along its route, but I'd quickly learned that it was impossible to get lost. With the sound on one side and the Atlantic Ocean on the other, all side roads would eventually lead you either to the water or to 58.

The sign announcing Fort Macon State Park appeared after a short stretch of road featuring small hotels, pastel-colored homes on stilts, and a few clusters of condominium and time-share properties. I drove past the official access point to the public beach on the right and the entrance to a Coast Guard station on the left before reaching the main parking lot. As I'd expected, it was crowded, but I was able to pull into a spot when a large SUV topped by strapped-down boogie boards left.

Despite its importance as a surveillance point, the fort itself was not visible from the parking lot. From previous visits I knew that only when someone walked out the back of the brick visitors' center and up a hill could the true size and structure of the fort be seen. Removing my sunglasses, I strolled into the center and made my way to the information desk, where Ellen was waiting.

"Right on time," she said, tying the ribbons of her straw hat under her chin. "I've eaten what little I brought for lunch, so let's head outside and take the walkway to the beach. I've already changed my shoes," she added, pointing her foot. Her flexible plastic water shoes were black with fuchsia stripes, matching the flowers on her short-sleeved cotton sundress.

"Stylish as always," I said, with a woeful glance at my own battered sandals. As I followed her out the front of the building, the sunlight blinded me for a moment, and I had to quickly slip on my sunglasses while we crossed the parking lot to one of the paths leading to the beach.

"Not too many people out today," I said as I pulled off my sandals and dangled them from my fingers. Walking in the drifted sand near the dunes was hard enough without the added problem of shoes. I glanced over at Ellen, admiring her good sense in choosing footwear meant for the pool or beach.

"Not here, maybe. But this isn't really the official beach access. That's closer to the entrance of the park."

"Oh right, I saw that coming in."

"That's where most people park, if they can. There's boardwalk access to the beach there, and a lifeguard on duty during the day, at least in season. But when that lot is full, people park at the fort. Which isn't great for our visitors, but what can you do?"

"There is a path here," I observed, my gaze focused on the expansive view of sea and sky.

"Yes, there are a few unofficial paths, and really, it's impossible to monitor, so we don't even bother. Although visitors are warned not to swim over there." Ellen motioned toward an area to our left, where the beach curved around at the end of the point. "The Beaufort inlet and ocean merge there, and there's a jetty, so it can be quite dangerous. It isn't even safe for wading. But a lot of shell hunters walk the beach in that area. Supposedly it's the best place for that."

"You're not a shell collector?" I asked, gingerly picking my way through the hot, dry sand.

Ellen glanced at me as she adjusted her hat. "I'm not a collector of anything, except the art pieces I use to decorate my house. I did too much traveling when I was working, I guess. It's hard to collect much random stuff when you don't have a permanent home for many years."

We'd reached the hard-packed sand near the water, which was blessedly cool against my bare feet. I paused for a moment, breathing in the heady scent of salt air, before following Ellen. "I can imagine. But I bet it was exciting, traveling all over the world when you were younger."

"Sometimes. I enjoyed learning about new places and people. But it was exhausting too." Ellen cast me a wry smile. "I wasn't usually traveling to tourist destinations, you know. With location work, you can end up in all sorts of out-of-the-way areas."

"Dangerous?" I asked, my gaze captured by a sand dollar half buried in the sand.

"Occasionally." Ellen stopped walking as I bent down and lifted the fragile white disk from the ground. "Ah, a whole one. That's rare. I usually only find bits and pieces."

I gently shook the sand off the shell before carefully slipping it between the tissues I'd stuffed in the outside pouch of my purse. "It's good luck, I hope. I could use some of that right now." As I pulled my fingers away, they slid across the bulge of the suede journal I'd stored in the main section of the purse.

"I'm not much for superstitions, but I suppose it is considered lucky." Ellen turned her head to look out over the ocean.

I followed her gaze, staring at the darker blue ribbon of water that separated the clear sky from the rest of the greenish-gray sea. The waves were low, rolling in gently instead of crashing, but still stirring up a froth of white foam along the shore.

"It's so amazing to think how it just goes on and on," I said, staring at the horizon. "You have to wonder at the sheer bravado of the earliest sailors, just heading for that edge, never knowing where it would lead."

"Especially since some of them thought they might fall off," Ellen said dryly. She turned to me. "Now—I believe you wanted to talk through some ideas you had about who might have killed the unfortunate Mr. Delamont?"

"Yes." I considered sharing the journal and photo first but decided that could wait. "I suppose there's really nothing I can add to the investigation that the police haven't, or won't, uncover, but it just helps to talk it out. Especially since some of the people involved . . ."

"Are your friends?" Ellen sent me a sidelong glance. "You and Julie Rivera are close, I believe."

"We are. And I confess that part of my urge to investigate this murder is so I can clear her from any suspicion." I detailed Julie's hidden connection to Lincoln Delamont as we strolled along, the lacy edge of water lapping at our feet. "The truth is, she mentioned having some secret boyfriend, but she never told me his name, even though apparently they'd been engaged in a relationship for a while. Mostly online, but still."

Ellen grabbed the brim of her hat as the breeze blew it back. "She was probably afraid you'd judge her, since Delamont was legally still married."

"She should've known I wouldn't have, although I might have warned her that she was being foolish—"

"Hmmm, that sounds a bit judgy to me." Ellen flashed me a bright smile before continuing. "But aside from that, do you really think she has the temperament to stab someone?"

"Not really. Except maybe in self-defense. I have wondered if Lincoln might have asked her to meet him at the carriage house and she was, oh, I don't know, worried for her own safety." I shrugged. "It seems he'd been physically aggressive with her once or twice before, and I can picture him becoming quite abusive if he didn't get his way."

Ellen thrust her hands into the pockets of her sundress. "But can you picture Julie staying with such a man after he did anything drastic? Even if it was a newish relationship and she was still giving him the benefit of the doubt?"

"Not really. Not for long. Although she did put up with some stuff that I . . . well, never mind," I said, not wanting to completely betray Julie's confidences. Ellen and I had hit a patch of saturated sand that made my feet sink in with each step. I had a momentary, irrational flash of fear, as if I'd just stumbled into quicksand, and moved a few paces away from the water, where the ground felt firmer. "And then there's the other side of the triangle."

"Yes, Jennifer Delamont. The wronged wife." Ellen joined me on the firmer sand. "Given what you've said, I expect it wasn't the first time she'd uncovered her husband's infidelity."

I couldn't let that pass. "Julie swears they weren't actually having an affair."

"Yet." Ellen stood still and turned to me. "But I'm sure that was only because Julie is sensible, not that Delamont was honorable."

"Probably," I admitted. "Anyway, Jennifer does seem to have been beaten down by that marriage. If she had to endure a lot of betrayal over the years, I suppose she could've snapped. Alicia actually heard them fighting the evening before Lincoln was killed. As did Kelly Rowley, come to think of it."

"Then there's the daughter, who was angry over her father's refusal to support her dreams of stardom." Ellen glanced over at me. "You of all people should understand how dramatic every-thing can feel at her age. I'm sure you saw plenty of students acting out over similar things."

"Yes, but the idea that she murdered her own father . . ." I straightened and thrust back my shoulders before relaying the story of the discovery of the fake purple gem in the azaleas. "I have a hard time imagining Tara stabbing anyone, but there is proof she was near that area at some point in the evening."

"And could have lost that trinket in a struggle," Ellen said.

"Possibly."

Ellen's expression grew thoughtful. "When you saw her later, was she still in her costume?"

"Yes."

"Any visible bloodstains?"

"No, Tara's costume was perfectly clean and dry." I widened my eyes. Why hadn't I thought of that? The killer would likely have been splattered with blood, even if they'd been careful. "And Tara's costume was a light amber color, which would've really shown bloodstains, even minimal ones. Come to think of it, I didn't see Jennifer Delamont until later, when she was already in her street clothes. And Pete Nelson whipped his costume off as soon as I asked everyone to come inside."

"Something to look into. I can't imagine Pete murdering a stranger, but perhaps he had some previous, unknown connection to Delamont."

"That's entirely possible. It wasn't Lincoln's first trip to Beau-fort. And Pete is an argumentative sort." I took a deep breath and added, "I also noticed that Alicia wasn't wearing her customary apron after I got back from the store. And, of course, no one really knows how long Scott Kepler was gone or when he returned to the carriage house."

"But does Scott have a motive?"

I twitched my lips. "Unfortunately, yes," I said, and I recounted my discussion with the author.

"You think he might have wanted revenge for Delamont cheating his father?"

"It's a possibility, don't you think? Especially since Scott seems to think the scam contributed to his father's fatal heart attack."

Ellen held up one hand. "Which means we have motives and opportunity for Julie, Jennifer, Alicia, and Scott," she said, ticking off the names on her fingers. "There's also a suspicious clothing change for Pete, although we don't have any sense of a motive there. At least not yet. Meanwhile, Tara seems to be in the clear, based on her appearance after the murder. Anyone else?"

"Damian Carr," I said reluctantly. "Again, I don't know what his motive would have been, but he did have the opportunity, and he has a temper."

Ellen nodded. "I've heard he's a bit of a firebrand."

"Yes, and he lives so close to Chapters he could've walked from his apartment. Everyone saw him leave in a huff, but he could've returned a little later, climbed the back fence, killed Lincoln, and returned home without ever being seen."

"Which also means he could've easily changed his clothes before the police called on him."

"I suppose so." I shoved my drooping sunglasses up onto the bridge of my nose. "Alicia, Damian, and Julie would've known where the key to the carriage house was kept too, although I guess any one of the guests could have figured that out ahead of time. They do have access to the kitchen, even when Alicia and I are out."

"And, of course, Scott had a key," Ellen said.

"Right. As for the knife—the block sits on the counter, so again, it wouldn't have been hard for anyone to scope out a knife to use as a weapon ahead of time."

Ellen dug the toe of her water shoes into the sand. "Back to square one? It seems we can't really narrow down the list of suspects yet. Although I believe I'd eliminate the Sandberg sisters."

"And maybe Sandy Nelson. Her husband has a temper, but I've never heard her even raise her voice." I tapped two fingers against my lips. "Then there's the Rowleys. I can't imagine why either one of them would want to stab Lincoln Delamont, but I admit I don't really know much about them."

"Did they stay in costume?" Ellen asked.

"Yes, but . . ." I frowned. "Kelly left her cloak outside. She said she collected it later, but there's still that little wrinkle of suspicion. And Todd's costume was a dark, voluminous type of material that might not have shown stains unless you were really looking for them."

Ellen held up three fingers on her other hand. "So they stay on the list. On the second page, perhaps, but worth further investigation. That brings us to eight possibilities. Quite a challenge."

"Yes, I don't envy the police having to handle so many suspects."

Ellen pursed her lips. "I'm sure they've dealt with that before, although perhaps not involving a murder. I don't think there's been a murder in Beaufort in over thirty years." She pointed at her watch. "But, interesting as this is, we probably should head back. I don't want to make my volunteer partner wait too long for her lunch break."

"That's fine," I said, but held my hand to stop Ellen from striding off. "One thing before we start back. There's something else I wanted to ask you, if you don't mind."

"As long as you aren't asking for an excessive amount of money from the trust," Ellen said, with a lift of her well-groomed eyebrows. "I take my management of the trust seriously, you know."

"No, it isn't anything like that. This is something I found when I was poking around in the attic this morning. Two things, actually." I reached into my purse and fished out the journal.

"Awfully hot day to be digging around in an attic." Ellen's gaze snapped to my hand. "Were you hoping to find evidence of Isabella's innocence?"

"Or guilt. I really just want to know. But I didn't actually find any proof either way." I held up the journal and waved it under Ellen's nose. "But I did find this."

As Ellen ducked her head, the wide brim of her straw hat cast a shadow over her face. "And this is?"

There was a wariness in her tone that made me examine her face more closely. "A book full of gibberish. Or so I thought at first. But now I wonder . . ." I held out the journal. "Take a look."

Ellen gingerly pulled it from my fingers. After flipping through the first few pages, she expelled one sharp breath before snapping it shut and thrusting it back at me. "Yes, it appears to be a journal. Written by Isabella. I recognize her hand. But, as you say, it makes no sense."

I crossed my arms over my chest. "I don't know about that. I think it's in code. And there's one more thing. Check out the photo I placed between the pages."

Ellen shot me a questioning look before opening the journal again. This time she located the photograph. "That's Isabella in the garden at Chapters. Well, before it was Chapters, of course."

"But who's the guy? I've never noticed him in any other family photos."

"I have no idea." Ellen shoved the photo back between the pages and handed the journal to me. "You must remember, I didn't move here until long after that picture would've been taken. It was probably just a friend, or even someone Isabella dated for a time. Although I don't think she had many serious relationships, she did keep a gentleman or two on call for plus ones at parties. She was quite the social butterfly, you know. Always attending or giving parties. She liked to have an appropriate male escort always available, even later, when I knew her. I can easily imagine her dating a variety of men when she was younger."

"I thought it might have been her benefactor, or sugar daddy, as you called him."

"I really don't know. Sorry." Ellen yanked her hat farther down her forehead. "We'd better get moving or I'll be late." She took off, almost loping across the hard-packed sand.

I increased my stride to stay beside her. "Okay, but what about that strange writing in the journal? It looks like it's a code. It made me think . . ."

Ellen slowed her pace and shot me a sharp glance. "What? That Isabella was some sort of spy or something? Really,

Charlotte, I know you love books and stories, but sometimes your imagination gets away from you. This isn't some suspense novel."

"You have to admit it's odd, especially with the date inside the front cover. It was one of the years when Isabella was out of contact with my family, in case you didn't know. Which made me wonder if she was engaged in some sort of covert operation or something." I lifted my hands. "I know, I know. I've read too many spy thrillers."

"Oh, I grant you it probably is a code. But I'm guessing it was some personal code that Isabella created so she could write frankly about her life without worrying about anyone ever reading it." Ellen strode along the water's edge, her eyes focused straight ahead. "She could be fanciful like that."

I straightened my sunglasses and marched in step with her. She was probably right—I was imagining things. Looking for conspiracies and crimes where there were none. "That makes sense. More sense than someone who lived most of their life in Beaufort being a spy. It's not like she worked somewhere where they dealt in secrets. Not even at a company where she could've engaged in industrial espionage."

"Exactly," Ellen said, as we turned away from the water and plowed through the deeper sand to the path. "Honestly, I doubt that investigating Isabella's colorful but decidedly ordinary past is worth much of your time. Now this murder, on the other hand . . ."

"We have plenty of suspects, that's for sure. I just wish Julie wasn't one of them. It would help if I knew more about where everyone was and what they were doing closer to the time that

Lincoln was killed." I paused to slip on my sandals before stepping onto the hot asphalt of the parking lot. "I thought I'd visit the Sandberg sisters this afternoon. They probably know something about that."

"Good idea. They tend to keep an eye on everything. I'm sure they'll have at least a little information on the movements of the people at the party."

"That's what I thought." I paused as we reached the parking row that held my car. "I should let you get back to work. Thanks for agreeing to speak with me today. It does help to talk over all the options."

"Happy to help." Ellen patted my arm. "Just don't worry yourself to death over this. Yes, it's a tragedy, and I'm sorry it happened at Chapters, but I'm sure it will be sorted, sooner rather than later. The Beaufort police are quite capable, you know. They'll find the culprit."

"I'm sure. I just want to know who to avoid." I offered her a brief smile. "I don't want to end up like those foolish female characters in horror films—locked in a cellar with a murderer."

Ellen tapped her forehead with her finger. "Good thinking, Sherlock."

"I keep telling you, I'm Watson," I called after her as she turned away.

She just waved her hand over her head and kept walking.

# Chapter Fifteen

After driving back from Atlantic Beach, I parked my car at Chapters and called the Sandberg sisters to make sure they were home before I walked the few blocks to their house.

A charming bungalow situated on one of the side streets between the Beaufort waterfront and Broad Street, their one-story, wood-framed house didn't have a historic designation plaque. But it was still an older home, with white clapboard siding and a covered porch. Aqua shutters framed the tall windows that flanked the cobalt-blue front door, and white wicker furniture provided an inviting seating area on the wide front porch. As I climbed the wooden steps, I admired the pink geraniums planted in ivory ceramic jars placed at either end of each tread. Ophelia Sandberg's gardening expertise was renowned in Beaufort. Her backyard was filled with blooming shrubs and flowers, and she often provided fresh flowers for local businesses, including Julie's bookstore and Pete and Sandy's café.

Bernadette greeted me at the front door. "Have you had lunch yet?" she asked as she ushered me inside.

I lied and said I'd already eaten, knowing that saying *no* would drive the sisters into a flurry of food preparation. "But I'd love a glass of water," I said, as I took a seat on a sofa covered in seashell-patterned chintz.

Ophelia popped her head around the corner of the kitchen door. "We also have lemonade and tea."

"Lemonade, then," I said, and was rewarded with a broad smile.

I expected the drink would be accompanied by some type of dessert, so I wasn't surprised when Ophelia bustled out of the kitchen, holding a glass of lemonade in one hand and a small china plate in the other. "Sugar cookies," she said, placing the items on the white side table next to the sofa. "Just out of the oven ten minutes ago."

"They look delicious," I said, and they were. I nibbled on one of the cookies while Ophelia and Bernadette settled into two armchairs that faced the sofa.

Allowing my gaze to wander, I experienced the emotion I always felt when I visited this house—envy. Despite Chapters' historic beauty and charm, it sometimes seemed too large for comfort. This bungalow, with its pale-jade walls and white cotton curtains edged with lace, felt more like a home than my rambling house. The airy rooms were filled with wicker plant stands and simple, whitewashed wooden furniture. Watercolor seascapes and vases overflowing with Ophelia's flowers offered pops of color.

"You said you had some questions for us," Bernadette said. "About the other night, I suppose?"

I took a swallow of lemonade before answering. "Yes. I was away from the house for a bit, getting ice. Which means I'm not sure where everyone was at the time of the murder. I thought maybe you could clear that up for me."

Ophelia shared a look with her sister. "The thing is, we probably aren't going to be too much help with that question. We were inside Chapters most of the time you were gone, I'm afraid." She tugged the hem of her pink-and-lilac floral-print skirt over her knees. "I'd misplaced my reading glasses, you see."

"Again," Bernadette added, stretching out her stocky legs. Unlike Ophelia, who was dressed for a garden party, Bernadette wore khaki shorts and a plain white polo shirt.

Ophelia fiddled with the lace trimming the collar of her ivory silk blouse. "Now, Bernie, you've been known to lose track of a few things too."

"But not every day." Bernadette met my interested gaze with a shrug. "It's true, though. We were in the garden for a bit, but then Fee realized she'd misplaced her glasses when she tried to read one of your flower markers. So it wasn't too long after you drove off that we headed into the house to search for them. We'd just arrived back outside on the patio when you called everyone into the parlor. So I'm afraid we can't help you with where everyone was while you were gone. But"—she kicked off her sandals and put her feet up on the tufted hassock in front of her chair—"we may have some other information that could prove helpful."

I set down my glass and slid to the edge of the sofa. "Oh? Like what?"

"Well, earlier in the evening, right before dinner actually, I overheard Lincoln Delamont having a rather heated conversation with your chef. I think you were in the dining room talking about Tey and the inspiration for the dinner menu at that point."

Ophelia smoothed down a flyaway strand of her fire-engine-red hair. "It was more like an argument, from what you told me, Bernie."

"They were fighting?" I asked. "What about?"

Bernadette narrowed her eyes. "I'm not sure. I was coming back from the powder room when I heard raised voices in the library. I thought that was odd—"

"You stopped to listen, right?" Ophelia asked.

"Just peeked in to see who it was." Bernadette cleared her throat. "I was worried it might be some strangers, wandering in while we were all preoccupied with the party."

I tightened my lips to prevent a smile. Bernadette had been curious, as I would've been, but since she was always accusing her sister of being too nosy, I assumed she didn't want to admit that. "You saw Damian Carr and Lincoln in the library? That *is* odd. I'd have thought Damian wouldn't have left the kitchen at that point, and anyway, he told me they didn't know each other."

"Seems like they did. At least well enough to have a disagreement," Bernadette said. "But, unfortunately, I didn't really hear what it was about. I didn't linger long. I thought it best to beat a retreat before they noticed me."

Ophelia demurely crossed her ankles as she leaned forward in her chair. "Bernie mentioned all this to me later, after we both overheard Lincoln embroiled in another argument, this time with his wife."

"Another confrontation on the same night? He was a contentious guy, wasn't he?" I sat back and grabbed another cookie. *A replacement for lunch*, I told myself.

Bernadette nodded. "I wasn't surprised to find out he'd been killed. Seemed like the type to make a lot of enemies."

"What was the argument with his wife about?" I asked, reaching for my glass of lemonade. The cookies, while delicious, were a little dry.

"Poor Mrs. Delamont was berating him for flirting with Julie Rivera over dinner. And he was, you know." Ophelia cast me an apologetic look. "Julie didn't seem to be encouraging him, but still . . ."

I wasn't about to share what I knew on that subject. "Jennifer Delamont was having words with Lincoln about it? When exactly was this?"

"Just after you'd driven off," Bernadette replied. "They were standing right outside the garden, near the holly hedge, so they weren't in the middle of things. As I mentioned earlier, Fee and I had just wandered that way to check out your flowers. Anyway, the argument didn't last very long. Lincoln stormed off— practically knocked Fee down as he passed us."

Ophelia pressed her hand to her cheek. "It's true. He bumped right into me and kept walking without saying a word."

"He headed off in the direction of the carriage house and disappeared behind the hollies," Bernadette said, flicking a short lock of her steel-gray hair behind her ear. "That was the last we saw of him."

Finishing off my lemonade, I waved off Ophelia's question about needing more before I replied. "Which means Lincoln was involved in at least two arguments before he was killed." *Three*, I thought, remembering that overheard conversation between him and Julie. But I wasn't about to mention that to the Sandberg sisters. I was there to gather information, not spread rumors.

"We told the police all of this, of course," Ophelia said. "I hated to add your chef and Mrs. Delamont to their list of suspects, but one can't lie to the authorities. I just don't think that's the proper thing to do."

"No, you were right to tell them," I said. "It's better that they have all the facts. And if someone is innocent, they have nothing to fear."

"Not so sure that's always true." Bernadette's tone betrayed a distrust I'd never have expected from her.

"You don't think justice is always served?" I asked, keeping my own tone light.

Bernadette snorted. "Hardly. Depends on who you are sometimes, doesn't it?" She cast me a baleful glance. "Sorry, but I've seen some things that make me a bit cynical."

"When you were at the university?" I asked, remembering that Bernadette had worked as a nurse at one of the University of North Carolina campuses.

"Yes. Students got treated differently sometimes, depending on their backgrounds and . . . other things."

I leaned my elbow on the arm of the sofa and rested my jaw against my balled-up fist. "But I don't get the sense that the Beaufort police will be unfair. They seemed very professional."

"Hopefully you're right." Bernadette lifted her feet off the hassock and kicked it away from her chair. "Sure we can't get you more lemonade?" she asked, pointing at my empty glass as she stood up. "I need to check on something in the kitchen anyway."

"Bernie's making dinner in the Crock-Pot," Ophelia said. "Chicken and vegetables."

"No, no, I'm fine. And I don't want to keep you much longer, but"—I grabbed my purse off the floor—"there is one more thing I wanted to ask you about."

"What's that?" Bernadette paused in the kitchen doorway.

"Nothing to do with the Delamont case," I said, fishing the suede-covered journal out of my purse. "This concerns Isabella."

Bernadette leaned against the doorjamb as she looked me over. "Something from the past?"

"Yes, a mystery I stumbled over when I was searching through my great-aunt's things." I rose to my feet and held up the journal. "I found this, and a photo I've slipped inside it, in the attic. Both are puzzling, and I thought maybe you could shed some light. You were both acquainted with Isabella for years." I waved the journal. "Honestly, you're the only people I know in Beaufort who knew her before she converted Chapters into a bed-and-breakfast."

Ophelia squinted as she stared at the object in my hand. "Is that some sort of book?"

"It's a journal or diary, I think. But it's written in code." I crossed the room to show the journal to both sisters. "Any idea why Isabella would've done that?"

Bernadette stepped forward and took the book from my hands. "Just to be inscrutable, I suspect," she said, as she flipped through a few pages. "She liked to promote an air of mystery, didn't she, Fee?"

"Oh my, yes. It was like she was always playing some sort of game. One where only she knew the rules." Ophelia fanned herself with one hand, as if this thought had heated her face. "I mean, don't get me wrong—I liked her very much. Bernie did too, didn't you, Bernie?"

"Um, yes, I suppose." Bernadette met my inquiring gaze with a lift of her square chin. "But she did like her little secrets. It was like she never grew out of playing games of pretend."

"You think this code was something she used for . . . what, exactly?"

"Probably just to amuse herself," Bernadette said, handing the journal back to me.

Ophelia, her eyes sparkling, glanced from her sister to me. "Or to hide the details of all her romantic relationships. She always had a man or two on the string, you know."

"No, I don't. She never brought any of her male friends along when she visited my family. In fact, she never even mentioned them." I slid the photograph out from between the journal's pages. "Like this guy? Was he one of her boyfriends?" I passed the picture to Ophelia.

"Oh yes, I remember this one," she said, handing the photo to her sister. "He was the British fellow, wasn't he?"

"British, my backside," Bernadette said, with an audible sniff. "He had a British accent all right, but I always thought that was put on." She cast me a sharp glance. "You'll probably think I'm being fanciful, but I suspected he came from somewhere other than the British Isles. I've worked with a lot of nurses and doctors from England over the years, and he just didn't fit the profile somehow."

"You thought he was an impostor?" I asked, staring at the photo again after Bernadette passed it back to me.

"I was never sure about that. I mean, maybe he was who he said he was. He had some sort of very ordinary name. Paul something, I think." Bernadette shook her head. "So maybe his name wasn't fake, or anything like that. I just never thought he was actually British."

"Yes, Paul Peters," Ophelia said, her expression more serious than usual. "Come to think of it, there *was* something a bit off about him. Remember, Bernie? We used to say he was always a little too formal or guarded or something. Like he could never really relax."

"Wound too tightly, is what I used to say," Bernadette replied. "I'm surprised Isabella didn't ever mention him to your family. He was one of the few who was around for more than a month or two."

"Now, Bernie, be fair. She had some she dated off and on for a few years." Ophelia sent me an apologetic smile. "But I'm afraid it's true that Isabella tended to be a bit flighty as far as men were concerned."

"Which is probably why she didn't ever talk about her relationships with the family," I said. "At least not openly. She may have shared some things with my grandma, who would've kept any confidences. They were sisters, after all."

Ophelia and Bernadette shared a knowing look. "Yes, there is a code of silence in that case. Usually," Bernadette said.

I slipped the photo back inside the journal. "But you say the guy in this picture was a more lasting relationship?"

"Oh yes. He would pop up from time to time for as long as we knew Isabella. Until she started up the bed-and-breakfast, that is. Never saw him again after that," Ophelia said.

I tightened my grip on the journal. This information supported my supposition that the man in the photo was my great-aunt's mysterious benefactor. *Or blackmailer*, I reminded myself. "Did they seem close, Isabella and this Paul Peters guy? Did it seem like she cared for him, and he her?"

Bernadette pursed her lips. "Hard to say. Isabella was so flirtatious and charming with everyone. It was almost impossible to tell if she liked one person better than any other."

"I always thought he cared more deeply for her than she did for him. I don't really have anything to back that up. Just a feeling I had," Ophelia said.

"Interesting." I pressed the journal to my chest. "Well, thanks for helping me unravel a bit of the mystery. Too bad we don't have a key to the code, but I suppose that's gone forever."

"Maybe. But you might want to search the library. I walked in on Isabella once and caught her studying some sort of document with strange writing in one column and regular words in another." Ophelia plucked at the lace on her collar and cast me an embarrassed smile. "She had it opened up on the desk, but folded it as soon as she caught me staring. She wasn't expecting me, you see. I was returning a vase I'd borrowed and showed up earlier than we'd planned. Anyway, I saw her shove the document inside a book. Can't remember what book it was, sadly, and she probably changed it out once I left anyway. But maybe she left the key to that code buried somewhere in the library? I do recall the strange writing resembling what you just showed me in that journal."

"Worth a look, I suppose," I said, groaning inwardly at the thought of searching through every book in my great-aunt's extensive library.

"You never told me about that," Bernadette said, with a sharp glance at her sister.

Ophelia fluttered her hands. "Oh, I just thought it was one of Isabella's little games. Nothing to talk about, really." She offered me an abashed smile. "Truthfully, I thought she was just planning some sort of treasure hunt or something for one of her parties. She liked to do that sort of thing, you know."

I didn't, which made me realize, once again, how little I actually knew about the great-aunt who'd left me a valuable legacy. *Why me?* I thought, resolving to solve that mystery someday too.

"Well, thank you for the refreshments and the information," I said, crossing back to the sofa to retrieve my purse. "But I should let you get back to your own business. I'll just say good-bye and show myself out." I shoved the journal into my purse and slung the purse strap over my shoulder. "And just so you know—despite all this real-life mess, I do intend to hold a couple of the planned special events this week. There's a cocktail party Thursday night, and the final book discussion on Tey's works scheduled for Saturday night."

"I thought you had planned a murder-mystery party for Saturday," Ophelia said. "One of those things where we would play detective."

"Yes, I had, but . . ." I cleared my throat. "I decided that might be in poor taste, given the circumstances."

Bernadette nodded and offered me a smile. "Good thinking, and don't worry, we'll be there. For both events."

"Okay, see you Thursday, then, if not before." I waved good-bye as I headed out the door.

Pausing on the front porch, I considered the sisters' comments about Lincoln Delamont. He'd gotten into arguments with both his wife and Damian, as well as had a confrontation with Julie, on the night he was killed. Which meant that my friend was not the only one who should be listed high on the suspect list.

*It shows a pattern of combativeness*, I thought as I descended the porch steps and made my way to the sidewalk. *And speaks to Lincoln's tendency to bring out the worst in people. So perhaps there was someone unrelated to Chapters' staff or guests who wanted him dead.*

It was a hope I intended to cling to as long as possible, anyway.

# Chapter Sixteen

Taking a detour on my walk home, I headed for the waterfront. Right off the boardwalk, a long wooden building housed several businesses, including Julie's store, Bookwaves.

Peering into the picture window of the bookstore, I saw only silent shelves and shadows and remembered Julie's comment about the store being closed on Mondays. So much for a chance to talk with her again in person.

I strolled along the boardwalk, appreciating the bright splashes of color the flowers in the over-the-rail flower boxes lent to the grayed timber railing that separated the walkway from the boat slips. As usual, the harbor was filled with boats of all types and sizes, from small dinghies to sailboats boasting towering masts. The Rowleys' yacht, the *Celestial*, was docked at the end of one wharf. Its pristine white hull glittered in the bright sunlight, outshone only by the chrome fittings. Indigo and turquoise stripes swept from bow to stern in an undulating pattern that mimicked the waves.

Leaning on the top rail for a moment, I wondered how it would feel to have enough money to buy something so beautiful—and so expensive to maintain. I supposed owning a yacht was like most things—if you had to ask how much it would cost, you couldn't afford it.

Not that I had any reason to complain, since I owned property that was worth over a million dollars. Yet I was almost always short on cash. I pushed a lock of hair behind my ears. That wouldn't be the case if I sold Chapters, of course. I could make a great deal of money, and without a mortgage to pay off, it would all be profit.

But I had no intention of doing that. Great-Aunt Isabella had bequeathed me the bed-and-breakfast for some reason. Perhaps because she'd realized that, since I was widowed and childless, I'd be the one family member willing to uproot their life to move to Beaufort.

*Or maybe*, I thought, as I turned away from the railing and resumed walking, *it was that conversation I had with her after Brent's funeral. When she caught me in my old kitchen, weeping silently, unable to continue to make small talk with the people who'd come to pay their respects.*

*When she told me that what I needed was a new start, somewhere far from the home I'd shared with my husband. When she said that sometimes you have to reinvent yourself in order to survive.*

I thrust my hands into the pockets of my shorts, allowing my purse, swinging from its shoulder strap, to bang against my thigh. Isabella had been over ninety at that point, yet she was still talking about new beginnings. I only hoped I could remain as positive throughout my life.

Reaching the end of the boardwalk, I crossed Front Street and walked a couple more blocks to reach another side street. Since I couldn't talk to Julie, I decided to stop by the Dancing

Dolphin café and question Pete and Sandy Nelson about what they'd seen at the costume party.

*Of course*, I reminded myself, *you need to be careful. Pete is still on the suspect list.*

But he wasn't at the top of my list, and even if he had been, I doubted he'd take any action during daylight hours, especially with Sandy present. Reaching the old house that had been converted into the Dancing Dolphin, I realized that since it was past two o'clock, the café would be closed. But since Pete and Sandy lived above the restaurant, they might still be at home.

I walked around to the wooden staircase that hugged the side of the house. Having visited Pete and Sandy before, I knew the staircase led to the upper level of the building, where they'd created a spacious apartment.

Knocking on the peacock-blue door, which matched the house's wooden hurricane shutters, I considered the best way to broach the subject of whom they'd seen where at the party. I knew Pete had been in the house, arguing with Damian in the kitchen, right before I left, but he had headed back outside before I went to get the ice. So I hoped that either he or Sandy could tell me more about the movements of the other guests while I was gone.

Sandy answered the door. "Charlotte, what are you doing here?" she asked, wiping her hands on the apron she was wearing over her T-shirt and shorts.

"Sorry. I was out walking and thought I'd stop by. Just to talk through some stuff related to the party."

"To the murder, you mean." Sandy opened the door wider and motioned for me to enter. "I guess that's been on all of our minds a little more than we'd like."

As I walked into the apartment, a blast of cold air from a nearby vent washed over me. "Big change from outside," I said, clutching my upper arms with both hands to quell a sudden shiver.

"Oh, I know. Pete keeps it so cool in here. He says he needs that after standing in a hot kitchen most of the day, but I think he just likes it cold." Sandy shook her head as she directed me to one of the fan-backed wicker rockers in the living room. "I tell him all the time he'd be better off in Antarctica than Beaufort, but he just says there isn't much call for a café there." Sandy flashed me a smile as she headed for the kitchen.

I sat down, allowing my gaze to wander. The Nelsons had removed most of the walls on this upper floor, creating an open-concept living space. A wide island, with bar stools creating seating along one edge, separated the large, white-on-white-toned kitchen from the dining and living areas. Everything was meticulously clean and bright, with only a few decorative elements lending color to the rooms. I knew from previous visits that beyond the kitchen lay a large bedroom with an en suite bathroom, as well as a guest bathroom and an office that doubled as a guest bedroom.

A perfect amount of space for two people, especially since these two people spent much of their time working in the café below. I sighed, again coveting the coziness of the space. Like the Sandberg sisters' cottage, this setup was more to my liking than my much older, rambling house. *But*, I reminded myself, *Chapters is your business, not just your private home. Even if Isabella did live there, all alone, for many years before she converted it into a bed-and-breakfast.*

That was something I found hard to imagine. When filled with guests, Chapters didn't feel too large and echoing, but when no one was there . . . I set my purse on the polished wood floor beside my chair. At least in the slow winter months, I had Alicia living at the bed-and-breakfast with me. We didn't share a lot of confidences, but she was another human being I could talk to from time to time. For many years, Isabella had been totally alone.

*Or was she?* I forced a smile as Sandy returned with a glass of water.

"You want anything else, you just ask," she said, pulling up another wicker chair to face me. "And Pete will be out in a minute. He was taking a little nap. He needs that sometimes, after the lunch rush."

"I can imagine," I said, after taking a sip of the water. "It's hard work, running any type of restaurant."

"Yes, but we love it. Usually." Sandy settled in her chair. "Although I sometimes wonder how long we'll be able to keep up the pace. We're only in our mid-fifties now, so it isn't too tough, but as I told Pete, I don't plan to be doing this when I'm in my seventies."

"And who do you think will take it over?" Pete appeared in the doorway to the master bedroom, rubbing at his right eye with one finger. "Neither Shawna nor Liza will likely move here to run a café."

"No, of course not. They have their own families to think about now." Sandy leaned forward, and added in a conspiratorial tone, "Second grandchild is due in the fall. Liza this time. We're thrilled, of course."

"That's nice. I guess it's a time for such news. I just found out my younger sister's wife is having a baby too."

"Oh, how lovely," Sandra said, clapping her hands.

"When I talked to her the other evening, Mel sounded so happy. She's been waiting a long time for this, so she's thrilled. As are my parents, of course." I waited until Pete had taken a seat in the rocker next to mine before diving into my inquiry. "Changing the subject to something less pleasant, I just wanted to check with you both about a few things."

Pete shot me a sharp glance. "About the party?"

"Yes. I know you don't have all the answers, but I thought perhaps you'd seen something that might help me understand the situation better." I lifted my shoulders in a *what can you do?* gesture. "I have to live with some of the guests, you know. I'd like to be sure I'm not under the same roof as a murderer."

Sandy shared a look with her husband. "Well, as to that, we are a bit concerned for you, honestly."

"Why's that?" I took a long swallow of water before setting my tumbler on the glass-topped wicker table next to my chair.

"That Scott Kepler fellow," Pete said. "He's still at Chapters, right?"

"Yes, and in the house proper now, since the carriage house isn't available."

Pete drummed his fingers against the arm of his chair. "That's . . . unfortunate, in my opinion."

"What do you mean? Surely you don't suspect Scott of being the killer."

"He doesn't seem like the type, but"—Sandy twisted the hem of her apron between her fingers—"we've just wondered, because Pete says he saw Scott arrive back at Chapters some time before he said he did."

I sat up, swinging the rockers of my chair so far forward that I had to slam my heels against the floor to stop their movement. "You did?"

"Yeah." Pete scratched at the side of his nose; his gaze focused on the string of cobalt-blue glass balls caught up in a fisherman's net that hung on the opposite wall. "I heard him tell the police he had just arrived back at the carriage house right before he discovered Lincoln Delamont's body. But I saw him messing around the side of the carriage house at least ten minutes before that."

"Near the old garden bin?" I asked, recalling Alicia's mention of the trench coat and hat found stuffed in it.

"Looked like it. I couldn't really see what he was doing, 'cause those hollies blocked the view, but I did see him walk back there and then heard something like a door opening. Might've been the lid to that storage box, I guess."

I sank back against the back of the rocker. "But he was on the property at least a little while before he claimed he was?"

"Yep. And then there's the stuff we heard him saying once." Pete turned to look at his wife. "You remember that conversation, don't you, Sandy?"

"Like it was yesterday," she replied. "Although I guess it was a year or so ago now." She met my inquisitive gaze with a little lift of her chin. "We weren't eavesdropping or anything. It's just that Scott has been a regular customer at the Dolphin when he's in town. While we don't claim him as a friend, we have chatted a few times when he was getting breakfast or lunch."

"What did he say that makes you think he might have had some hand in Lincoln Delamont's death?"

"It wasn't so much what he said, but how he said it. He mentioned Delamont, you see, and not in flattering terms." Sandy released her grip on her apron and smoothed the wrinkled fabric over her knees.

"Really ticked off, is what she means," Pete said. "Lots of anger in his tone."

"Because Lincoln swindled his dad?"

Pete gave me the side-eye. "That was it. How did you know?"

"He mentioned something about it to me. Just briefly," I said, considering my next words. "Did he say anything threatening?"

"Not really. That Delamont fellow had simply stopped by to pick up a sandwich he'd ordered over the phone, so he wasn't in the Dolphin long. But Kepler spied him at the register and asked who he was. I guess he maybe had an inkling of what the guy looked like, or something. When Sandy told him it was a visitor who was a bookdealer, Kepler lost his temper just like that." Pete snapped his fingers.

Sandy nodded. "It was like night and day. I was chatting with Mr. Kepler and thought he was very pleasant; then as soon as I said *bookdealer*, he sat up and slammed his fist onto the table." She fanned her face with one hand. "Scared me to death."

"I poked my head out of the kitchen after I heard the bang and noticed Kepler's face. He looked so enraged, I headed over to his booth." Pete gave his wife a little smile. "Had to protect my girl, you know."

Sandy waved this comment off. "Oh, I knew I wasn't in any real danger. Mr. Kepler calmed down quickly, but not before he said a few things about Lincoln Delamont being a swindler and crook."

Pete leaned forward, clasping his hands together on his knees. "Yeah, but that initial anger was pretty dramatic. We've wondered, ever since the other night, if maybe Kepler had it in for Delamont, and used the confusion of the party to kill him."

"Which makes us worry a bit about him staying at Chapters with you and Alicia and poor Mrs. Delamont and her daughter still there," Sandy said.

"Oh, I don't know. I can't picture Scott Kepler as a killer." I fiddled with a loose piece of wicker poking out of the arm of the rocker. *Even though he admitted he laid some of the blame for his father's death at Lincoln's door . . .* I shook my head to clear this thought. While it was true that Scott had a motive, so did others. Perhaps even Pete Nelson.

"Did you know him, then? Lincoln Delamont, I mean," I asked, fixing Pete with an intense stare. "Had you encountered him in Beaufort before?"

"A few times. He visited several times over the past few years, and had a few meals at the Dolphin before. Not always alone," Sandy added, with a swift glance at Pete.

"With a woman. Well, different women, actually," Pete said.

"Anyone you recognized?" I asked, thinking of Julie.

"No, they weren't locals," Pete said, speaking so rapidly that I wondered if he was telling the truth. "Or if they were, they weren't ones who often frequented our café."

Sandy shifted her feet. She looked so uncomfortable, I decided not to press her about whether they'd ever seen Julie lunching with Lincoln at the Dancing Dolphin. "Never his wife and daughter, though?"

Pete wrinkled his nose and sniffed, as if the thought of Lincoln's behavior disgusted him. "Nope."

"We didn't even know he was married, much less had a child, until the other night," Sandy said. "He was either alone or with some woman or another. Ones we didn't know," she added, a little too quickly.

"A real ladies' man." Pete's expression darkened to a glower.

I glanced over at him, curious at his obvious distaste for Lincoln's behavior. Of course, it wasn't praiseworthy, but I was sure Pete had encountered many other less-than-honorable men in the course of running his restaurant. Why did Lincoln's behavior disgust him so?

"When did you first see him in Beaufort?" I asked as a thought flashed through my mind.

"About five years ago, I guess," Sandy said. "I remember Liza talking about him once, and she's been gone for around three years." Sandy looked at me with a smile. "She only worked at the Dolphin over the summers until she finished college. Then she moved on to bigger things."

Pete stirred in his chair. "I think she only met him the once."

I cast him a side-eyed glance. I'd never met Liza, but I knew from photographs that she was a lovely girl. Although I remembered Ellen commenting that she had been a bit wild, at least until she'd left Beaufort to marry a naval officer.

Just the sort of girl Lincoln Delamont might've hit on, despite their age difference. I surreptitiously studied Pete, noting the tension in his jaw. I knew Pete was very protective of his girls. Had Lincoln incurred Pete's wrath by messing around with his daughter? There had been something in Ellen's voice when she had mentioned Liza that had made me wonder if there was more to the girl's story than just a little natural teenage rebellion.

And Julie *had* mentioned a woman who'd contacted her to warn about Lincoln's proclivity for violence. It was entirely possible that Liza had seen Julie dining with Lincoln at the Dolphin during one of her visits home. Was Liza one of Lincoln's former girlfriends?

*Victims*, I thought. *And if Lincoln had mistreated Liza in any way, that alone could have been Pete's motive for killing the man.* I tightened my lips and decided to ask Ellen to share more, if she knew it, about Pete's daughter's past.

Sandy, who seemed oblivious to this undercurrent, stood. "Sure I can't get you something else to drink? Or a snack?"

"No, no." I grabbed my purse and rose to my feet. "I should be getting along anyway. I know you must be tired, and I need to think about helping Alicia with some dinner for our guests." I twitched my lips into a semblance of a smile. "There's not many of them left, so I thought we'd offer some additional meals, if they're interested."

We said good-bye and I beat a hasty retreat, my mind racing with thoughts of Scott or Pete as the killer. *Either one might have had a motive and opportunity*, I thought, as I descended the stairs to the street.

I definitely needed to discuss my latest information, and my suppositions, with Ellen. Maybe she could help me make sense of it all.

*Or maybe,* I thought, setting off at a fast pace for Chapters, *there is no sense to it at all. Maybe I'm just chasing an imaginary butterfly, like Shandy often does. Running in circles that lead nowhere.*

I thrust back my shoulders as I reached my block. I couldn't let my muddled thoughts derail my pursuit of the truth, especially if I could help Julie in any way. My sleuthing was still worth the chase, despite all the dead ends and detours.

# Chapter Seventeen

Having given Alicia the day off, I was prepared to make breakfast for the few remaining guests, but soon discovered it was unnecessary. As I fiddled with the percolator, Jennifer Delamont wandered into the kitchen to inform me that she and Tara were taking off before breakfast. They'd been given permission by the authorities to leave the Beaufort area for the day, and planned to drive into Wilmington to consult with a lawyer on several matters concerning Lincoln's death. Scott, my only other guest, had also refused my offer to make him breakfast, simply requesting one of Alicia's cinnamon rolls and coffee.

"I want to take some additional photos of the area before I dive into more research at the Maritime Museum's library," he'd told me.

So I was left with more time on my hands than I'd expected. Pondering Ophelia Sandberg's comments about my great-aunt hiding things in her books, I decided to search the library. Not that I could go through every volume in a morning, but I could at least make a decent start.

In the library, I stood in the middle of the room and surveyed the shelves covering all four walls. The idea of taking down every volume and checking for hidden papers or other secret documents was daunting, but I knew the best way to accomplish any major goal was to break it into smaller components. I couldn't allow myself to become overwhelmed by the sheer magnitude of my task. Instead, I'd simply choose one section of shelving and make that my goal for the morning.

*There's no rush*, I reminded myself as I climbed the rolling ladder to start at the top left edge of the shelving section. *Whatever Isabella's secrets, they've remained hidden this long without causing any harm. Or, at least, none you know about. Surely they can keep for weeks or even months longer.*

It was two hours later before I discovered anything inside the books other than their bound pages. Shoved inside a first edition of Agatha Christie's *Murder at the Vicarage*, I found a stash of folded onionskin paper. *The type of thing that was once used for international correspondence*, I thought as I backed away from the shelves, clutching the slender packet of papers.

Sitting down at the desk, I carefully opened the papers and spread them across the leather-bound blotter that covered the wooden surface.

I didn't recognize the handwriting, but it was obvious from the sloppiness of the black ink scrawled across the translucent paper that the author had dashed off this letter in a hurry.

*My dear Bella*, it said, before devolving into an account of the weather in some unnamed country. Paragraphs devoted to banal descriptions of rainstorms and snow showers were followed by equally boring depictions of meals and visits from people only designated by the first initial of their names. My eyes glazed over as I read scintillating passages such as: *Mr. K stopped by to ask my opinion on the best way to fertilize roses.*

I slumped down in my chair with a sigh. Why Isabella would keep such drivel, much less hide it between the pages of her books, was beyond me. Flipping to the end, I noticed that the letter wasn't even signed with a full name—just a flourish of one more initial. Squinting at the letter, I realized that it was a capital *P.*

*P for Paul?* I sat up and stared at the pages again. Ophelia and Bernadette had identified the man in the old photograph as Paul Peters. Was this a letter from my great-aunt's long-term companion?

Reading more carefully, I noticed the use of repeated words and phrases, and how they were often used to start a sentence. Perhaps, like Isabella's journal, this seemingly innocuous letter was written in code. Pulling my cell phone out of my pocket, I dialed Ellen Montgomery's number.

She answered on the third ring, but when I mentioned uncovering some new information about Isabella's past and asked if I could stop by her house in a few minutes, she informed me she had a long-standing commitment that would take up most of the day.

"How about tomorrow instead? I can free up my entire morning if you like," she offered, obviously sensing my disappointment.

I agreed to this plan before we hung up. Carefully folding the letter, I slid it into my pocket, then stood and wandered into the kitchen. Absently opening one of the standing freezers, I contemplated my options for lunch. I was startled out of my reverie by a series of sharp raps on the back door.

"Hello," I said, opening the wooden door but keeping the screen door closed and latched.

Kelly Rowley stood on the cement stoop, clutching a leather-bound book to her breast. "Oh hi, Charlotte. I just stopped by to return this." She held up the slim volume, which I recognized as a copy of Hemingway's *Old Man and the Sea*.

"Sorry, I'm here by myself this morning, so I wanted to be a little cautious." I unlocked the screen door and held it open. "Please, come in."

After Kelly entered the kitchen, I hesitated for a moment before latching the screen door again. Of course, it would be easy enough for a determined attacker to break through that door, but at least we'd hear them before they got inside.

*Listen to yourself,* I thought. *Imagining someone trying to attack you in your own kitchen on a Tuesday morning.* I shook my head as I followed Kelly over to the table tucked under one of the room's tall windows. A battered oak piece I'd found in the attic when I'd first moved in, the round table was so small that it accommodated only two chairs. But that was enough for its purpose. Alicia and I typically ate our meals there, often alone, since our schedules didn't always coincide. We reserved the dining room for our guests.

"Mind if I sit down?" Kelly asked, her hand resting on the rounded back of one of the wooden chairs.

"Of course not. Please have a seat." I waited until she sat before motioning to the smaller refrigerator that held our nonalcoholic drinks. "Can I get you anything?"

"Just water," Kelly said, slipping a loose tendril of hair behind one ear.

As I grabbed a tumbler from a cabinet, I noticed that Kelly had lost that sleek but simple elegance I had admired upon meeting her. Today she'd yanked her golden hair into a messy ponytail, and instead of her usual classy slacks and blouses, she'd thrown on a pair of rumpled cotton shorts and a knit top with a neckline so stretched out that it kept sliding off one of her slender shoulders.

I placed a fisherman's rope coaster on the table in front of her before setting down the ice water. "Thanks for bringing back the book," I said, as I took the other chair. "But you could've waited until the end of the week. If you're still reading . . ."

"No, no." Kelly gulped down some water before continuing. "Besides, it was Todd who'd borrowed it, not me. He didn't mean to take it out of the house, of course, but when we had to pack up and move back to the yacht so quickly . . ." Kelly's lashes, surprisingly pale without their usual touch of mascara, fluttered over her light eyes. "Apparently it got mixed in with some of his own stuff in his briefcase. He didn't notice it until last night when he was going through his things."

"Well, thanks." I picked up the book and slipped it into my lap. "As it turns out, I was just headed for the library when you stopped by. I'll mark it *returned* in the guest checkout card file for you."

"Thanks. We didn't want to forget and leave town without bringing it back." Kelly looked me over. "I hope you're doing okay. It must be tough, dealing with all this on your own. I have Todd to lean on, thank goodness. Don't know what I'd do without him."

I squared my shoulders. *Kelly's just trying to be sympathetic, not unkind.* "I admit it would be nice to have someone who could support me, and me them, of course. But unfortunately, I'm alone now."

"Yes, I remember you saying something about your late husband, so I assumed you were a widow." Kelly's gaze softened. "My sympathies. He must've been relatively young when you lost him."

"Not quite forty," I said, in the detached tone I'd learned to employ whenever I discussed Brent.

"That is tragic." Kelly cleared her throat. "And I mean that sincerely. You see, I lost my parents when I was young. Never really got over it, despite trying for many years." She stared down into her water glass as if it held the answer to a particularly puzzling riddle. "Oh, I learned to cope and have a full life and all that. But"—she looked up at me, her eyes haunted—"you never totally get past it, do you?"

"No, not entirely." I pressed my hand to my heart. "And maybe that's okay. I wouldn't want to forget or not care anymore. Would you?"

"No, never." Kelly took another swallow of water as her gaze swept over the kitchen. "Ms. Simpson is out?"

"Yes, I gave her the day off. She has some family in the area. I thought she might want to get away and visit with them, especially since we don't have the usual number of lodgers this week."

"That was thoughtful of you," Kelly said, setting down her glass and fixing me with a troubled stare. "But since she isn't around at the moment, maybe it's a good time to tell you something that's been worrying me."

"Concerning Alicia?" I fought to keep my tone light.

"Yes." Kelly slid one finger around the rim of her tumbler. "I saw her, you see, while you were gone the other night. Outside, I mean. Near the carriage house."

"Really?" Aiming for a nonchalance I didn't feel, I sat back in my chair.

"You were out getting ice, I think you said. Anyway, after you drove off, I heard a door slam and noticed Ms. Simpson had stepped outside. I was standing at the edge of the patio, over near that holly hedge. When I saw her marching with such deliberation toward the carriage house"—Kelly, her elbows resting on the table, templed her fingers—"I admit I was curious."

"Did you see her enter the carriage house?"

"No. As I said, I was on the other side of the hedge."

"But did you also notice when she left the carriage house area?" I gripped the edge of the tabletop. "She had to have done so before I returned, as she was in the kitchen when I got back."

Kelly shook her head. "No. Todd called me over to take a look at something in your garden." She met my inquisitive gaze without blinking. "He doesn't know as much about plants as I do, so he's always asking me to identify things he finds interesting."

"I see." I drummed my fingers against the table. "Were you in the garden long?"

"Not really. I mean, I was, but not with Todd. I waited while he went to grab us more drinks." Kelly ducked her head. "But he got waylaid by someone who wanted to talk or something, or that's what he told me later."

"You were in the garden until I called everyone inside? That was not long after Scott found the body."

"Yes." Kelly lifted the tumbler and pressed it to her lips. She audibly inhaled and then took a drink before glancing at me over the rim of the glass. "By the way, I also saw Mr. Kepler return. It was a little sooner than he told the police."

"Oh?" I worked my jaw to release the tension clenching my facial muscles. This fit what Pete had told me yesterday, which wasn't a comforting thought. "Did you see what he was up to? I mean, did he enter the carriage house as soon as he returned to Chapters?"

"No, he was doing something outside. Near that garden storage container at the side of the carriage house."

*Messing around the bin. Just like Pete told you.* I shoved my fingers through my hair, tugging a little to feel a twinge of pain. I wanted to remind myself to stay alert, to watch my words. "You saw him clearly?"

"No. I just heard rustling, and when I glanced in the direction of the noise, I noticed a shadowy figure moving around in the space between the hedge and the side of the building." Kelly cast me an apologetic smile. "You can see through from the other end of the hedge when you're in the garden, you know. But it was dark, so I couldn't make out who it was. Until the clouds moved away for a second and the moonlight cast some light. His height, and that reddish hair of his is distinctive, so I figured it must be him." Kelly shrugged. "I didn't think too much about it at the time, because he was staying in the carriage house. I assumed he had a right to be there."

I clasped my hands together on the tabletop. Kelly's comment confirmed Sandy and Pete's assertion that Scott had returned some time before he had claimed to have discovered Lincoln's body. "You told the authorities about that, I hope."

"Not yet." Kelly cast me an abashed smile. "I should have, I know, but things were so crazy the other night, it just slipped my mind."

I dropped my hands into my lap, resting them on the tooled leather cover of the Hemingway book. "You should tell them." Since I'd always liked the man, I didn't enjoy the cloak of suspicion this threw over Scott, but truth was truth.

"I will. As a matter of fact, the Beaufort police asked Todd and me to come in to the station later this afternoon for another round of questions, so I'll definitely share the information then." Kelly pushed back her chair. "Now, I should be running along. I'm sure you have things you need to do."

I almost said I didn't, but rose to face her instead. "Well, thanks again for returning this." I held up the book. "And I hope you and Todd will consider participating in the two remaining events I've scheduled for this week—a cocktail hour on Thursday evening, and another discussion on Tey and her books on Saturday night. Thought that was better than the murder mystery event I originally planned," I added with a grimace.

"I agree, and yes, we will definitely try to attend." Kelly bobbed her head as she offered a good-bye, before heading toward the back of the kitchen.

"Need to unlatch it," I called out to her as she fumbled with the screen door.

Kelly waved and exited, allowing the door to slam behind her.

I hesitated for only a second before crossing the room. This time, I left the screen door unlatched, closing and locking the heavy back door instead. Leaning my forehead against one of its silky wooden panels, I considered the possibility that Scott Kepler had stabbed one of my guests to death.

Unlike most of my other guests, Scott was likely to return to Chapters on a regular basis. Adding in his obvious interest in

Julie, I knew I had to face him, to find out for sure if he had killed Lincoln Delamont. Or, barring that, to at least get a better sense of whether I felt he was capable of such a thing.

Stepping back, I considered my options. Scott had told me he'd be working most of the day at the Maritime Museum, which was only a short walk from Chapters.

It was a journey I had to make, even if I might not like what I found when I reached my destination.

# Chapter Eighteen

The Maritime Museum was located on Front Street. Another section of the museum that I loved to visit, the Harvey W. Smith Watercraft Center, was located directly on the waterfront, across the street. It featured boat-building demonstrations and exhibits. But I knew Scott would probably be working in the museum proper, as that building housed a small research library along with its exhibits.

Walking into the museum, I resisted the urge to examine the items on display that chronicled the history of the *Queen Anne's Revenge*, the flagship of Edward Teach, better known as Blackbeard. I knew from previous visits that Blackbeard had run the ship aground in 1718 in the waters of Beaufort Inlet, just off Fort Macon. Although the pirate and his crew escaped, the ship sank and was not rediscovered until 1996. The actual wreck site was owned by the state of North Carolina, as it fell within the three-mile state waters limit. Many of its archeological finds were displayed in the Beaufort Maritime Museum.

I rummaged through my purse to find my wallet. Although admission to the museum was free, I always liked to drop a few dollars into the donation box. The museum's preservation of history and commitment to educational programs was work I admired.

Walking past a few exhibits in the main hall, which resembled the interior of a great ship with its high, open-timbered wooden ceiling, I made my way to the area that housed the museum's research library. It also had a two-story ceiling and included a second level along one side of the room, accessible only by staff using a wooden staircase that looked like it belonged on an old sailing ship. The first level, with its tall bookshelves topped with a ledge displaying ship models, a large study table, and an inviting fireplace flanked by wingback armchairs, was available for use by visitors.

Scott was seated in a leather-upholstered, curved-back wooden chair at one of the tables, numerous volumes open on the table in front of him. He looked up as I entered the room.

"Why, Charlotte, hello. What brings you here?" he asked as I sat down.

"Curiosity," I said, meeting his inquiring gaze squarely. "To be honest, I've recently heard a few things that don't quite match what you told me about your movements on the night Lincoln Delamont was killed." I leaned forward, resting my arms on the table. "I wanted to clear up the confusion. For my peace of mind, if nothing else."

"Oh?" Scott casually closed his laptop. "What stories has the rumor mill been grinding out?"

"That's just it—I know it could simply be people spreading gossip. And also, anyone could be mistaken about what they saw, given the confusion of that evening." I gripped my forearms with my hands. "That's why I wanted to ask you about it directly."

Scott leaned back in his chair and studied me for a moment before speaking. "Or they could be deliberately muddying the waters. Throwing suspicion on someone else to protect themselves."

"I've considered that as well, but"—I fixed him with the stare I'd perfected to bring an unruly classroom to order—"two different people have mentioned that you arrived back at Chapters some time before you discovered Lincoln's body. They also said you were *messing around*, as they phrased it, near the side of the carriage house before you went inside."

"Oh, that." Scott shrugged. "Yes, I lingered outside for a little while before I headed inside. But it wasn't for any nefarious purpose, I assure you. Just something silly, actually."

"What do you mean?"

"I'd picked up a few things while I was out during the day, thinking I might join the party. Even though I wasn't really part of the Tey celebration, it just seemed like it might be fun to surprise you and the guests by appearing in costume."

*To surprise Julie, I bet you mean*, I thought, as I narrowed my eyes and continued to stare at him. "What does that have to do with you loitering outside?"

"Okay, so I found an old trench coat and fedora at a consignment shop and decided I'd just throw the coat over my regular clothes, slap on the hat, and appear as Tey's character Alan Grant. I figured a trench coat and fedora would work for a detective from the thirties and forties." Scott cast me an abashed smile. "A foolish idea, I know."

"Those were *your* items the police found in the garden bin?"

"Yes. Sorry for the confusion, but I explained the situation to them once I realized they'd taken the coat and hat away for analysis."

I slid back in my chair, dropping my hands into my lap. "But why stuff them in the bin?"

"That was just convenience. At first, when I came up with my plan, I thought I'd don my costume outside instead of bothering to unlock the carriage house. But then, after I'd already shoved the bag in the bin, I realized I had my laptop and figured I'd better store it. I just thoughtlessly left the clothes bag in the bin when I headed inside."

"Where you found Lincoln."

"Yes, unfortunately." The lines bracketing Scott's mouth deepened. "I totally forgot about the coat and hat until I heard the police had found them."

I looked him over. His explanation made sense, and he appeared perfectly sincere, but then, if he had killed Lincoln, he'd had time to come up with a plausible story. I frowned as another thought occurred to me. If Scott had been outside the carriage house earlier than I'd originally thought, he could've glimpsed the killer. If it wasn't him, of course.

"Did you see anyone fleeing the scene?"

"No. As I told the police, I didn't see or hear anything suspicious. Not until I entered the carriage house—yes, the door was unlocked, which should've been my first clue that something wasn't right—and went inside. But whatever happened obviously occurred before I returned to the property, because all I saw was Lincoln's body."

*That would explain the missing key*, I thought, before placing my hands back on the table. "And the police know all this?"

"Of course. I'm only sorry I forgot to mention the items earlier. It would've saved the authorities some time. They could have eliminated them as evidence right away."

"I'm not sure they would've taken your word for it," I said, using my fingertip to trace a question mark on the tabletop.

"No, you're right. They'd probably have sent them off for analysis anyway." Scott rested his chin on his hand and studied me. "You look unconvinced. You don't really think I had anything to do with Delamont's death, do you?"

I lifted my hands. "Your story sounds reasonable, but I know you do have a history with the man, which gives you a motive."

"My dad, you mean."

"Lincoln Delamont swindling your dad, to be more precise."

Scott nodded. "Not an impossible stretch to imagine someone killing over that, I suppose. But even though I was angry with Delamont for his unsavory business practices, and have always wondered if his actions might've affected my father's health, I promise I didn't kill the guy. Besides"—Scott pointed his finger at me—"I believe you also have a motive, if what I've heard about Delamont threatening you with blackmail is true."

"How did you . . . ?" I shook my head. "Never mind, I should've known that rumor would get around."

"As rumors do."

"Yes, unfortunately. But despite that, I also swear I didn't stab the guy."

Scott's gaze swept over me. "It seems we're at an impasse on that topic. Why don't we set aside our mutual suspicion and talk about something else?"

As I surveyed his pleasant face, I had to admit that I wanted to keep talking, but not about Lincoln's murder. My gut told me he was innocent, and while that wasn't proof, I was more interested in his feelings for Julie and in determining whether or not he was a good match for my friend. "Is this for your book?" I gestured toward the pile of texts on the table. "I assume this is all research for that project."

"Yes, it's never ending." Scott flashed me a smile. "Or at least it feels that way."

"I guess that tends to be true, especially for nonfiction."

"If you want to get it right, and I do."

"Which is good." I noticed tension tightening his jaw. It reminded me of our discussion the night of the murder. It seemed mentioning his writing made him a little uncomfortable, and I thought I might know why. "Despite your dad's success, you really have no desire to write fiction?"

"More like *because* of it. As I said the other night, I don't want to fight in my father's arena. Dad may have passed away, but I'm sure some reporter or blogger would dig up our connection and compare my fiction to his." Scott lowered his lashes, veiling his brown eyes. "I'm pretty sure I'd come up short in that analysis."

"You don't know that for certain."

"But I do. Dad was such a famous literary figure, well respected by his peers. His books were not only best sellers; they also won prestigious literary awards." Scott glanced up at me. "Quite a shadow to live under as a writer, let me tell you. I do okay with my historical tomes, but I'm nowhere near his level. And if I tried to equal his success in fiction . . ." His lips twisted into a sarcastic smile. "Well, let's just say I don't plan to subject myself to that humiliation."

"But you obviously make enough to write full-time, which most authors can't do." I shrugged. "Or so I'm told by my writer friends."

"That's only because I inherited enough money from Dad to supplement my earnings. Otherwise, I'd need a full-time job on top of the writing." Scott flicked his hands as if casting away a piece of trash. "I'm lucky, I know. Even if I occasionally resent my father's success, it's allowed me to live the way I do. And help support my daughter."

I sat up straighter. "I didn't know you had a family."

"Not much of one. Well, not exactly. Both parents dead, no siblings. And divorced years ago," Scott said. "But I do have one child, Abigail, or Abby, as I call her. She's ten."

This added a new wrinkle to the possibility of him being a suitable companion for Julie. Fortunately, I knew she liked children, which should make this a plus rather than a problem. "You see her often?"

"Oh yes. As much as I can. My freelance schedule helps with that, since her mom's a lawyer. Which means she often needs me to take care of Abby. Which is fine by me." Scott shifted in his chair. "In fact, Abby's been pestering me to let her visit Beaufort, and I'd hoped she could accompany me on this trip." He raised his eyebrows. "Thank goodness that didn't work out."

"Yes, that's a blessing. I'd hate to think of her mixed up in this. It's bad enough that Tara Delamont is caught in the middle of it."

"That is a shame. Even worse if she is the killer."

I tapped the table with one finger. "I don't think she is, honestly. Because of her costume, for one thing."

"Oh? What would that have to do with anything?"

"She was still wearing it later, when not everyone else was, and there wasn't any blood on her rather light-colored gown, or any evidence that there ever had been," I said.

"Good point." Scott looked me over. "You're a pretty smart cookie, aren't you? I hadn't thought of that. But a stabbing would result in some blood spatter, I suppose. Unless it was a professional assassin, and I doubt we're dealing with that."

"Which also makes Julie an unlikely suspect, since she never changed out of her costume either," I said, thinking I should throw my friend's name into the mix. Scott was looking at me with a new level of interest that I wanted to quash. Not that he was flirting, but there was a new intensity in his gaze, and I wanted to make it clear I wasn't trying to encourage such a thing. I thought he was a better match for Julie, and besides, I didn't want to encourage him, or any man, in anything beyond friendship. Not yet. I wasn't ready for that. Maybe I never would be.

"That's true, although she was wearing a color that might not have shown the stains, especially if it was a minor splatter," Scott said. "But don't worry, I don't suspect Julie as the murderer. I just can't imagine her hurting, much less killing, anyone."

"Exactly." I gave Scott a warm smile. "I think you like her a little, don't you?"

"I confess I find her interesting as well as beautiful." Scott tipped his head and gave me a wink. "Since you're her friend, I hope that meets with your approval."

"It does, unless . . ."

Scott's eyebrows quirked. "I killed Lincoln Delamont? Trust me, I didn't, although I must confess I didn't shed any tears over the guy's death."

*You'll be even happier that he's gone when you find out the truth about Julie's relationship with him.* Of course, I didn't voice this thought, choosing to offer Scott a warm smile instead. "I understand. I just feel sorry for his wife and daughter, to be honest."

"Me too. Even if it was his wife who killed him, I suspect she had good reason. And the girl . . . well, it has to be tough, losing someone suddenly like that."

"It is." Unexpectedly, tears welled in my eyes. I fished a tissue from my purse and dabbed at my eyes. "Sorry, still get choked up sometimes, and it's been three years."

"Your husband?" Scott asked, his tone gentle.

I stared at the hands I'd gripped together on the tabletop. "Yes, I'm sure you've heard me mention Brent once or twice."

"I have, and I admit I was curious, but I didn't want to pry." Scott closed one of the open research books and set it to the side. "He must've been rather young, unless he was some years older than you."

"No, we were the same age. He'd be forty-two today, just like me." I pulled apart my interlaced fingers and shook out the tension in my hands. "He was thirty-nine when he died."

"I'm very sorry to hear that. Was it an accident or an illness?"

"An act of God, or so they tell me." I met Scott's inquisitive gaze squarely. "He was vice principal for a middle school in the town where we lived. I taught in a high school in the next county, so we didn't work together, although we met when we were both teaching at another school." I took a deep breath. "Anyway, Brent was always very devoted to his job and his students. He really loved those kids." I smiled wistfully at the memory. "So one day, when a tornado warning went out for the area near his school, he jumped into action."

"The school didn't have a warning system of some kind?"

"They did, but Brent knew there was a classroom, one of those stuck in a trailer due to lack of space, whose alarm hadn't worked properly during the last drill. He told the office staff he was heading out to make sure they'd gotten the warning." I gripped the edge of the table with both hands. "That was the last time any of them ever saw him."

"So sorry," Scott murmured, his eyes filled with sympathy.

I coughed to hide the trembling in my voice. "Brent managed to shepherd that class into the main building and secure them in a windowless room before the tornado touched down. The only thing was, with the rising wind, they found that someone had to hold the door shut outside so that it could be locked from the inside. Anyway, that's what the teacher and kids told me later."

"They survived, then?"

"They did. Brent's actions saved that entire class and their teacher. But apparently, before he could find shelter for himself, the roof in the hallway came off and he was swept away." I squared my shoulders. It was never easy to tell this story, especially when I had to face the pain, and shock, in a listener's eyes.

"Oh God, that's terrible." Scott blinked rapidly but couldn't halt the single tear that trickled down his cheek. "He was a true hero, though."

"Yes, yes, he was. And the town recognized that. They gave him a hero's funeral, and even renamed the school for him. And they were very kind to me, too. Helped me out any way they could."

"As they should have."

"It was still above and beyond. The town even paid for a memorial plaque dedicated to Brent in the local park. So anyway, like you said about your conflicted emotions about your dad, the truth is, I wasn't as grateful as I probably should have been." I pushed my hair behind my ears with both hands and then pressed my palms against my temples. "I understood the town's devotion to Brent's memory, but honestly, I just wanted out of there. I'd been reduced to the 'widow of the hero,' you see. It was done in kindness and to honor Brent, but I felt trapped by the town's reverence for his sacrifice." I dropped my hands. "Sounds horrible, doesn't it?"

"No. That makes sense. You weren't being appreciated for who you were, or liked for yourself."

I nodded. "Exactly. And even though I did, and do, love and admire my husband for his bravery and sacrifice, I am now alone. He'd done a heroic thing, but that still meant he'd left me. Selfish, I know."

"But understandable. I had a similar feeling about my dad. I loved him but wanted to be my own person. When he was alive, I was always questioning whether people I met really wanted to know me for me or were hanging around just as a way to connect to him. And I always felt guilty about that."

"Something we have in common." I absently ran my fingernail over the deckled edges of one of the books on the table. "Anyway, when my great-aunt left Chapters to me in her will, I jumped at the chance to start over. Even if I had to give up my teaching career. But honestly, I didn't quite know what I was getting into," I said, allowing my hand to rest on the book's cover.

"I guess, for starters, that you didn't expect a murder on your doorstep."

I offered him a wan smile. "No, I definitely didn't see that coming."

Scott reached across the table and covered my hand with his. "Well, hopefully this will all be cleared up soon and you can get back to your normal life."

"Thanks," I said, sliding my hand away. Not because it felt wrong. No, it was actually nice to feel a man's touch again.

But in addition to my reluctance to encourage more than friendship with any guy, there was also my belief that Scott's real interest was Julie. A situation I wanted to encourage, not complicate.

*Not to mention*, I reminded myself, *that Scott is still a suspect.* Despite his seeming honesty and the ease of our conversation, I had to remain on my guard.

Because if life had taught me anything, it was that just wanting something to be true didn't make it so. No matter how secure I felt, Brent's death had taught me that everything could change in the moment between one breath and the next.

# Chapter Nineteen

A crash startled me from sleep. Throwing a lightweight robe over my short pj's, I grabbed my cell phone off my nightstand, filched a walking stick from the umbrella stand in the corner of my bedroom, and stepped cautiously out into the main hall.

The noise was coming from the kitchen. I glanced upstairs, where everyone else in the house slept. No one but me appeared to have been awakened by the clatter. Fingering the phone in my pocket, I tiptoed to the kitchen door.

One glance reassured me that there was no intruder—only a girl seated at the small table under the window.

"Tara, what are you doing in here at this hour?" I asked as I crossed the kitchen. Surveying her tangled hair and bleary eyes, I wasn't surprised by the empty split of spumante lying beside her bare feet.

It had obviously rolled off the table—the source of the sound that had woken me. I released my grip on the cell phone in my robe pocket and leaned over to pick up the small blue bottle.

"And what's all this?" I asked, shaking the bottle under her nose. "You're too young to be drinking alcohol."

Tara straightened, tossing her heavy mane of hair behind her shoulders. "I've had wine at home plenty of times."

"But this isn't your home, it's mine. And I don't allow underage drinking here." I waved my hand over the empty cracker sleeves and bits of cheese littering the tabletop. "And while I don't mind my guests having an occasional snack, I prefer they ask first."

"I was hungry," Tara said, fixing me with a glare that would've frozen the blood of most adults. But I'd taught high school for far too long to be intimidated by such tactics.

"Fine, but either Ms. Simpson or I would've fixed you something if you'd asked." I pointed to the clock. "Earlier in the evening, of course. Not at three in the morning."

Tara dropped her head into her hands. "Couldn't sleep. I can't ever seem to sleep anymore."

I noticed the shaking of her narrow shoulders. "I'm sorry." I pulled out the other chair and sat down across from her. "I know this is a terrible time for you. But drinking won't really help, you know."

"I know." Tara straightened and met my sympathetic gaze. "It's just . . . today was especially awful. I wanted to blot it all out."

"What happened? I know you and your mom spoke to a lawyer today. Well, yesterday, actually," I added, with a smile I hoped would ease the girl's anxiety.

Tara yanked her fingers through one of the knots in her curly hair. "Yeah, and it made me realize that I did something stupid.

Said something, I mean. To the police. It was the truth, but . . ." She shook her head. "So dumb."

"Telling the police the truth isn't stupid," I said.

Tara grimaced. "It is if it ends up getting my mom in trouble."

Her eyes were rimmed in red. I frowned and swept aside a scattering of cracker crumbs. "Was this something to do with a piece of trim from your costume?"

Tara shot me a sharp look. "Yeah. How'd you guess that?"

"I saw the officer find it, caught up in an azalea bush near the carriage house," I said, thinking it best not to mention that I was the one who'd first noticed the fake gem.

"It popped off my gown when I was trying to look inside." Tara's direct stare dared me to question her further.

I'd take that challenge. "You were at the carriage house close to the time your dad was killed, then."

"Right after you drove off to get something. Some more drinks or whatever it was you told the police."

"Ice," I said mildly. It seemed that Tara wanted to talk, despite her belligerent attitude, and I had no intention of stopping her.

"Yeah, anyway, a little before that I overheard my dad talking to some woman." Tara wound one lock of her hair around her finger. "I didn't see them. They were behind that big hedge. But I recognized Dad's voice."

"And the woman?"

"Couldn't tell who it was. I mean, I knew it wasn't Mom, but all I could figure out was that it was some female. They were whispering, you see."

"But you heard what was said?"

Tara squinched her face, as if the memory pained her. "Unfortunately. Dad asked the woman to follow him into the carriage house. The woman agreed, although she didn't seem too thrilled about it. Then I had to scramble out of there, because they were moving out from behind the hedge and I was afraid they'd see me. Once I heard a door open and close, I figured they'd gone inside."

"You tried to look in the carriage house windows to see who it was?"

Tara nodded. "I just wanted to know for sure. I thought it was probably your friend, that Julie person. Figured that, anyhow, 'cause Dad was flirting with her at dinner." Tara cast me a disdainful look. "Yeah, I noticed. So did my mom."

"Sorry," I said, not sure what else to say.

It didn't matter anyway, as Tara was now on a roll, the words bubbling out like water from a spring. "I crawled behind that bush to try to look in the window but couldn't see anything 'cause the curtains were drawn. There was just a little slit I could peer through, but even though I did try, it was too dark inside, so"—Tara lifted and dropped her shoulders in an exaggerated shrug—"no go."

"You didn't stick around to see who else might've entered or exited the building?"

Tara wiped her mouth with one hand before answering. "No. Somebody else showed up and I heard the carriage house door opening, so I ran out the back opening of the hedge, into the garden. I was able to see who came out of the carriage house, though. It was my dad. I guess the woman stayed inside to hide because of who showed up to confront dad."

I leaned forward, resting my arms on the table. "Your mom?"

Tara lips trembled as she nodded. "Yeah. She looked so pissed, I was afraid to stick around."

"And you told the police all this?"

"Uh-huh. When they questioned me about that fake jewel off my costume." Tara dashed away her welling tears with the back of one hand. "But now I think I did something wrong. Cleared myself but got my mom in trouble. At least it seemed like that lawyer thought so."

"You had to tell the truth," I said, keeping my tone gentle. "That was your responsibility."

"But my mom had every right to be mad!" Tara blurted out. "I mean, Dad had humiliated her in front of all those other people. Letting all those strangers see him dis her. Carrying on with that woman the way he did. I was angry too. Doesn't mean either of us killed him."

"No, it doesn't." I sat back, compassion tightening my chest. The girl had obviously been through a lot, and not just on the night her father was murdered. "Did he do that often? Humiliate your mom, I mean?"

"All the time." Tara looked off to one side as she swallowed back a sob. "He always put her down. Acted like she was stupid or something. Treated her like she was nothing, and she . . . put up with it."

*Until maybe she didn't.* I refused to voice this thought aloud, instead reaching my hand across the table. "You defended her, I bet."

"A lot of the time." Tara glanced back at me. She stared at my hand for a moment before wiping her fist under her nose.

"Did she get angry about it when he wasn't around?"

"Sometimes. Not that I blamed her. I thought she should've slapped him or kicked him in the nuts or something. I would've, if he'd treated me like that."

"They argued, though?"

"Sometimes. But Mom always backed down."

"I imagine she kept the peace partially to protect you," I said, my own eyes welling with tears.

"Yeah," Tara said morosely.

"But that isn't your fault, and neither is telling the police the truth."

"I guess. It's just that"—Tara sniffed back another sob—"if something happens to my mom, I'm all alone, you know. Well, there's my grandparents, but that isn't the same."

"I'm sure it won't come to that," I said, knowing in my heart it was a lie. If Jennifer Delamont had murdered her husband, she would go to jail and Tara would be left without any parents. "But couldn't you stay with your grandparents for a while? I mean, if you had to."

"I guess. But it's only Mom's parents. My dad lost his parents long before I was born." Tara bit her lower lip. "That's what he always said, anyway."

"You didn't believe him?"

Tara's eyelashes, beaded with tears, fluttered as she met my gaze. "I guess I did. But he didn't seem to want to talk about them much. Like maybe they didn't get along or something, even though he did inherit a lot of money from them."

"I imagine that's how he was able to set up as a rare-book dealer."

"Guess so. I know he didn't make a fortune off his business later, 'cause Mom was always worried about that. But he had investments, or something. That's what we mainly lived on, according to what I overhead my parents say." Tara pursed her lips. "Dad handled all the financial stuff. Mom didn't know much about it, which made her nervous. She even got a job not long ago. Working as a teacher's aide at an elementary school. Doesn't pay that much, but she seems happier, having some money of her own."

*Because she was afraid Lincoln was a crook?* I considered whether Jennifer Delamont might've been planning a split from her cheating spouse before his untimely death. "It's always good to have something of one's own."

"Yeah, that's what Mom says. She told me I should always keep some money in my name, even when I get married." Tara shot me a conspiratorial look. "But I'm not really sure I ever want to do that. Get married, I mean. Doesn't seem like such a good deal to me."

I swallowed back a swear word. The poor kid had obviously been disillusioned by her difficult family life. "It can be wonderful, but you have to be with the right person. My husband and I were very happy together, so I know it's possible."

Tara's eyes widened. "But he died?"

"Yes." I fought my urge to weep, unsure whether it was sparked by my loss or Tara's situation. At any rate, indulging my own emotions wouldn't help the girl.

"That's sad. Seems unfair too," Tara said. "People who love each other shouldn't lose each other."

"Sadly, life isn't fair," I said.

"That's true." Tara motioned toward the table. "I'll clean up this mess if you want."

"No, I'll get this. You go to bed." I shoved back my chair and rose to my feet. "You're my guest," I added, in a softer tone. "And even if you weren't, I'd want you to get some rest."

Tara stood to face me. "I'll try. Thanks for listening," she added, with a tremulous smile. "And not treating me like I'm a brat."

"If anyone has a right to act out, you do," I said. "And honestly, you haven't done anything too terrible. But"—I shook my finger at her—"don't get into the booze again, okay?"

"Okay." Tara's smile, faint but earnest, reassured me that she'd abandoned her claims about my connection to her father's murder.

*Which she probably never believed*, I thought, as the girl left the kitchen. *No doubt that was all an attempt to shield her mother from any suspicion.*

Because now there was even more reason to suspect that Jennifer Delamont, humiliated for the last time, had stabbed her dismissive, philandering husband.

# Chapter Twenty

I cleaned up Tara's mess, then wielded a handful of paper towels and bottle of cleaner to attack some other areas of the kitchen. Not because they really needed cleaning—Alicia kept the space practically spotless—but because I was too full of nervous energy to go back to bed.

Shoving a rolling metal cart to one side so I could reach the edge of one counter, I noticed a crumpled piece of paper on the floor. I picked it up and realized it was some sort of letter. That was odd. Alicia wouldn't have just tossed something like that, and I always handled any mail or paperwork in my office.

I carried the letter to a counter that had a light fixture built into the cabinet overhead. Flicking on the light, I smoothed out the paper so I could read the contents.

The information printed in the upper right corner was my first clue. It was the name and address of a prestigious restaurant in Beaufort. I glanced at the date. It seemed the letter had been written in early May.

The salutation, *Dear Mr. Carr*, surprised me, until I remembered that Damian had worked a gig at Chapters around that time. He'd obviously received the letter and read it here while cooking for us, then tossed it away for some reason.

That reason wasn't hard to imagine once I'd read through the entire letter. It was a polite, but firm, rejection of Damian's application to work at the restaurant as a sous-chef. Despite commending his cooking skills and experience, the owner had felt compelled to turn down Damian because, as he put it, a friend and restaurant patron had warned him about Damian's "volatile temper."

I leaned over the counter, staring at the rumpled page. Damian had been trying to land a full-time position as a chef for some time, so I knew this had to have been a blow. No wonder he'd balled up the letter and tossed it aside. He'd probably meant to pick it up later, but had simply forgotten it in the rush of preparing a special dinner for one of Chapters' events.

"You're up late. Or is it early?"

I turned to face the speaker. "Both, I guess. Hope I didn't wake you."

"I woke myself. I had a nightmare about being lost in the dunes, which I guess was because I was thirsty. The tepid water from the bathroom wasn't cutting it, so I thought I'd grab a cold bottle from the fridge." Alicia padded into the kitchen in a fluffy lavender robe and matching slippers. "What's that you're studying so intently? Worrying over the bills in the middle of the night now?"

"No, I found this behind that cart, which I guess hasn't been moved in quite some time." I waved the page through the air. "It's a letter to Damian from a restaurant in town."

"Oh?" Alicia narrowed her eyes. "I'm guessing, from the condition and where you found it, that it wasn't an offer of employment."

"The opposite, I'm afraid."

Alicia crossed her arms over her chest. "Another rejection? No wonder he tossed it aside."

"Yes, but this didn't have anything to do with his cooking skills. The owner says he's been warned off hiring Damian because he's heard too many negative things about his bad temper." I fixed Alicia with a stern stare. "You wouldn't happen to have had a hand in that, would you? I'm aware that you have some long-standing connections with a few of the restaurants in town."

"Me? Why would I do that?" Alicia cast a sharp look at me as she brushed past on her way to the refrigerator. She grabbed a bottle of water and leaned back against the closed door of the fridge.

"Because you dislike Damian. Admit it. You're not a fan."

Alicia gulped some water before responding. "That's neither here nor there. I think he's an arrogant little twerp, but I'm not going to go out of my way to trash the guy's career." She took another long swallow of water. "Besides, I don't have that much influence over anybody. Much less some owner of a fancy restaurant."

"Well, someone apparently did."

"Yeah, more likely that Lincoln Delamont fellow. May he rest in peace," Alicia added, without any real sympathy.

"Why would he have done that? Damian told me he didn't even know the guy."

Alicia cut me off with a wave of her hand. "Honestly, do you think Damian always tells the truth? Of course, it was before your time, but I remember him talking about Delamont creating a stink at some restaurant a few years back. Apparently, Damian was filling in for the chef, who'd broken his arm Jet Skiing. The way Damian told it, he got to the restaurant and discovered the chef hadn't ordered in some ingredients for the specialty of the house, so Damian had to make do."

"Why would that cause a problem?"

Alicia tapped the now-empty water bottle against her palm. "Oh, Delamont claimed he'd made a trip to that restaurant for the house special, and when it wasn't what he expected—because Damian had to substitute stuff, you see—he threw a fit. Chewed Damian out in front of the other patrons as well as the owner."

"I suspect Damian did not take well to that sort of treatment."

"Heavens, no. They had a regular knock-down, drag-out. Verbally, at least."

I met Alicia's amused gaze with a roll of my eyes. "I can imagine, unfortunately."

"I bet you can. Anyway, Damian was really steamed about it. I remember Isabella having to calm him down so he'd be in the right frame of mind to create some cakes for one of her book club teas. This was a day later too, so I guess he'd been stewing about it all night and morning."

I stared back down at the letter dangling from my fingers. "But there's probably not a connection . . ."

Cutting me off again with a loud sniff, Alicia tossed her bottle into the recycling bin. "Yeah, well, I heard Damian muttering about Delamont when he was fixing the food for your War of the Roses dinner. It was after he caught a glimpse of him in the dining room, I guess. Anyway, he banged a few pans around and muttered something about Delamont being a 'nasty snitch' who 'screwed things up for other people.'" Alicia tapped the side of her nose with one finger. "Which makes me wonder if your blackmailing bookdealer was the one who soured that restaurant owner on hiring Damian. He might not have lived here, but he did know some people in town pretty well, from what I've heard through the grapevine."

"It could be, I suppose." I laid the letter back on the counter. "Which means I should share this with the authorities. Even though it doesn't mention who told the owner not to hire Damian."

"But the police can probably find that out easily enough. All they have to do is question the person who sent the letter."

"I guess you're right." I stared at the letter, wishing, in a way, that I'd never found it. I hated throwing more suspicion on Damian. *But if he did kill Lincoln Delamont, he needs to be brought to justice for that crime.* I shook my head. Somehow, the more I heard about Lincoln, the less I felt like finding his murderer. Even though I knew that didn't constitute rational thinking.

Of course, at four in the morning, who was rational? I shrugged off my indecision, folded the letter, and stuck it in the pocket of my robe. "I'll give it to Detective Johnson tomorrow," I told Alicia, who was eyeing me with suspicion. "I mean, we don't know this letter connects Damian to Lincoln, do we?"

"Nope. Although if it was Delamont who messed up Damian's chance at that job . . ." Alicia allowed that thought to dangle as she walked past me. She paused in the doorway to glance back at me over her shoulder. "That could be a strong motive for murder, don't you think?"

What I thought was that her possible desire to protect Isabella Harrington's reputation offered an equally valid motive, but I didn't voice this aloud. Instead I just bid her good-night.

I waited until I heard her footfalls on the stairs before I left the kitchen. But I didn't immediately head back to my own room. Instead, I wandered into the library, figuring I might as well check another couple of shelves. I doubted I'd fall asleep at that point, and there was no sense in just lying in my bed staring at the ceiling. Searching the books for more of Isabella's hidden notes or letters seemed like a better use of my time.

My search didn't yield anything until I opened a copy of Dorothy Sayers's *Murder Must Advertise*. Since she was one of my favorite authors, I had my own dog-eared copy that I'd read several times, but I'd never opened this one. Flipping through it, I discovered another folded sheet of onionskin paper tucked between chapters ten and eleven.

I didn't bother to read it this time, instead sliding it into the pocket with Damian's letter and heading back to my bedroom.

Placing Damian's letter on my dresser, I crossed over to my bed and slumped down onto the firm mattress. I opened the newly discovered document, expecting another innocuous but possibly coded message from the mysterious Paul.

But this was a note written in Isabella's hand. After smoothing out the folds on my knee, I read an account of some party she'd attended, deducing from the references to popular music and clothing that it had been written in the early seventies.

All of which was vaguely interesting, in a historical sort of way, but seemed otherwise too bland and inconsequential to be connected to my great-aunt's other, more mysterious documents.

Until I ran across a name that made me gasp and release my hold on the letter. The flimsy paper fluttered from my fingers and drifted to the floor near my bare feet. I didn't bother to pick it up. My mind was processing a discovery I knew would require additional thought.

And careful questioning of the person mentioned in the document. An individual I trusted, who had claimed she'd not known Isabella in the 1970s. Someone who'd always told me, and others, that she'd first met Isabella after moving to Beaufort in the eighties.

A woman identified in Isabella's letter only by her initials, but lauded as a friend and confidant. Someone my great-aunt respected for her knowledge of the world, which she traveled for her job as a film-location scout.

I picked up the letter and stared at the damning paragraphs again. No, I had not been mistaken. Isabella's script was florid but the initials were clear enough—an *E* and an *M*.

My neighbor, Ellen Montgomery.

# Chapter
# Twenty-One

I never fell back to sleep after my discovery in the library, which meant I was in a daze on Wednesday morning. After helping Alicia serve breakfast to an equally bleary-eyed Tara and her mother as well as Scott, I stumbled back to my room and fell across my bed.

Fortunately, I'd mentioned my ten o'clock meeting to Alicia while we made breakfast, so she banged on my door when I didn't appear again by nine thirty.

"Said you needed to be someplace by ten," she said, when I cracked open the door.

I muttered something that I hoped sounded like "Thanks." After grabbing a quick shower, I didn't bother blow-drying my hair before I threw on a cap-sleeved lavender silk blouse, white cotton slacks, and a pair of beige canvas espadrilles.

Shandy greeted me, fervently barking as he bounced up and down behind Ellen's front door. I tapped the oval window set in the door and told him to hush, but of course that had no effect.

Ellen appeared and used one foot to gently hold the Yorkie to the side so I could enter the house.

"Oh hush, Shandy. You know who this is," she said, as she closed the door behind me.

Indeed, the little dog stopped barking as soon as he sniffed my scent. Bounding forward, he licked my shoe before rolling over to offer up his belly.

I bent over and scratched his fuzzy tummy. "You're a mess."

All four of Shandy's paws waved in delight. "I probably shouldn't reward you for bad behavior," I said indulgently.

"It doesn't matter. I always do. Guess that's why he doesn't behave," Ellen said.

Straightening, I faced off with her.

Something in my expression must have given me away. Ellen pursed her lips and looked me up and down before motioning toward the adjacent front parlor. "Let's sit in here." She marched into the room, Shandy trotting at her heels.

I fingered the three letters I'd stuck in the pocket of my slacks before settling into one of Ellen's comfortable armchairs. "I do have some new information."

"So you said." As soon as Ellen sat in the armchair that faced mine, Shandy jumped up into her lap.

I sank back against the suede cushions of my chair and allowed my gaze to wander over the room. Although Ellen had retained many of the Victorian features of her home, including the wainscoting, deep moldings, and hardwood floors, she hadn't decorated to match. Her furniture was a comfortable blend of casual and modern, in muted tones accented by pale wood. I suspected Ellen had chosen this simple palette to set off the vivid paintings and other works of art that enlivened the space. From previous conversations, I knew she'd collected many of the art pieces during her travels. Everything from Indian wall hangings to Asian ceramics and German cuckoo clocks lent the house an eclectic and exotic air that matched Ellen's own personal style.

*Mysterious*, I thought, narrowing my eyes as I stared back at Ellen.

She met my gaze with a confident smile. "You mentioned something about a document you found in one of Isabella's books. Would you like to share that first?"

"No, before we get into that, I think I'd rather discuss this letter I found in the kitchen last night." I pulled the documents from my pocket and extracted the letter to Damian, laying the others on the French wine barrel that had been cut in half and topped with glass to serve as a side table. "It's a letter Damian Carr received from a restaurant in Beaufort. A rejection letter, sadly."

"For a chef position?"

"Yes. Well, sous-chef, but at this place that's still a coup." I held up the letter. "The thing is, Damian lost the job because of his temperament, not his cooking skills. Someone warned off the owner, claiming Damian was difficult to work with. Alicia seems to think that maybe Lincoln Delamont was involved."

Ellen absently stroked Shandy's back as she continued to hold my gaze. "How is that possible? Delamont wasn't in the restaurant business, at least as far as I know."

"No, but he apparently knew this owner." I explained Alicia's theory about Lincoln bad-mouthing Damian due to their previous altercation. "I guess that gives Damian a strong motive for murdering the guy."

"Which means he stays on the suspect list."

"Unfortunately. I've bumped Jennifer Delamont up to the top of the list, too." I offered Ellen a brief summary of my discussion with Tara. "It wouldn't be surprising for a woman who's been treated with disdain for so many years to finally snap."

"Especially if she'd always been belittled, and then had her narcissistic jerk of a husband shove his latest girlfriend in her face."

"Exactly." I glanced over at the two other letters. "It's one thing to keep up appearances if everything remains a secret, but when you realize you can't pretend anymore"—I looked back at Ellen, noticing with interest the wrinkle that had formed between her brows—"it can set off unpredictable repercussions."

"Very true." Ellen lifted one hand off Shandy's back and pressed it against the padded arm of her chair. "Which means now we have Jennifer Delamont with motive and a definite opportunity, if what her daughter says about encountering her near the carriage house is true. But there's also Damian Carr, who appears to have a strong motive as well."

"And could've walked to and from his apartment easily enough," I said. "Likely without being seen."

"Yes, I imagine he knows the area well enough to move about unobserved." Ellen tapped the arm of her chair. "I'm friends with the owner of that particular restaurant. Perhaps I should give him a call and see if I can find out if it was indeed Delamont who convinced him to reject Damian."

"Oh, I don't know. Shouldn't I share the letter with the police first? They could question him officially."

Ellen lifted her hand and flicked it, as if tossing away something. "If you feel you must. I just thought that if we discovered that Delamont was not involved in Damian's loss of a great job opportunity, it would spare the young man another interrogation by the police."

"There is that." I studied the older woman for a moment, wondering just how willing she was to bend the law. "If you can call the owner and find out anything, great. I'll hold off giving Detective Johnson the letter until I hear from you."

"Good. No use causing more trouble for Damian. It's all just speculation right now, isn't it?" Ellen flashed me a bright smile.

"Yes, but . . ." I allowed my words to trail off. Ellen was right—it was just a theory at this point. A theory that had felt solid last night but seemed less certain in the light of day.

"Very well. I'll let you know as soon as I find out anything, one way or the other." Ellen examined me, her forehead crinkling. "It sounds to me like you've removed Tara Delamont from the suspect list. Am I right?"

"Yes. I just don't think she's involved. Not after you mentioned that clue about her costume, and what she told me last night." I frowned. "But then there's Scott. He did explain why he was outside earlier than he first claimed. Apparently, he was planning to appear in costume at the party and stashed a coat and fedora in the garden bin for that purpose."

"Or so he says." Ellen quirked her eyebrows. "Be honest, Charlotte. I know you like the guy, and I suspect you hope he can be Julie's rebound, if not more, but that's an odd story. And rather convenient. I mean, after the police found that coat and hat, he had to say something. They were likely to connect those items to him eventually."

I slumped in my chair. "I suppose so."

Ellen waved her hand through the air. "Playing the logical detective, we can't rule him out. He does have a motive, if what you told me about his issue with Delamont's treatment of his father is true."

"You're right. Although I can't imagine him killing anyone, I guess we have to leave him on the suspect list. Along with Julie," I added glumly.

Ellen's face expressed sympathy. "I know it's hard to consider your friends as killers. But you know, over the years I've learned that the most unlikely people can do some astonishing things."

I drew in a deep breath. "You've said that before, and I think I have to agree with you." Setting aside Damian's letter, I picked up the two documents I'd discovered in my great-aunt's library. Rising to my feet, I unfolded the one the man who'd called himself Paul Peters had sent Isabella. I slipped the other letter back in my pocket. "Like this letter, for example," I said, strolling over to Ellen's chair. "What do you make of this?"

Ellen took the thin paper from my hand. As she shifted to reach for a pair of reading glasses on the side table next to her chair, Shandy yipped and leapt down onto the floor. He cast me a bright-eyed glance before trotting out of the room.

"And this is . . . what?" Ellen asked, perching the glasses on her nose.

"Something I found in one of the books in Isabella's library." I took a few steps back. "A letter signed with the initial *P*." I examined Ellen's face for any flicker of recognition. But she might as well have been playing high-stakes poker for all I could glean from her expression.

"Really? And why is this so important?" Ellen sat back and stared at me over the rims of her glasses.

"Because," I said, walking back to my chair, "the Sandberg sisters told me about a man they'd met in Isabella's company. A Paul Peters, they said." I flopped back down in the armchair. "They also identified him as the man I saw in that photograph I found of Isabella in her garden. The one I showed you at the beach. It was a picture from back in the sixties, if my guess is correct."

"I imagine Isabella received many letters from friends. Why does this one interest you so?"

"Because it seems . . . odd. It's very banal, but there are these repeated phrases that seem shoehorned in." I tipped my head and met Ellen's intense stare without flinching. "Almost like they were conveying a hidden message. Like that journal I found, only a different type of code."

Ellen glanced down at the letter. "I think you're imagining things. It's just a letter from a friend, talking about the weather and such." She lifted the document by one corner and dropped it on the table beside her. "It wouldn't be surprising that a man she knew wrote to her from time to time. People used to write to their friends, you know, before social media became such a thing."

"I think they were more than friends."

"What makes you say that? Just because he appeared in some random photo with Isabella?"

"No, because Bernadette and Ophelia, who actually met him, told me they assumed the guy was one of Isabella's lovers."

Ellen shoved the eyeglasses back up her nose. "One of them? Did they think she had so many, then?"

"Don't you know?"

"Heavens, no. How could I? I wouldn't know anything about her personal life during that time period, and she certainly didn't appear to have any male companions later in life. You must remember—I didn't meet Isabella until I moved here in the 1980s."

"Yes, about that." I slipped the other letter from my pocket and shook it. "I found something last night that seems to contradict that story. Another document hidden in one of my great-aunt's books."

Ellen looked me over, her eyebrows drawing together. "And what did this missive say?"

"That you knew Isabella before you moved here, for one thing. Unless there were two film-location scouts working in the seventies with the initials *E.M.*"

Ellen's frown turned into a glower. "She wrote something about that in a letter?"

"Yes, she talks about a person with those initials. I assumed it was you. She writes that she'd have to run the details of some trip by you because you know so much about traveling the far reaches of the world."

"Did she indeed." Ellen took off the glasses and dangled them from her fingers. "How inconvenient of her. But then, she always was a bit reckless."

"You did know her before you moved here, then?" I held my breath, waiting for her response.

Ellen swung the glasses for a moment before answering. "Yes. But perhaps not quite in the way that you imagine."

"In what way, then?"

"It was business." Ellen dropped the glasses on the side table and rose to her feet. "She was involved in some projects I supervised."

"I don't understand." I placed the suspicious document on the side table next to the other letter before standing.

"No, and I can't explain. Not now. I would need to . . ." Ellen cleared her throat and snatched up Damian's letter. "Here, take this too. I'll make that call to the owner as soon as I can. If he confirms that it was Lincoln Delamont who suggested that he reject Damian's job application, then perhaps you should share it with the police. But otherwise I would simply discard it."

I stepped close enough to take the letter from her extended fingers. "I take it you aren't going to explain your previous connection to my great-aunt?"

"Not today. Maybe another time." Ellen's gaze swept from my head to my feet and back again. "For now, I'd suggest not digging any deeper. At least not where Isabella's past is concerned."

I turned away to grab the third letter. "Because I might find out information you don't want me to know?"

"No, because you might discover certain facts you'll later wish you hadn't."

I faced her, steeling myself to make my stare as stern as hers. "All right, I'll show myself out. Just let me know when you hear something from that restaurant owner."

"I will." Ellen trailed me, staying close behind me as I strode into the front hall, where we discovered Shandy asleep on a rug in front of the door. He lifted his head and yawned.

"Sorry, fella," I said, "but you need to move so I can exit."

Ellen leaned down and hoisted the sleepy dog up in her arms. "Trust me, Charlotte, I will tell you the truth, if I can." Her voice was so soft that I could barely hear it over the squeak of old wood as I yanked open the door.

I cast her a questioning look. "Good-bye, Ellen. When, or if, you can talk more, just let me know. Although, to be honest, I think I may have an inkling of what you're hiding."

Ellen flashed me a smile that was as brittle as it was brilliant. "I think you may have missed your true calling."

"Unfortunately?" I paused, one foot over the threshold.

"No, I would say you are actually quite fortunate in that regard." Ellen grabbed the edge of the wooden door and held it ajar as I allowed the screen door to slam behind me. "Trust me," she called out as I crossed the porch, "in this case, missing your calling makes you the lucky one."

# Chapter Twenty-Two

When I returned to Chapters, I slipped the three letters into my sock drawer before changing into older clothes and spending the rest of the day helping Alicia clean. We usually did some cleaning every day, but except for taking care of the occupied guest rooms, we'd let things slide a bit this week. It was past time to catch up.

The physical work was just what I needed to keep my mind occupied and quell some of my anxiety, but I was definitely tired by dinnertime. Both Scott and the Delamonts were out for the evening, so after a light supper, I retreated to my room.

I considered reading one of the many books on my "to be read" list, but decided I couldn't give any of them the attention they deserved. Instead, I climbed onto my bed and opened my laptop. After checking emails, I conducted a few random searches on my great-aunt's name. Finding nothing other than mentions related to the bed-and-breakfast business, I switched to looking for information on some of my recent guests.

Of course, there were mentions of Scott in connection to his books, but what caught my attention was an article about the

Rowleys. Even thought it was a puff piece in a lifestyle magazine, my curiosity drove me to read the entire thing.

There wasn't that much of interest—just descriptions of their homes and their yacht, along with a few paragraphs chronicling Todd Rowley's meteoric rise as a leader in the world of high-tech entrepreneurship. But one element from Kelly's past made me pause to read more closely. While most of the coverage focused on her running career, there was a mention of her family that surprised me. I'd assumed Kelly had married into her money, but apparently her parents had been quite wealthy in their own right. Reading on, I realized that my first impression of Kelly as some-one who'd not always lived a life of wealth was actually correct—after her parents died when she was only eleven, the entirety of their estate had passed to her older brother, who was twenty-one at the time. The article went on to congratulate Kelly for rising above this trauma, and financial setback, to carve out a career as a celebrated athlete.

I leaned back into the pillows I'd piled against my headboard. The subtext of the article indicated that Kelly's brother had not taken care of his sister. At least, not financially. That was odd, but then, where money was concerned, sometimes familial feel-ing went out the window.

There was a lot more information on Todd, as well as on Kelly's track-star days, but nothing that would suggest that either one of them would stab a stranger to death.

Not that I expected the Internet to spell out that sort of con-nection. But sometimes, I'd found, it was possible to read between the lines and develop a picture of someone from the footprint they'd left on the Web. Researching a few of my students' parents in order to get a better sense of their homelife, I'd correctly identified a few as emotionally absent, or overly strict law-and-order types, or . . . *reckless*, I thought, remembering Ellen's statement about Isabella.

That thought spurred me to look up references to Ellen Montgomery. These were numerous, but most were false hits, unconnected to the woman I knew. Of course, Ellen had retired from her career as a film-location expert rather young. I frowned as I ran some calculations in my head. Unusually young, actually, which raised another red flag. I'd never really thought about it before, but given her current age, she'd only have been about forty when she moved to Beaufort. That was extremely early to retire, even if someone had made a fortune, and I doubted that a film-location expert, no matter how good, made that much.

I slid my forefinger over the bottom edge of my laptop. It was funny how Ellen's age when she moved to Beaufort hadn't seemed odd to me until now. But when we met, she'd already been in her seventies. I supposed I hadn't really thought it through, since it had seemed reasonable that she'd been retired for some time. I'd never bothered to run the numbers and consider the oddity of her moving to Beaufort, supposedly retired, when she was barely forty.

Setting the laptop on my nightstand, I climbed off the bed and wandered over to the bedroom window overlooking the backyard.

There were no tiny lights sparkling in the vines covering the pergola that evening, but the automatic spotlights still illuminated the patio with crisscrossing ovals of light. I allowed my gaze to slide over to the darker area near the carriage house. Hopefully, the building would be turned back over to me in a day or two. I wanted to thoroughly clean the space. *Scrub it down with bleach, if necessary*, I thought, my lips tightening as I contemplated trying to remove any remaining bloodstains from the weathered wood floors.

One of the azalea bushes swayed, as if brushed by something in passing. Creating a spyglass shape with my hands, I leaned forward to peer into the darkness. An animal, I thought, before my eyes discerned a distinctly human form moving away from the shrub.

I didn't think twice. All I knew was that some stranger was poking about on my property. After slipping on a pair of sandals, I grabbed a sturdy walking stick from my umbrella stand and dashed out of my bedroom to reach the back door.

Once outside, I slowed my steps to silence my approach. A rustle of branches made me suspect that the intruder was still on the premises. Lifting the walking stick in a defensive posture, I advanced on the carriage house, determined to reveal the trespasser.

As I moved close to the azalea bushes, I heard a whooshing noise. I spun around to face the holly hedge and, startled, dropped the walking stick. But as my gaze tracked the sound, I realized it had been made by an owl, flying out of the hedge and sweeping up into the night sky.

My shoulders slumped as I exhaled a sigh of relief. I leaned over to retrieve the walking stick, only to see it slide away from my fingers. Before I could turn to see who had grabbed it from behind, the stick whistled through the air.

A blow sideswiped my head and struck my shoulder. I fell to my knees, bracing myself with my palms. Choking as the scattered leaf meal filled my mouth and nostrils, I barely registered the sound of footfalls. My attacker was fleeing the area—the reverberation of the wooden rails of my back fence confirmed it.

They had leapt the fence and gotten away before I'd had a chance to catch a glimpse of them.

I sat back, spitting out fragments of twigs and leaves. Lifting and rolling my injured shoulder, I was relieved to feel it move freely. It would be sore, of course, probably excruciatingly so. But at least it seemed to be in its proper place, and unbroken.

Blinking to focus my eyes, I noticed something glinting at the base of one of the azaleas. I crawled forward to examine the object more closely and realized, with a strange sense of detachment, that it was a knife.

*Not just any knife*, I told myself as I recognized the handle. *But the one stolen from the knife block in the kitchen.*

The murder weapon.

I staggered to my feet, using the discarded walking stick to brace my trembling legs. Obviously, the intruder had not been a random trespasser. It was the murderer, returning the knife to the scene of the crime.

The knife flashed, its metal surface sparkling, when I poked it with the tip of my walking stick. Wiped clean, no doubt, along with the handle. I sniffed, identifying the scent rising from the murder weapon as a strong cleaning solution or solvent.

I backed away, my gaze still fastened on the knife. I knew I needed to alert the police, but was afraid to leave the scene in case the killer felt emboldened enough to return.

Footsteps crunched the gravel behind me. Swinging the walking stick with my good arm, I turned to face whoever had stepped up behind me.

"Whoa!" Scott held up his arms, crossed to protect his face. "What's going on? I just walked back from having dinner on

Front Street, but I swear I haven't been drinking that much." He grinned and dropped his arms. "No need to fight me off."

"I thought you were the person who struck me," I said, lowering the walking stick while tightening my grip on it. Scott had just appeared, or had he? I rubbed my eyes with the back of my free hand.

"Struck you?" Scott looked me over with concern. "Someone was here just now?"

"Yes, an intruder. I saw them from my bedroom window and came out to investigate . . ."

"You should've stayed inside and simply called the police."

"I know, but I wasn't exactly thinking straight. Anyway, when I got out here, I didn't see anyone. Then I heard a noise and looked away for a moment, and whoever it was hit me and ran." I rubbed my shoulder. "Nothing broken, and they missed my head, so I think I'll be fine."

"But still." Scott moved closer, placing one hand on my forearm. "Sure you're okay?"

"Yes, but we do need to call the police." I grimaced as the pressure of Scott's fingers sent a fission of pain up my arm.

"Well, sure." Scott stepped back, dropping his hand. He reached inside the inner pocket of his light jacket to extract his cell phone. "I'll do that right now." He punched in some numbers before looking back at me. "You really didn't catch a glimpse of the person who hit you? Didn't see anything that could help identify them?"

I shook my head, realizing as I did so that I wouldn't have told him even if I had. Because there was still a possibility he was involved . . .

*Or Jennifer Delamont*, I thought, as Scott talked to the police dispatcher. *Or Damian, who knows this house and grounds well enough to sneak in over the fence.*

"They're on their way," Scott said, as he pocketed the phone. "Can I help you inside? You look like you need to sit down."

"Yes, but we can't yet. Not until the police arrive." I gestured toward the bottom of the azalea bush. "The intruder left that behind."

Scott's eyes widened as his gaze followed my pointing finger. "Is that your missing kitchen knife?"

"Yes. And it wasn't there before tonight, or the police would have discovered it days ago."

"What are you saying? That the killer came back to simply drop the murder weapon at the scene?"

"Wiped clean of any evidence." I touched the side of my nose. "Take a good whiff of the odor rising from that shrub."

Scott sniffed. "Solvent."

"That's what I thought." I blinked as Scott's tall figure swam in front of me. Maybe I wasn't quite as calm as I'd assumed. "You know, maybe I do need to sit down or something," I said as I wavered slightly, leaning hard into the walking stick to prevent my knees from buckling.

Scott sprang forward, catching me by my upper arms. I squeaked as his fingertips dug in close to my injured shoulder but still allowed myself to fall into his arms.

*He might be the murderer*, my brain warned me, but my shaking limbs didn't care. I rested my head against his shoulder, grateful for any support at that moment, knowing that without it I'd have collapsed and fallen to the ground.

I was so exhausted, so weary of secrets and lies and violence, that even if he had been a serial killer, I wouldn't have moved away.

# Chapter
# Twenty-Three

A team from the Beaufort police department arrived within minutes. After collecting the abandoned knife, they searched the area, but found no additional evidence. Not only was the ground too dry and thickly layered with dead leaves and twigs to really hold a clear impression of footprints, but my own scrambling about had also made obtaining such evidence difficult. I apologized, but the police brushed this off. They were more concerned about my health, calling in an EMT I swore I didn't need. But I submitted meekly to an exam while I answered their questions about the intruder to the best of my ability. It was the least I could do.

Once I was pronounced clear of any serious injury, Scott escorted me inside and sat me down at the kitchen table.

"You have anything stronger than wine?" he called out from the pantry.

I suggested the brandy I'd stored in the upper cupboard I used as a liquor cabinet. Scott brought me a glass, along with one for himself, although the one he placed in front of me held decidedly more liquor.

I eyed it dubiously. "You might have to carry me into the bedroom after I down that."

"I thought it might help you sleep," he said, sitting down across from me. "Better than a hammer to the head, anyway."

"Hmm . . . that's a bit grisly, considering the circumstances, don't you think?" I took a drink, hoping my lack of a reaction to such a large swig wouldn't convince Scott I was a lush. I wasn't, but Brent had loved his brandy and cognac, collecting the finer varieties. I'd sampled enough glasses with him in the past to inoculate me against the coughing or sputtering response of a novice.

"Sorry, sometimes I blurt out stupid things when I'm on edge," Scott said, the humor fading from his expression as quickly as it had appeared.

"No need to be nervous," I said, wondering if Scott's reaction was heightened by guilt. If he'd killed Lincoln . . . Staring into his earnest face, I found this hard to believe, but I knew I should remain on guard. "The police didn't find anything other than that knife, and with one of their cars patrolling the area all night, I doubt the intruder will return."

"Too bad you couldn't see who it was." Scott leaned back in the chair until the front legs rose off the floor. "That could've closed the case right then and there."

I circled the rim of my glass with one finger. "As I said, I didn't see anything. I couldn't even tell if my attacker was male or female."

Scott sat forward with a lurch, banging the chair legs down onto the ceramic tile floor. "I guess it will remain a mystery, then."

"Perhaps. But maybe the police will glean some information from that knife, even if it was wiped clean."

"Doubtful." Scott polished off his brandy in two gulps. "Well, I suppose I should head on upstairs. Unless you do need me to help you to your bedroom."

"No, I can manage," I said, after another swallow of brandy. "But thanks for your support outside. I might've hit the ground again otherwise."

"You're quite welcome." Scott stood, holding up his empty glass. "I can wash this if you want."

"No, that's okay. Just set it in the sink. I'll put both tumblers in the dishwasher later." I gave him a wan smile. "Health regulations, you know. Need that hot-water cleansing on any dishware."

"Oh, right. Not like my house, where a quick rinse will sometimes do." Scott flashed a grin before crossing to the sink.

"No, I'm afraid we have to be a little more thorough." I used the table to brace myself as I rose to my feet. "Good night, Scott."

He paused in the kitchen doorway to look back at me. "'Night, Charlotte. Hope you sleep well."

"I'll be fine," I said, although I was actually afraid sleep, good or otherwise, would elude me once again.

Scott gave me a little one-finger-to-the-forehead salute before striding into the hall.

I shuffled over to the sink and deposited my empty glass. *Alicia will probably wonder what I was up to*, I thought, as I headed for my bedroom. Then it occurred to me how odd it was that she hadn't heard the ruckus and appeared downstairs.

Of course, if she had killed Lincoln, and then tried to toss away the now-pristine knife, only to encounter me . . .

I tried to clear my mind of such fancies but couldn't shake how easy it would've been for someone with keys to all the doors at Chapters to circle around the house and quietly enter through the front door. Someone like that—someone like Alicia—could've climbed the stairs and been safely tucked into their bed even before the police arrived, not to mention before I reentered the house.

Of course, if whoever it was had sneaked out the front door and left it unlocked, it could have been a guest like Jennifer Delamont. Or Damien Carr, who lived so close and knew the area, could've easily entered the backyard and fled without being seen.

*And*, I reminded myself, *it was rather convenient for Scott to show up at just the right time to assist me.* Sure, he'd claimed he'd just walked back from dinner, but I had no way of knowing how long he'd been back before he appeared behind me.

I kicked off my sandals and slumped down on my bed. Slipping off my blouse, I grimaced at the dark bruise that discolored my shoulder. It hurt now, but I suspected it would be even more painful in the morning. Sighing, I staggered back to my feet and changed into an old, worn-soft sleep shirt before crawling into bed.

Sleep, when it came, was fitful and full of dreams I couldn't remember when I woke.

Which, judging by the lingering wisps of fear and sorrow flitting through my mind in the morning, was just as well.

\* \* \*

Despite the pain and lingering malaise tormenting me on Thursday morning, I decided to leave Chapters after we served breakfast. I wanted to indulge my desire to investigate my great-aunt's mysterious past.

*Of course*, I admitted, as I drove out of the historic area of town, taking Live Oak Street toward the Beaufort branch of the Carteret County Public Library, *it's also a good diversion. Heaven knows I need something to distract me from thoughts of murderous guests or staff.*

Given the dearth of information online, I thought perhaps the reference department at the library would yield better results. I knew from previous visits that the library held microfilmed copies of a local newspaper, the *Carteret County News-Times*, and that they also maintained vertical files that contained newspaper clippings, pamphlets, and other materials related to the history of the region. That type of resource might yield some mention of Isabella's activities in Beaufort in the 1960s and '70s, especially if she'd hosted and attended high-profile social events.

At the library, I was ably assisted by one of the librarians on duty, who unlocked the vertical files and pulled several folders for me once I explained the type of information I needed. I decided to start with the files, saving scrolling through the microfilm for another day.

Flipping through the material was like stepping into a time tunnel. Newspaper articles of social events were interspersed with programs from school and community theatre productions and flyers advertising regional events. Peering at the grainy photos, I was transported to another time, when the Internet did not exist and newspapers, pamphlets, and other hard-copy materials were the only way, outside local TV or radio coverage, to share community information.

The surprising thing was how often I spotted Isabella Harrington's distinctive face and figure in the group photos of important social events. Occasionally the coverage included parties held at the house that later became Chapters. Reading the captions and accompanying articles, I realized that Isabella had spent a good deal of time mingling with the wealthiest families in the county, as well as with senators, foreign ambassadors, and other high-ranking dignitaries.

It seemed clear that my great-aunt had been one of those "hostess with the mostess" types—to borrow a phrase from the late, not-so-lamented Lincoln Delamont—at least during her younger years. Not something I would've gleaned from any family discussions or from any conversations I'd had with her when she'd visited my parents and grandparents. Even though these files showed she'd moved in exalted social circles, she'd never once mentioned knowing the rich and famous. Yet here she was, her vivacious beauty captured by the camera as she rubbed elbows with some of the most powerful people of the day.

Which made me wonder, once again, where the money she'd lived on had come from. I knew from my own modest efforts at entertaining that the costs of hosting the types of parties documented in some of these clippings would've been astronomical. Even in the 1960s and '70s, entertaining national and world leaders would've required a significant output of cash.

"And there you were, with no visible means of support," I mused, touching a picture with the tip of my finger. Isabella looked back up at me, her smile as enigmatic as ever.

After a few hours, my aching shoulder demanded relief. I thanked the librarian and left, pondering the information I'd discovered.

Perhaps Lincoln Delamont had been right, at least in part. Maybe Isabella had stolen enough valuable items from her employers to stake a claim on a lucrative enterprise. Something she was involved in during the years she was out of contact with my family. Something that had allowed her to then buy a home in Beaufort and live there for many years before converting the house into a bed-and-breakfast.

*Probably not a legal enterprise, though*, I thought, as I drove back to Chapters, *given her lack of a career or any inheritance, and yet her evident wealth. Not to mention her refusal to talk about her past, even with us, her family.*

As I walked from my car toward the kitchen door, I was met by a vehicle leaving the parking lot. Peering into the car, I was surprised to spy Tara Delamont in the back seat.

The passenger's side window rolled down, and an older woman poked her head out.

"Hello, Ms. Reed. Glad we caught you, especially since Jennifer took off for a walk right after saying good-bye to Tara. We're Jennifer's parents, and we've been given permission to take Tara to stay with us until our daughter is free to leave Beaufort."

I peered in at Tara, who was slumped down in her seat. "Is that right, Tara?" I asked, although the older woman looked enough like Jennifer to ease my fears.

The girl nodded before looking away.

"Jennifer can explain more later if you want," said Tara's grandmother. "We just thought it best to get Tara away from this situation. The police had no objections," she added, her brow creasing with worry lines.

I offered her a sympathetic smile. It was a difficult spot to be placed in—worried about their daughter as well as their grand-daughter. *And maybe*, I thought, *knowing only too well why Jennifer might have wanted to kill their son-in-law.*

"I'm sorry to see Tara go, but I certainly understand," I said, waving good-bye as the woman rolled up her window.

When I stepped out of the driveway to allow the car to leave, a series of sharp yips caught my attention. Ellen, walking at a fast pace behind the bounding Yorkie, waved the hand not gripping the leash at me.

"Hello, Charlotte. How are you today? I heard about your little dustup last night."

I stopped short at the back-door stoop. Of course she'd heard. Ellen always seemed to know everything that went on at Chapters. Narrowing my eyes, I waved her over.

"I'm fine. But I do have a few questions I'd like to ask, if you have a minute."

"Happy to oblige. Just let me take Shandy inside and I'll meet you in the garden."

"I was thinking inside." I gestured toward Chapters. "Everyone's out, except for Alicia, and she told me she was going to spend the day cleaning upstairs, so we should have the library to ourselves."

Ellen shaded her eyes with one hand and stared at me for a moment. "All right," she said slowly. "But I still need to take the dog back to the house."

"No rush. I'm just going to head inside and wait in the library. I'll leave the back door open for you." I turned away and marched up the two steps of the back stoop. Holding the screen door open with one foot, I focused on unlocking the deadbolt on the wooden door. When I glanced over at Ellen, she'd already disappeared into her own house with the dog.

I dropped my purse off in my bedroom before heading for the library. Taking a seat in one of the room's armchairs, I sank back against the leather upholstery and contemplated my next move.

Because I knew Ellen had information that would explain my great-aunt's past. All I had to do was to figure out how to get her to share it with me.

Resting my elbows on the chair's padded arms, I templed my fingers and tapped one thumb against the other. I'd called Ellen a "Sherlock" to my "Watson" in jest, but now I suspected I'd been more prescient than I'd ever suspected.

My seventy-five-year-old neighbor was, to all appearances, simply a retired film-location scout with a love of small dogs and a taste for exotic fashions. But I now suspected she was much more than that. Someone cleverer than her carefully cultivated old-lady-who-gardens persona. Someone more devious.

Someone, perhaps, far more dangerous.

# Chapter
# Twenty-Four

E llen joined me in the library several minutes later.
"I locked the back door," she said, as she sat in the armchair facing mine. "I thought that was best, all things considered."

I rubbed my sore shoulder. "You're right. Thanks."

"First things first." Ellen stretched out her legs. Her purple-and-lime-green-print wide-legged pants clashed violently with the muted tones of the Oriental rug. "I did talk to the owner of that restaurant, and he confirmed our suspicions regarding Damian. It appears that Lincoln Delamont was the person behind Damian losing the position."

"Which does give Damian a legitimate reason for wanting him dead."

"Yes, I'm afraid it does." Ellen looked me up and down, her eyes narrowing. "But this isn't why you wanted to talk to me, is it? I imagine you want to ask me more questions related to Isabella's past."

"Yes, and I hope you can be more forthcoming this time."

"You're in luck, then." Ellen ran her fingers through the vividly colored streaks of hair at her temples. "I've just received approval from the higher-ups to share a few things with you.

Now that so much time has passed, most of the information is no longer of any importance, anyway."

"What sort of higher-ups?"

"My old bosses. Well"—Ellen tipped her head and offered me a sardonic smile— "not so very old, as it turns out. They seem to keep getting younger as I continue to age."

"That happens," I said, clutching the arms of my chair with both hands. "Not to pry, but are you actually retired? I mean, if you still have to check with bosses . . ."

Ellen held up one foot, seemingly intrigued by the laces of her magenta sneaker. "One never actually leaves my old job. Not completely. I continue to have to clear certain things with the powers that be."

"Still secrets you need to keep?"

"Definitely." Ellen dropped her foot with a thump. She studied me with her piercing blue gaze before speaking again. "Tell me, what is it you suspect? That I was working for U.S. intelligence?"

"That's my first choice." I released my grip on the chair and crossed my arms over my chest. "Were you ever really a film-location scout?"

"Oh yes, I did the work. Even though that was just my cover for other activities, I had to do enough to make it appear legitimate." Ellen fingered the hem of her lime-green silk tunic. "I was quite good at that job, actually. And, of course, it offered an acceptable reason for jetting off to all sorts of strange and out-of-the-way locations."

"Including trips that had nothing to do with movies or TV?"

"If you're asking if there were some advance scouting expeditions that were more about other matters, then, yes."

"You were a spy." I'd never expected to address these words to anyone, but I knew they were appropriate in this case.

Ellen waved this remark aside. "Intelligence officer is the more appropriate term."

"It all comes down to the same thing, doesn't it?"

"I suppose. But I assure you I wasn't skulking about wearing lapel-pin cameras or carrying death-dealing umbrellas. Nor did I chase people down dark alleys in foreign countries."

"What exactly did you do? Something tied to my great-aunt, it seems."

"I'm afraid my precise duties are one of the secrets I still can't reveal." Ellen pulled her legs back in against the chair. "But yes, I was connected to Isabella. I was her handler, as a matter of fact."

I lowered my arms and clasped my hands in my lap. "Great-Aunt Isabella was a spy too?"

"Yes, and a very good one. Although a bit of a loose cannon sometimes." Ellen lowered her eyelids, shadowing her eyes. "That's why I was sent to Beaufort, you see. To keep an eye on her after . . . Well, I suppose I'd better start at the beginning, or none of this will make any sense."

I slumped against the back of my chair. "I think you should."

"Very well." Ellen straightened and leaned forward, her hands gripping her knees. "You know that after she graduated from college, Isabella went to work at an estate in Virginia."

"Yes, and our family always wondered about that."

"Oh, that was totally legitimate. Like I mentioned before, it was a difficult time for women, even university-educated girls like Isabella, to find jobs. Especially after all the men came home after the war. She took the job as a maid as a stopgap, to make some money while she looked for something else. But she'd been noticed at college. By a professor who kept in touch."

"I assume he also worked for the U.S. intelligence community?"

Ellen shook a finger at me. "*She* did. Anyway, while Isabella was working at the estate, the family hosted several young men from England. Friends of their sons, who'd been attending university classes in Britain before the war cut short their studies."

"One of whom was the man captured in the photograph with Isabella, Paul Peters?"

"Bingo." Ellen looked me over, a little smile playing about her lips. "See, I knew you missed your calling."

I lifted my chin to meet her intense gaze. "Would you have tried to recruit me, if you'd met me when I was younger?"

"In a heartbeat. But that is neither here nor there." Ellen settled back in her chair. "The thing was, Paul Peters was not what he appeared to be."

I recalled Bernadette Sandberg's suspicions about the man. "He wasn't British?"

"Hardly. Although he was meticulously trained to pass as a typical Oxford or Cambridge grad, he was actually born elsewhere."

"Russia," I said, not bothering to make it a question.

"Back then we would've said the Soviet Union, but yes."

"I assume this was all part of the Cold War."

"Yes, and it was indeed chilling for those involved." Ellen rubbed at one of her temples. "Anyway, Isabella met Peters at the estate. Sometime around 1950. He was supposedly in the U.S. to conduct some postgrad research."

"What was his field?"

"Linguistics. And yes, he had an actual degree and taught in various universities in England over the years."

"But you think he was visiting America for more than research?"

"Of course, because he was definitely a Soviet spy. A sleeper—one who'd been put in place in England long before the war. As a small child, actually. He was placed with a British couple with strong Communist sympathies." Ellen tugged on one of the amethyst earrings dangling from her ears. "The intel I read suggested he'd cultivated his American friends at the university for this precise purpose. His goal was to use these acquaintances later, to try to gain intelligence on the U.S. as well as Britain."

"And then he met Isabella at his friend's estate, and . . . what?"

"He was instantly smitten and pursued her relentlessly." Ellen narrowed her eyes. "It wasn't that he thought he could gain any information from her; he simply fell in love."

"Which you used against him."

"Yes. But only after Isabella alerted us to the situation. Oh, Isabella was flattered, at first. But like you, your great-aunt was no fool. She began to suspect something was off about Peters and did some sleuthing. When she discovered his true identity—I don't actually know all the details about how, because that was before my time—she immediately contacted her former college professor."

"Who asked her to spy for the U.S.?"

"It was a little more complicated than that, but essentially, yes."

I wrinkled my nose in concentration. "Wait—did she actually steal anything from the estate?"

"She did, but it was all part of her cover story. She made sure Paul Peters knew about it, you see. Told him some story about how she was desperate, how she needed money so badly that she'd do anything—"

I couldn't prevent a swear word from flying from my lips. "He recruited her to spy for the Soviets?"

"Yes, for money. And knowing about her so-called theft— the items were quietly returned a year later, by the way—Peters thought he had an additional hold over her."

"But she was actually working for you?"

"Well, not me, exactly. I was a child at the time. I was assigned to be her handler many years later. But yes, she was secretly working for the U.S."

I sputtered something unintelligible before collecting myself enough to speak again. "She was a freaking secret agent?"

Ellen's smile twisted into a grimace. "She was."

I stared wildly about the library. "And Chapters? And her books?"

"The money was provided by the U.S. government. Compensation for her services, as well as an excellent cover for her activities." Ellen shrugged. "As far as the world was concerned, she was a wealthy social butterfly. She circulated in high society, hosting and attending events that brought together some, shall we say, interesting people. Parties that Paul Peters often attended as well, thinking he was being offered the opportunity to gather valuable information sought by his own handlers."

"But he was being played, I suppose."

"Like a fiddle. Oh, we shared a few insignificant true facts. Just enough to keep him on the string. But more importantly, we also fed him information that we wanted him to transmit back to the U.S.S.R."

"Disinformation, you mean."

"Exactly." Ellen folded her hands neatly in her lap. She looked like nothing more than a trendy grandmother, but I could spy ice in her eyes. "It was quite a successful little operation for many years. Although poor Isabella . . ." Ellen exhaled a deep sigh. "She had to pretend to love him, you see. He was mad about her from the beginning, but I doubt she ever felt the same. Still, it was useful, him loving her as well as believing he was running her. I think his feelings blinded him to many things, which ultimately proved good for Isabella, and us."

A thought flashed through my mind. My great-aunt, always living alone . . . "But she couldn't pursue any other serious relationship."

"No. Peters didn't want to live with her. I suppose he thought that much intimacy might blow his cover. Also, he was away a lot—he actually lived in England, where he kept up appearances as a university lecturer. I also have it on good authority that he took a few clandestine trips to his real homeland." Ellen shifted in her chair. "But he was a jealous man. He didn't make much effort to find out what Isabella did when he was away, so we all overlooked her short-term flings, but he definitely would've known something was off if she'd embarked on a serious romantic relationship."

"He sent her coded letters."

"One of which you found. She shared those with me when I was her handler, of course, but she didn't mention keeping a coded journal." Ellen raised her eyebrows. "That was definitely against protocol. But then, Isabella wasn't one to religiously follow all the rules."

"Do you want the journal? I mean, maybe you or someone you know can crack the code."

"I would like to have it, but I doubt we'll bother to try to read it. Those events are too far in the past to matter now. But I suppose it might be best if it's kept locked up somewhere."

I twitched my lips into a smile. "Just in case it proves that aliens did land at Roswell and the government has been covering it up all this time?"

Ellen laughed. "Wrong time period. More like we faked the moon landing. Which we didn't," she added, waving one hand through the air. "Anyway, just give it to me whenever you want. I'll find a proper home for it."

I studied her intelligent face for a moment. "You retired very early, if my calculations are correct. You would've only been about forty when you moved here in the eighties. Why was that? Were you still Isabella's handler?"

"No, she'd retired at that point. Paul Peters died, and we saw no point in trying to set her up with anyone else. Besides, she'd already been in the game for far too many years. The agency felt it was time she was out. They allowed her to keep the house free and clear, and do whatever she pleased with the property. Of course, she decided to turn it into Chapters and run it as a bed-and-breakfast. Not that she really needed the money, as there was still enough in the trust that had been set up for her use to last through her lifetime. I think she was simply bored."

"But why send you here if Isabella was no longer working for your agency?"

Ellen stirred uncomfortably in her chair, fixing her gaze on a point over my shoulder. "It was just something that worked out for everyone. I did retire rather young. Not by choice. I'd been injured, you see, during another operation. Quite badly, I'm afraid. I lost my nerve for the game after that, even for a desk job. So the agency offered me a deal—a free house and stipend if I'd move to Beaufort and keep an eye on an important former asset."

"I think I understand why you agreed, but why did they think Isabella needed to be watched?"

Ellen shrugged. "As I said, she was always a little reckless. A free spirit who could be unpredictable. I believe they were afraid she'd get restless and engage in a little espionage on her own. She still had many contacts within Russian organizations, as well as a few others, from her work with Peters."

"Surely they didn't think she'd turn traitor at that point?"

"They shouldn't have, but they did." Ellen smiled grimly. "As if Isabella would've ever betrayed her county. Despite her sometimes wild behavior, she was a true patriot. The truest I've ever known, if I'm honest."

"It does sound like she was willing to sacrifice a great deal."

"And she did. No one can understand the constant anxiety and pressure one is under unless they've lived it." Ellen wiped the back of her hand across her forehead, as if the memory still pained her. "But anyway, I was more than happy to accept a deal that only required me to keep tabs on Isabella and report back to my superiors periodically. Knowing Isabella, I knew I'd never need to do more."

I stood, shaking out one leg that had fallen asleep before I dared to take a step. "Thank you for sharing all this. I assume you want me to keep it to myself?"

"If you don't mind. It's all ancient history now, but I think it best if your family and others retain their current memories of Isabella. Besides"—Ellen grinned—"I might get kicked out of the garden club if they knew the truth about my past."

"I doubt that, but I promise to stay silent." I crossed to face her as she rose to her feet. "Why *did* you tell me, by the way?"

She met my stare without blinking. "Because I was afraid you'd dig up too much, or too little, and make the wrong assumptions. Knowing how determined you are, I thought you might stumble onto part of the story and draw the wrong conclusions. I didn't want you to suspect Isabella of betraying our country. She doesn't deserve that. If nothing else, she deserves your respect. So I decided I'd rather you know the truth."

"Thanks." I looked her over, noting the weariness tugging down the corners of her lips. "I guess you've been carrying this around for some time."

"I have. It's a relief to share it, I admit." Ellen glanced over my shoulder. "Ah, hello, Alicia. How are you today?"

"Just fine, thanks," Alicia called out from the hall. "Sorry to interrupt, but if we plan to hold that cocktail party tonight, you'd better get a move on, Charlotte."

I slapped my forehead. "Darn, how could I forget? Sorry, Alicia, I'll be with you in a minute."

Alicia waved her hand over her head and muttered something as she walked off down the hall.

I glanced at Ellen. "We're holding one of the week's planned events tonight. Just a little cocktail party outside on the patio. Some of the guests said they'd attend, despite everything, and I thought it might be a good time to . . ."

"Play detective?"

"Yes. Speaking of that, you're welcome to attend. It would be an opportunity to continue our investigation, especially now that I know you possess a very particular skill set."

"I'd like that," Ellen said.

"Good, and mark Saturday evening down on your calendar too. That's the final event for the week—another discussion of Josephine Tey and her books."

"All right, I'll attend both. Especially since I'm worried you might need backup."

"And who better?" I held up my hands as Ellen made a tutting noise. "Seems that you were trained for stuff like this."

"I was, although I'm afraid I'm a bit out of practice. But I'll do my best."

"Six o'clock tonight. Seven on Saturday." I gave Ellen a mock salute. "Until then, comrade."

She touched her forehead with one finger. "Prepare the barricades, *mon amie*. We shall fight to reveal the truth. Which is always a heroic goal."

I shot her a sharp look. "Those are odd words coming from someone who's had to hide so much of it."

Ellen laid one hand on my forearm. "That's how I know."

# Chapter
# Twenty-Five

As the cocktail party got under way, I stumbled across Julie commiserating with Alicia.

"Yeah, they've questioned me a couple more times too," Julie said, glancing over as I entered the kitchen.

Alicia, at the sink, had her back to me. "If you ask me, it could just as easily have been Charlotte as either of us."

Julie shushed her as I cleared my throat.

"So that's what you think of me?" I asked. "I know you sometimes question my hospitality skills, but that seems a little extreme."

Alicia spun around to face me. "Sorry, but you have to admit you have as much of a motive as anyone."

I waved off her apology. "Don't worry. I understand why you'd keep me on a suspect list. But since I was attacked by someone who's probably the real killer, and I haven't been questioned again by the police, I think they've cleared me."

Alicia placed her fists on her hips. "Is that so? Even with the blackmail connection?"

"Blackmail?" Julie's gaze darted from me to Alicia and back again. "What's that all about?"

233

I shrugged. "Lincoln might have suggested that he had some dirt on my great-aunt, that's all."

Julie's feathery eyelashes fluttered over her dark eyes. "Really? You never mentioned anything like that to me, Charlotte."

"No, I didn't." I crossed over to the counter that held a tray containing several green glass tumblers and a pitcher of ice water. "I wanted to get to the bottom of his accusations before I said anything. Find out the truth first," I said, pouring myself a glass of water.

Alicia tapped her foot. "You mentioned something about his threats to me."

"Because I wanted to know if you had any information that would validate or disprove Lincoln's claims. I was pretty sure you wouldn't know anything about it," I added to Julie. "It was something from Isabella's past, and you didn't even meet her until a few years ago."

Julie toyed with the delicate gold chain encircling her wrist. "Lincoln might have told me something."

"Yes, but I didn't know you were involved with him until later."

"And by that point, everyone figured I might have killed him?" Julie tossed back her heavy fall of dark hair.

Alicia nodded sagely. "The thought crossed my mind, for sure. Once I heard you'd been involved with the man. A woman scorned and all that."

"Well, to be honest, you're on *my* list." I cast Alicia a sharp look. "Since you did know about Lincoln's threats to expose some dirt from Isabella's past."

"You think I'd kill to protect her reputation?" Alicia snorted. "I did care about the crazy old broad, but I wouldn't murder anyone for her sake."

*No, but maybe for your own*, I thought, narrowing my eyes as I met Alicia's defiant stare. *Because if a scandal shut down Chapters, you'd be out of a home as well as a job.*

"Since we obviously can't solve this right now, I think I'll go join the rest of the suspect pool on the patio." Julie shot Alicia a hurt look as she swept past us. She allowed the screen door to slam behind her.

"Guess I ticked off your friend. Sorry," Alicia said, as she turned back to the sink.

"Do I need a new housekeeper and cook?" I asked, not bothering to temper the sharp edge to my tone. I was irritated with Alicia's treatment of Julie, who'd always been nice to the brusque housekeeper. *Nicer than me*, I thought, with a little pang of remorse. My relationship with Alicia had never been more than cordial, probably because I'd always felt a sense of resentment from her. I'd always suspected that she thought she should have inherited Chapters instead of me. *Which isn't*, I realized, *entirely out of line. She was the one who spent over thirty years of her life working here, and then I just sail in, not knowing anything about running a bed-and-breakfast . . .*

"Naw, not planning to quit anytime soon." Alicia glanced at me over her shoulder. "In fact, I bet I'll still be here after you've thrown in the towel." She pulled a metal serving tray from a cabinet and banged it down on the counter. "Not exactly what you expected when you inherited the place, is it?"

As I stared at her back, I noted the tension hunching her shoulders. Given her admittedly legitimate resentment, I wondered if she'd have no problem lying to me about the knife, her movements on the night Lincoln Delamont was killed, or anything else.

I thrust back my own shoulders and marched over to the sink. "If you do know anything more about the murder, you'd better have already told the police. They will find out eventually, you know."

"Don't know any more than I told you," Alicia said without looking at me. "Now, I need to get some snacks together to take out to that crowd. Unless you want them drinking on empty stomachs, which I don't advise."

"I'll leave you to it, then," I said, before making a quick exit. I should've stayed to help, but I didn't feel inclined to do so. Besides, at this point, I suspected Alicia would be happier with me gone.

Outside, I made my way over to the patio, where the guests were clustered in small groups. Next to the table we'd set up as a bar, I spied Ellen deep in conversation with Bernadette and Ophelia Sandberg.

After wishing them a good evening, I turned to the bar, where Damian was fixing the drinks. "You really are a bartender, I see," I said, when I caught his eye.

"I know enough to be dangerous," he replied. "Don't need a license in North Carolina, but I went ahead and got one when I took a certificate class a while back, because it opened up more job opportunities. Like this one," he added, with a nod of his head. "Thanks for asking me, by the way."

"No problem." I looked him over, observing the bags under his eyes. *From too much work, or guilt?* I couldn't tell. "I hope you'll be able to work Saturday night as well. Just some hors d'oeuvres with drinks in the library."

I felt a little guilt myself, knowing I primarily wanted to make sure Damian was part of the group activities so that Ellen and I could examine him for any telltale signs of involvement in Lincoln's murder. *But if he did kill someone*, I reminded myself, *all's fair.*

I asked for a gin and tonic, then walked back over to join Ellen and the Sandberg sisters. As I did, I surreptitiously glanced around the patio. Surprisingly, Jennifer Delamont was present. Clutching a large glass of what could've been either water or vodka, she was engaged in a lively conversation with Todd and Kelly Rowley.

Julie, I noticed, was chatting with Scott and the Nelsons. As I expected, Scott was standing close to Julie, and the look on his face when he glanced at her told me my assumptions about his growing interest in her were correct. Which was great. *As long as he isn't the murderer*, I thought, taking a gulp of my drink.

"Hello, Charlotte," Ophelia said. "Thanks for trying to offer at least part of the events on this week's schedule."

I shrugged. "I felt I should try to do as much as possible."

Bernadette took a long swallow from her drink. "Looks like the gang is all here, although I haven't seen Tara Delamont yet. But I suppose she's too young for cocktails."

"Definitely too young, although that doesn't always stop them from trying." I remembered finding the girl with the empty spumante bottle a few nights before. "But actually, she's gone. She's staying with her grandparents right now. Which is probably for the best."

Ophelia widened her pale eyes. "I guess that means the police cleared her of any involvement in the murder."

"I suspect so, although they could call her back, I suppose. Face it, without her own funds and a car, she's probably not as much of a flight risk as an adult, especially if she's been released into her grandparents' care," Bernadette said.

"There is that. And it seems unlikely that the girl was involved in her father's death." Ellen looked at me over the rim of her glass. "At least, from what little I've heard."

"Just as well she's not around, since her mother seems well on her way to becoming falling-down drunk tonight," Bernadette said, motioning toward Jennifer and the Rowleys with her glass. "Probably best if her daughter's not here to see that."

Ophelia clucked her tongue. "Now, Bernie, cut the poor woman some slack. I'm sure she's under a tremendous amount of stress."

"Sure, especially if she recently stabbed her husband," Bernadette replied darkly. She downed the rest of her drink. "Think I'll get another. Anyone else?"

"I'm fine," I said, echoing Ophelia and Ellen.

As Bernadette strode off toward the bar, I sipped my own drink and threw out an innocuous comment about Ellen's garden, which, as I'd suspected, got Ophelia talking Ellen's ear off about her own flowers. That was one sure way to change the subject. I gave Ellen a raised-eyebrow look before slipping away.

"Good evening," I said as I joined Julie, who'd left Scott and the Nelsons to talk to the Rowleys. "Thank you all for coming. I know it isn't under the greatest circumstances . . ."

"Now there's an understatement." Julie flashed me a wry smile before she tossed back her drink and walked off to deposit her empty glass on one of the small tables we'd set up on the patio.

"We're happy to participate," Todd said. "Given the circumstances, you would have been within your rights to cancel the entire week."

"I hated to do that, especially since you had to stay in Beaufort anyway. It only seemed fair to offer a few of the activities you were promised. Just to try to keep things as normal as possible."

"And we appreciate that," Kelly said, staring at something over my shoulder. "Oh dear, that doesn't look good."

I turned to see Julie stalking up to the group that included Pete and Sandy and Jennifer. "Excuse me, maybe I'd better head over there."

"Yes, you might need to referee," Todd said, his pleasant expression growing grave.

I set my glass on a table and hurried over to stand between Jennifer and Julie, but I was too late.

"Your apology means nothing to me," Jennifer said, her words slurring into mush. "Should've thought of that before you started sleeping with my husband."

Julie, her arms akimbo, faced off with the older woman. "I never did."

"Doesn't matter, does it. Would've happened eventually." Jennifer swatted one hand through the air, as if Julie were a bothersome insect. "Happened plenty of times before, you know."

"No, I don't, and I'm not sure I should take your word for it," Julie said, widening her stance like someone getting ready to throw a punch.

Jennifer's laugh dissolved into a choking fit. Sandy made a sympathetic noise and moved closer, but Jennifer stumbled away before Sandy could pat her back.

Catching sight of me, Julie's haughty pose crumpled. "I just wanted to apologize," she said. "I didn't want to cause any trouble."

"I know," I said. "But maybe this wasn't the best time . . ."

"Not cause trouble?" As Jennifer flung out her hand, the tumbler she was holding flew from her fingers and crashed onto the flagstones.

All of the guests turned their heads at the noise. Ellen, handing her own drink to Bernadette, strode over to my side.

"What's all this, then?" she asked, fixing Jennifer with a stern glare. "I'm afraid you're drunk, Mrs. Delamont. Not that you don't have reason to indulge, but perhaps you should take a bottle to your room instead?"

"Who died and made you queen?" Jennifer, wobbling, gripped her upper arms with both hands. She stared at Ellen, blinking rapidly. "I don't even know who you are, do I?"

"Probably not," Ellen said. "I'm Charlotte's neighbor, Ellen Montgomery."

"Not even a guest," Jennifer said, before slumping down onto the patio. She stared up at Ellen with bleary eyes. "You think I killed him? My husband, in case you didn't know. Lincoln Delamont. He was stabbed just over there," she added, flapping her hand in the general direction of the carriage house.

"Yes, I've heard," Ellen replied, her voice suddenly gentle. *But firm.* I cut her a look. *A well-trained interrogator's tone.*

Scott swiftly crossed the patio to stand beside Julie. *A protective gesture*, I thought, as he addressed Jennifer in a stern tone. "Doesn't sound like you care all that much that he's dead."

"No, I don't. Why should I? He never loved me." Jennifer sat up straighter, folding her legs in a pretzel pose. "Oh sure, he pursued me in the beginning. All flowers and romantic dinners and sweet words. But that was his way—he loved the chase, not the person he was pursuing. After he achieved his goal, well . . ." She pressed one hand to her forehead. "Let's just say that once we were married, he showed his true colors. He treated me like dirt. Yeah, just dirt under his expensive shoes."

*Is this a confession?* I glanced at Ellen, who gave an almost imperceptible shake of her head. "I've got a broom and dustpan on my back porch," she said. "Would it help if I grabbed them to sweep up this glass?"

I nodded and she scurried off. Turning back to Jennifer, I held out my hand. "Come on, let's get you inside."

Jennifer stared up into my face for a moment before gripping my fingers and allowing me to help her to her feet. "Sorry," she muttered. "Sorry, sorry."

"It's all right, dear," Sandy said, elbowing her husband. "Pete, why don't we help Mrs. Delamont to her room? That way Charlotte can remain here with the other guests."

I demurred, but the Nelsons insisted on taking Jennifer inside. "We'll ask Ms. Simpson to make you some coffee, how about that?" Sandy said, as Pete wrapped his arm around Jennifer's shoulders.

"I guess that's our entertainment for the evening," Julie said as she watched the trio head into the house. She turned to me with an apologetic smile. "Forgive me for losing my cool with her earlier, Charlotte. I know we're all suspects, although it seems to me"—she motioned toward the back door—"that's your culprit right there."

"Maybe. But if so, it seems she had reason."

"I don't doubt that," Scott said, sliding his arm around Julie's waist. "You doing okay?"

"I'm fine, thanks," Julie replied, without pulling away. She looked up at Scott with a warm smile. "But another drink wouldn't hurt. How about you?"

"Sounds like a plan," Scott said. They turned and wandered off toward the bar as Ellen returned with the broom and dustpan. "Here, let me do that," I said, taking the broom from her hand.

"You sweep and I'll collect," Ellen said, squatting down with the dustpan.

After we gathered up all the broken glass, I motioned toward the holly hedge screening the carriage house. "No need to take it inside. There's a trash bin right behind the hollies."

I followed Ellen over to the bin, lifting the lid so she could dump the broken glass. "Oh, I was wondering—could we meet again sometime tomorrow? I'd like to talk over our impressions of this evening in relation to our suspect list."

"Of course, but I'm afraid I'll be volunteering at Fort Macon all day, so it will have to be later." Ellen tapped her chin with one finger. "Come to think of it, maybe you could do me a favor."

"Happy to, if I can."

"Well, my car needs a checkup, so I'm catching a ride to the fort with one of the other volunteers. Unfortunately, she has to run some errands after work. I was willing to ride along with her, but if you could come over around closing time and give me a lift home, I'd really appreciate it."

"No problem," I said. "I don't have any other events planned before Saturday night, so I can easily do that. What time?"

"The fort and welcome center close at five thirty, so around then would be fine." Ellen cast me a warm smile. "And thanks."

"Glad to do it," I said. "Maybe I'll even come a little early and take a stroll around the grounds and the fort. Get an extra walk in. That might be good for my mental state as well as my health." As I finished my sentence, a rustle made me turn on my heel to face the holly hedge. "Did you hear that?"

Ellen stepped up beside me. "I think someone was lurking there."

"Listening?" I looked at Ellen, who's expression had darkened.

"Perhaps. I saw a figure moving behind the hedge but couldn't see who it was."

I frowned. "We should go join the others. Maybe we can tell something from everyone's location."

"Doubtful," Ellen said. "But let's give it a try."

She strode off toward the patio. I followed, gripping the broom like a weapon.

# Chapter
# Twenty-Six

Of course, since all the guests were wandering about on the patio, we couldn't determine who'd been lurking behind the hedge. As Ellen whispered to me before joining Scott and Julie in a discussion of the newest Louise Penny novel, the sad fact was that any one of them could've easily strolled from the hedge to join the rest of the crowd without arousing any suspicion.

I carried the broom and dustpan to Ellen's back porch before rejoining the party. With Jennifer gone, conversations continued in a lighter vein, although no one seemed interested in lingering past seven thirty. That was fine by me. After helping Alicia and Damian clear away the food and drinks and clean the patio, I retreated to my bedroom.

Pulling out my folder on the Tey discussion scheduled for Saturday evening, I looked over my notes. I was actually surprised that all of the guests had agreed to attend Saturday's event. Perhaps because it was the last hurrah before the Tey week ended? *Or maybe*, I thought, *to put on a brave face and show they feel no guilt and therefore couldn't be the actual murderer.*

After making several changes to my notes, I returned the folder to my desk and got ready for bed. The snacks Alicia had made for the cocktail party would hold me until breakfast, and I certainly didn't want to socialize with anyone. Not even Julie. Scott had offered to escort both Julie and me to dinner, but I'd begged off, allowing Scott and Julie to head out without me. Which was, I had to admit, only partially due to my lack of interest in talking to anyone for the rest of the evening. This was a perfect opportunity for Julie to spend some time with a man like Scott, who was kind, intelligent, and more importantly, single.

*But also perhaps a killer*, I thought, anxiety fluttering in my chest. If I'd allowed my friend to be put in danger . . . But no, even if Scott had killed Lincoln, he'd have no reason to harm Julie. Although, in that case, encouraging their relationship was probably a bad idea.

I sighed and crawled into bed. After a solid hour of lying flat on my back and staring at the ceiling, I admitted defeat and sat up. Grabbing my copy of Sujata Massey's latest Perveen Mistry novel from my nightstand, I attempted to read a chapter, but even this fascinating depiction of a female lawyer in 1920s India couldn't hold my attention.

It wasn't the fault of the book but of the racing thoughts tumbling around in my brain. I hated to think Scott had been involved in Lincoln's death. In fact, it was hard for me to believe he was capable of murder—but then, I'd never even had a glimmer of suspicion that anything was amiss about my great-aunt, and she'd been an honest-to-goodness spy. So maybe I wasn't the best judge of such things.

Giving up my attempts at distraction, I turned off my night-stand lamp and rolled over in my bed. After counting about ten flocks of sheep, I finally fell into a fitful sleep.

*　　*　　*

I spent most of the day Friday working in Chapters' garden, something I'd neglected during the past hectic week. After ensuring that the weeds wouldn't continue to grow and swallow the other vegetation, like Audrey in *Little Shop of Horrors*, I grabbed a shower before driving over to Atlantic Beach to meet Ellen.

Fort Macon's park grounds stayed open until eight o'clock, so there were still people around, hiking the trails and using the public beach. But since the actual fort closed by five thirty, I found that area almost deserted by five o'clock.

I paused at the top of the paved path to appreciate a view of the restored early-nineteenth-century fort. The five-sided structure appeared to have been built in a deep depression in the earth, but this was an illusion created by the grass covering the top and sides of the outer walls, or covertway. Surveying the main entrance, called the sally port, I had the fanciful notion that the fort had sprung up from the earth like a lime-washed brick mushroom. But a full survey of the scene displayed the human ingenuity that had constructed this coastal defense station. Butted up against the inner walls, wide, open-air corridors formed a moat that was officially called the ditch. According to the history I'd read about the fort, this moat could be deliberately flooded to provide extra defense against invaders. It also functioned as a canal to absorb coastal flooding during hurricanes or tropical storms.

Today the ditch, bare of any vegetation except grass, was dry. It separated the inner section of the fort, with its vaulted rooms, or casements, that formed a pentagon around a central plaza, from the thick outer walls. Roofed by grass, the outer walls included dark chambers at each corner. Called counterfire galleries, they had been used by the fort's defenders to fire on any enemy troops trapped in the ditch. I'd never walked into one of these rooms, finding the steps leading down into them almost as intimidating as the darkness of the enclosed chambers.

I had often walked the ramparts, which were covered in grass and featured numerous cannon emplacements. Originally, cannons could be fired to protect the fort from enemy approaches on all sides, including from Bogue Sound, the Beaufort Inlet, and the Atlantic Ocean. Now only some of the cannons, restored by efforts of the Friends of Fort Macon, among others, remained. But visitors could still walk the grassy ramparts and look out over the water that surrounded the area on three sides.

As I strolled down the sloping brick-and-timber wagon road and across the wooden bridge that led to the arched main entrance, the inner walls of the fort, devoid of any openings except narrow slits used for defensive gunfire, loomed above me. I popped off my sunglasses in the short tunnel formed by the casements, but I slipped them on again as I walked onto the open-air plaza, more accurately called the parade grounds.

The row of casements that encircled the parade grounds had been used by the park to depict life in the fort from its earliest days to its use by the army in World War II. The museum displays included reconstructions of soldiers' quarters, the fort's kitchen, gunpowder magazines, ordnance storerooms, and other scenes from the fort's history. Not all the casements had been turned into displays—some were left empty. Although I enjoyed the informational displays, the vaulted brick walls and wood floors of the empty spaces affected me more deeply, as they showed the true beauty inherent in the construction of this 1834 complex.

I wandered around the grass-covered parade grounds, trying to imagine what it had been like, living and fighting there. Although I was sure it had been bustling back in the day, now the place felt barren, its grassy plaza home to only a cannon and the "hotshot" furnace that was once used to heat cannonballs to red-hot temperatures. With no one to man the ramparts, the wide brick-and-stone stairs that rose to the grassy inner ramparts above the ring of casements were empty. I glanced around, thinking how the entire space resembled a stage set for an outdoor production of a Shakespearean tragedy.

I walked into one of the empty casements, turning to look out over the parade grounds from inside the barrel-vaulted brick room. As my eyes adjusted to the dim light, I noticed a flash in another empty casement.

*Like sunlight glinting off a watch face*, I thought, and realized I wasn't as alone as I'd believed. The thud of footfalls on old wooden planks behind me confirmed this. Someone was walking between the casements, using the openings cut into the side walls at the back of each room.

These formed another sort of tunnel in the fort. I cast a glance at the opening in my casement as the steps drew closer. Something about the speed of the stranger's steps, and the isolation of the area, made me dash out into the parade grounds.

Glancing over my shoulder, I spied a lone figure, clad in a charcoal-gray hoodie and sweat pants, their face hidden by dark glasses and a black cloth that wrapped their mouth and chin. They popped out of the back connector in the casement I'd just left. I veered to the right, jogging through an open arched tunnel that led to the ditch. If I could make it around the fort to the main entry . . .

I looked for other visitors, but saw no one. Lengthening my stride, I reached the corner that led to the main entry and, more importantly, the path to the welcome center. But as I rounded the corner, I saw the figure appear on the ditch side of the tunnel to the sally port. I turned and, desperate, took the steep steps down into one of the counterfire galleries.

Darkness enveloped me, forcing me to pocket my sunglasses and run my hand along the walls to orient myself. The bricks felt rough under my searching fingers. I couldn't help but imagine encountering spiders and other scuttling creatures.

*Like you.*, I swallowed a hysterical urge to laugh. *Another scuttling creature in the dark.*

I listened for footsteps but heard nothing. My pursuer was probably waiting for me to emerge, like the unfortunate rodent in a game of whack-a-mole. I cursed my stupidity in panicking and running into this trap.

*The rangers will soon close the fort. They'll have to check the perimeter as well as everything inside*, I reminded myself as I fought to control my urge to scream. *Time to get outside, even if you have to fight your way past that hooded stranger. Whoever it was didn't look huge. You can at least make an effort to evade them and make another run for it.*

I fumbled my way back to the opening, where I cautiously peeked around the corner before climbing the stairs to reach the open area of the ditch. Seeing no one, I sprinted toward the main entry.

A figure once again stepped out of the main-entry tunnel. I screamed and stumbled, only to find myself caught up in a pair of strong arms.

"Miss, are you all right?" asked a sympathetic voice.

I looked up into the face of a park ranger. "Yes, sorry, sorry," I said, pulling away. Blinking, I fumbled for my sunglasses.

"Get spooked or something? I saw you fly up out of the gallery." The ranger looked me over, his expression kind but confused. "You aren't thinking you saw a ghost or anything, are you?"

"No, not a ghost. Definitely not." I shoved on my sunglasses and glanced around. "You didn't run into someone else here. Wearing a hoodie and sweat pants?"

"In this heat? I should hope not." The ranger tipped his hat back from his damp forehead. "But no, I didn't see anyone. Now, can I help you back to the welcome center? We're closing, you know."

"Yes, I know, and no, I'm fine. I'm actually meeting someone at the center to give her a ride home."

"Okay. I need to help my partner do one more check and secure the main doors, so if you're truly all right . . ."

"I'm fine. Really." I forced a smile before thinking about my pursuer hiding in one of the many secret places in the fort. "Just look out for that person, would you? They seemed to be following me, and their clothes were so odd, as you said. Anyway"—I brushed sweat-dampened strands of hair away from my cheeks and tucked them behind my ears—"be careful."

The ranger's kind expression grew troubled. "Someone was chasing you? Should I call the police?"

I considered enduring another interrogation by the authorities and shook my head. "No, I may have been imagining things. At least the chasing part, although I did see an oddly dressed visitor."

"All right, then." The ranger tipped his hat to me. "Take care, miss."

"Thanks, I will," I said, turning to stagger back up the path to the welcome center.

Ellen was already waiting outside the front doors. "Charlotte, is everything okay? You look like you've seen a ghost."

"No ghost," I said firmly. "Just a strange human." I motioned toward my car. "Let's go. I'll tell you what happened while I drive."

Once we were on the road, I explained my encounter, or at least what I could make of it, to Ellen.

"You think someone was stalking you?" she asked.

"It seemed like it. Although they didn't follow me down into the counterfire gallery."

"Perhaps they spied the rangers and hightailed it out of there."

"Maybe." I cast her a side-eyed glance. "We both thought someone was listening to our conversation last night."

"You think someone at the party overheard your plan to walk around the fort before meeting me?"

I shrugged. "It's possible, right?"

"Yes, which is . . . worrisome." Ellen scrunched the hem of her red-and-white-striped cotton top in one hand. "It really points to one of the guests at the party being our killer."

"Or one of the staff. Aside from me, I mean," I added, with a grim smile.

"True. Both Alicia and Damian were there as well."

A thought filtered through the chaos of my mind. "But not Jennifer Delamont. She was up in her room at that point."

"Which means she wouldn't have been our eavesdropper," Ellen said slowly. "That throws a spanner in the works, doesn't it? I'd pegged her as the primary suspect after that drunken display last night."

"Me too. But she wouldn't have known where I was going to be today . . ." I frowned. "Listen, do you mind if we make a stop before heading home?"

"Of course not. You're doing me a favor, anyway."

"I just thought maybe we could just run by the police department and see if Detective Johnson or anyone else is available to speak with us. I think we should share the events from the party and this latest incident. Agreed?"

Ellen nodded. "Sounds like an excellent plan. Especially now that it looks like someone is specifically targeting you."

"And I'm afraid you could be next," I said.

Ellen waved that aside. "Oh, don't worry about that. I can take care of myself."

A swift glance at her face assured me that yes, she probably could.

# Chapter
# Twenty-Seven

As we drove from Morehead City to Beaufort, I finally remembered a question I'd meant to ask Ellen but kept forgetting.

"By the way, since you've lived in Beaufort for quite some time and seem in touch with the local gossip, I wondered if you'd heard anything about Pete and Sandy's daughter, Liza, being mixed up in some sort of bad romantic relationship. Before her marriage, of course."

Ellen shot me a side-eyed glance. "I may have heard something from Isabella."

"She found out something from the book club?"

"Yes. Apparently, Pete broke down during one of their meetings. Sandy wasn't present, which Isabella said was a good thing. Anyway, they were reading *Anna Karenina* and got into a discussion about adultery and doomed love affairs, and it set Pete off. He fled the library, obviously distressed, and Isabella followed to make sure he was okay."

I tightened my grip on the steering wheel. "Did Pete tell her what was wrong?"

Ellen turned her head to stare out the side window as we crossed the bridge into Beaufort. "He said he was afraid Liza was involved with an older man. A much older, *married* man."

"I thought that might have been the case, because I heard something from Julie that ties in with that," I said, before telling Ellen about Julie's anonymous caller.

"You think Liza could've been in a secret relationship with Lincoln Delamont? That would definitely give Pete a motive to kill him," Ellen said, when I'd concluded my account. "He's very protective of his girls."

"Especially if Lincoln was abusive." I lifted one hand off the wheel and flexed my cramped fingers. "It just seems to fit. The caller claimed that Lincoln could be abusive, like she was warning Julie to be careful. And Julie didn't want to mention her name, which would make sense if it was Liza. Pete and Sandy are her friends. She wouldn't want to draw their daughter into the murder investigation if she could help it."

"And you said Julie claimed that the caller wasn't in the area now, which would also fit."

"Yes, Liza's actually living overseas at the moment." I glanced over at Ellen. "Her husband's in the Navy."

"That's right, Liza is married. Which is probably another reason Julie wants to keep her identity a secret."

"Probably." I flexed my other hand. "Even though it might help her own situation. But that's Julie for you—more concerned about others than herself."

"I expect Lincoln Delamont realized that and exploited it," Ellen said darkly. "He probably told her sob stories about his marriage and his past."

"I wouldn't be surprised," I said, remembering that Lincoln's parents had supposedly died when he was barely in his twenties. "Anyway, we don't know any of this for certain, but if it is true, it does make Pete a more viable suspect in Lincoln's death."

"Unfortunately," Ellen said. "It also makes me think that whoever killed him did the world a favor."

I flashed a wry smile. "Maybe, but perhaps we shouldn't share that with the authorities."

"Probably not our best move," Ellen said.

Parking on the street near the police department, I debated aloud whether this was a good idea. Just dropping in on the police had seemed sensible while we were driving back to Beaufort, but now I wondered if it would simply waste their time.

"Don't be silly," Ellen told me, as she strode into the station. "This a murder investigation. They'll want all the information they can get."

The friendly young woman at the information window confirmed Ellen's claim.

"Let me see who's available," she said. "If you like, you can wait in the conference room." She pointed across the hall to the only other door outside the locked perimeter of the actual station.

Sitting at the table in the conference room, I couldn't help but think how its modern blandness contrasted with the historic, mysterious air of the fort we'd just left. *Like leaping through time*, I thought, as the inner door of the room opened.

Detective Johnson walked in and grabbed a chair across from Ellen and me. "Hello, what can I do for you ladies today?"

"I hope we can do something for you," I said, before recounting the events of the cocktail party and my adventure at Fort Macon.

"You really believe someone was following you?" Detective Johnson arched her dark brows.

I shifted in the hard chair. "Yes, and I think it may have been someone from the party. Whoever was eavesdropping from behind the hedge. They'd have known where I planned to be, and when."

"But to play devil's advocate"—Detective Johnson tapped her pen against her legal pad—"you have to consider the possibility that the individual at Fort Macon was just a random stranger who gets a kick out of scaring tourists."

"I suppose," I said slowly, realizing I might have jumped to conclusions again.

"Those sorts of things do happen," Detective Johnson said. "More than you'd expect."

Ellen cleared her throat. When the detective's gaze slid over to her, she leaned forward, her expression intense. "That may be, but someone definitely overheard our conversation last night. I find that to be a strange coincidence, don't you?"

"Are you sure about that? The eavesdropper, I mean. Perhaps one of the guests was simply loitering at the edge of this holly hedge. It is near the patio." Detective Johnson sat back in her chair, her intelligent gaze studying Ellen.

"I'm absolutely sure. If you must know, I have experience with noticing such things," Ellen said.

"Oh? What would that be?"

I glanced at Ellen, waiting for her nod of approval before I spoke. "Ms. Montgomery used to work for a branch of the U.S. intelligence services."

Detective Johnson's dark eyes narrowed. "Is that so? I don't suppose you have any credentials on you?"

Ellen lifted her hands. "I'm retired. But I can give you a contact number, if you'd like to confirm my previous experience. Not all the details, of course," she added, with a sardonic smile. "But they'll have my name in their records."

"Interesting," Detective Johnson said, twirling the pen between her fingers for a moment before holding out her hand.

Ellen fished a card from her purse and slid it across the table. Glancing at it, the detective raised her eyebrows again before standing.

"Be right back," she said, as she headed into the station.

"I'm not sure she thinks my encounter at Fort Macon is connected to anything," I told Ellen as we waited for the detective's return.

"Oh, I think she is considering all the possibilities," Ellen replied. "She seems to be too intelligent to reject any leads out of hand."

Detective Johnson returned a few minutes later. "One of our officers is checking on your credentials, Ms. Montgomery. I hope you don't mind."

Ellen shrugged. "Of course not. Although I'm not sure what my former job has to do with anything."

"You never know," the detective said as she sat down. "We may need a consultant on some other matters. But back to the case at hand. You two seem to have been playing at investigating, which I'm sure is amusing, but as you can see, might also be dangerous. If your stranger at the fort did happen to be Lincoln Delamont's killer, you could have put yourself in harm's way."

I leaned forward, resting my elbows on the table. "The thing is, we know the eavesdropper wasn't Jennifer Delamont, since she had already been escorted to her room at that point, and I doubt she was in any shape to sneak back outside. Which blows my theory of her being the killer out of the water."

"That is, if there is any correlation between this eavesdropper and the individual at Fort Macon," Detective Johnson said. "And even if that's true, it doesn't mean that the same person killed Lincoln Delamont, now, does it? Chasing you around a historic site isn't really proof of anything."

I ground my teeth in frustration, but had to admit she had a point. There was nothing that absolutely linked any of these actions or events.

"True, it could be simple coincidence." Ellen straightened in her chair and looked the detective over in a way that made her appear more like an interrogator than a witness. "However, in my previous job I learned that seemingly unrelated occurrences could prove to be valuable clues. It's worth a little of your official investigation time, don't you think?"

"Oh, rest assured we'll look into it." Detective Johnson's gaze slid from Ellen to me. She appeared lost in thought for moment as she examined me. "Now, Ms. Reed, tell me a little more about your plans for the rest of this week. Any more events on the schedule?"

"Only one," I said, and described the Tey discussion planned for Saturday evening.

Detective Johnson stared at a point over my head. "And your guests have agreed to participate in this event?"

"Yes, all except Tara Delamont. But I believe you've already cleared her."

"We have." Detective Johnson appeared lost in thought for a moment. "You'll be talking about murder mysteries as part of this discussion?"

"That's what Tey wrote. Well, she also wrote plays and a few other novels too, but we won't be talking about those. We'll be focusing on the mysteries."

"Interesting. I almost wish I could join you. I'm particularly fond of Tey's *A Shilling for Candles*." Detective Johnson grinned. "I like a good mystery read myself."

"I guess that isn't surprising, although I suppose they aren't much like actual police work," Ellen said.

"Which is why I like them, to be honest. Real police work is quite different."

Ellen nodded. "Same in my previous profession. Days or months or even years of tedious legwork, research, and surveillance, punctuated by explosions of violent activity."

"Exactly." Detective Johnson tapped the pen against her jaw. "I wonder . . . just how far are you willing to go to help the police in this matter, Ms. Reed?"

Before I could answer, a young man poked his head around the door and gave Detective Johnson a thumbs-up gesture as he handed her Ellen's card.

"Well, well," the detective said, sliding the card back across the table. "The things you find out about people."

"They constantly amaze, don't they?" Ellen said, her expression mild as milk. "But now I'm curious about what you want

Charlotte to do. I hope it's not something that will place her in danger."

Detective Johnson looked from Ellen to me. "I would definitely try to avoid that, but I admit it might put her in a rather tricky position."

"What exactly are you talking about?" I asked. For the sake of Chapters' reputation, as well as clearing Julie and my own peace of mind, I was willing to take a reasonable risk, but I didn't want to agree to anything that might get me killed.

"Well, it just struck me that you are in an envious position to help us try to expose our killer. You are hosting an event where most of the original guests will be present. Except for Tara Delamont, of course, but as you said, we've ruled her out as a suspect." Detective Johnson cast us a knowing smile. "You didn't hear it from me, but the girl was able to prove that she was on her cell phone secretly talking with a boy—someone her parents had forbidden her to contact, which was why she was reluctant to tell us when we first questioned her. This call took place during the time we've pinpointed for Lincoln Delamont's murder. She even took some selfies right before the call, and they show a background that matches her room at Chapters. So we have records of her exact location, and she was nowhere near the carriage house."

"That's a relief," I said.

"I thought so too." Detective Johnson sat back, crossing her arms over her chest. "But we're still looking into her mother and some of the other guests and staff, and frankly, we seem to have hit a brick wall. We really have to allow the out-of-town guests to leave Beaufort if we don't get better intel soon, so I thought"—she tipped her head and examined me intently—"maybe this event of yours could help us gather some more information."

"How?" I glanced over at Ellen, who was staring at the detective with a furrowed brow.

"If you were to ask some specific questions related to Tey's books but also associated with aspects of Delamont's murder, maybe somebody would slip up and say something that could give us a new lead."

"You mean link the books to the real-life murder?"

"Subtly, but yes." Detective Johnson dropped her arms and leaned forward. "We could help you craft a few leading questions."

"But even if someone slipped up and said something compromising, that would be secondhand information," Ellen said. "Sure, Charlotte could testify to hearing it, as could some of the other guests—including me, since I plan to attend. But would that hold up? It wouldn't be a direct confession to law enforcement."

Detective Johnson's dark eyes flashed. "It would if Ms. Reed was wearing a wire."

"What?" I couldn't keep a squeak out of my voice. Yes, I wanted to help, but wearing a wire like some sort of spy wasn't what I'd had in mind.

Fortunately, I was sitting next to an actual spy. Who lifted one hand and said, "Hold it right there. I don't think that's something Charlotte should be asked to do. It's a lot trickier than they make it look on TV, you know."

"Yes, I'm aware. But it seems like the best way to get a handle on this case," Detective Johnson said, her tone apologetic. "At least, it's a golden opportunity for pushing these people to talk."

"That may be, but you want to do this right. I suggest"—Ellen extended her hand, palm up, as if offering a gift—"that you wire me instead. I will be there, and I have done this sort of thing before."

Detective Johnson stared speculatively at Ellen. "I suppose you have. Very well. That actually solves the problem of when and where to get someone hooked up. We can come to your house before you head over to Chapters and avoid the problem of the other guests noticing strangers wandering around the bed-and-breakfast."

"But won't you need to be nearby anyway?" I asked, my mind reeling from the idea that an undercover operation was being planned for my home.

"Yes, but we can be down the block in an unmarked van," the detective replied. "The state bureau of investigation can lend us equipment and any special expertise if we need it. The county sheriff's office will help too, if we ask."

I turned to Ellen. "Are you sure you're okay with this?"

"I am. Don't worry," Ellen said, giving me a pat on the arm. "I really have done this before. Many times, if I'm honest. It's been a while, but it's not something that one forgets."

"All right," I said. "I'll help with the questions if Ellen will wear the wire." Meeting Detective Johnson's approving gaze, I pointed a finger at her. "But you'd better promise to show up immediately if you hear anything threatening. I don't want Ellen, or anyone else, hurt."

"We'll have a team at the ready," Detective Johnson said. "First sign of trouble and we'll be there."

"Okay." I inhaled deeply. "I guess you'd better give me those leading questions."

"I'll have the team work on them tonight, and we'll email you as soon as they're ready."

"That should work," I said.

Detective Johnson rose to her feet. "Good. Just leave your email address with the receptionist. Now, I'll wish you a pleasant evening, and again, thank you." She looked at Ellen. "Leave your phone number at the front desk too, Ms. Montgomery, so we can set up all the details of fitting you up with the wire. And thank you as well."

"Always happy to be of service," Ellen said as the detective left the room.

I pressed the back of my hand to my forehead. "Have to check to make sure I don't have a fever," I told Ellen when she cast me a concerned look. "Because this whole situation has me feeling like I'm delirious."

"I know it must seem strange, but I'm confident you'll manage," Ellen said, as we exited the conference room. I provided the receptionist with my email, and Ellen left her number before we headed out the front doors of the station.

"Don't you find this all the least little bit overwhelming?" I asked as we walked to my car.

Ellen shook her head. "After what I've seen in my life? Hardly. Just another day at the office."

# Chapter
# Twenty-Eight

B y Saturday afternoon, my concern over my participation in what was basically a police sting operation had me so hyper that I decided to take a walk to the Beaufort docks.

Alicia encouraged me to go. Or rather, she basically told me to "get out of the kitchen." I guess my constant pacing was fraying her last nerve.

I acquiesced without complaint. Everything was set up for the evening's event, and Alicia already had to share the kitchen with Damian, so I knew I wouldn't be missed. Besides, strolling along the waterfront always calmed me.

When I reached the Front Street end of the boardwalk, I walked a short distance before I paused to once again admire the *Celestial*. Todd Rowley was on the deck of the yacht, polishing some of her chrome fittings. He returned my wave with a broad smile.

"See you tonight," he called out before I turned away.

Although I'd planned to continue my walk, the picture window of Bookwaves beckoned, and I climbed the few steps to the wooden porch of the building that housed Julie's bookstore. I paused for a moment to study the window display, which was filled with what Julie always called "beach reads."

When I pushed open the front door, a bright jangle of bells accompanied my entry. I hadn't visited the bookstore in several weeks and was amused to see that the front table held a varied assortment of titles, all of which featured predominantly red, white, or blue covers. *Get a bang out of your summer read*, the banner draping the front of the table said, a theme emphasized by the sparkling, firecracker-style decorations.

"Getting ready for the Fourth already?" I asked Julie as her head popped up from behind a range of shoulder-height wooden shelves.

"It's a huge tourist week." She stepped around the shelves to greet me. "I mean, the Big Rock week is busy, but not as many of those people are looking to buy books. The Fourth and the few weeks leading up to it are when I see more visitors who want something to read. You know, on the beach or while enjoying waterfront views."

"I guess that's right. Hard to read when you're managing a fishing line." I was happy to see that Julie looked less stressed.

She swept her hair back and whipped it up into a ponytail she tied off with the scarf she'd draped around her neck. "Sorry, even with the air on, I always get hot moving books."

"I'm sure. Having had to do that in Chapters' library several times, I know it's hard work." As I gazed at my friend, I shifted my weight from one foot to the other. I wanted to tell her about assisting the police with finding Lincoln's killer but knew I couldn't say anything. Although perhaps I could find a way to reassure her that her ordeal as a suspect would soon be over.

"Speaking of Chapters, you're coming to the Tey discussion tonight, I hope?"

"Yes. I told Scott I'd be there, so I guess I should come."

I widened my eyes. "Ah, do I sense some interest? Not that it's a bad thing. He's definitely into you, from what I've seen."

Julie glanced down at her hands, which she'd clasped tightly at her waist. "Now, don't start any rumors." Her tone was serious, but when she looked up at me, her eyes were sparkling. "He's an interesting guy, and we share a love of books. That's all there is to it."

"For now," I said. "Don't worry, I approve." My smile slipped as I considered one little wrinkle. "Unless the police prove he murdered Lincoln, of course."

Julie waved off this idea. "I can't imagine that. And anyway, you have me on your suspect list as well."

"Not really. I know the police may still think of you that way, but I don't."

Julee grinned. "You're allowing your emotions to cloud your logic, Charlotte. What if we were in on it together? Or maybe it was everyone at the party. Ever think of that?"

"No, that's one thought that hadn't crossed my mind. Besides," I added, with an answering grin, "we're in Beaufort, not on the Orient Express."

Julie picked up one of the thrillers from the front table. "But it would make an interesting twist." She flipped the book over and read aloud, "'You'll never see the final twist coming.'" She tapped one corner of the book against her other palm. "Bet I will, though. I've read too many popular titles recently, and they all have twists. At this point I can usually guess what's coming."

*But you probably won't guess that the police will be listening in to whatever is said at the party tonight*, I thought, as Julie placed the book back on the table.

I grimaced. I didn't like the idea of deceiving my guests, especially the ones I considered friends. But the truth needed to be revealed, one way or the other. It was the only way we could all move forward without the shadow of suspicion hanging over us.

Picking up another book from the table, I looked it over with surprise. "*My Cousin Rachel* in a brand-new edition? When did that happen?"

Julie shrugged. "Movie tie-in. You know how it is—people are suddenly interested in a classic again if it's made into a film."

"One of my favorites," I said, my fingers caressing the glossy cover.

"Was she a murderer or an innocent victim—dun, dun, dun," Julie said, her voice mimicking the sonorous tone of a movie trailer announcer.

"You have to admit it's a brilliant use of an unreliable narrator. And long before they became so popular, too."

"You love that sort of thing, don't you?" Julie tipped her head and examined me, her eyes as bright and unblinking as a falcon. "Stuff where you have to puzzle it out and come to your own conclusions."

"I do. I mean, you're talking to someone who adores Henry James's *Turn of the Screw* for that very reason. Are the ghosts real, or in the narrator's mind, or . . . ?" As I allowed my statement to dangle, the string of bells on the door jangled again.

"Oh, hi there," Julie said, gazing at the door over my shoulder. "How are you today?"

I turned to face Kelly Rowley.

"I'm good," she said, although I still thought she looked drained. "Hello, Charlotte," she added, with a tight smile.

"Hi. I just saw Todd out on the boat."

"Yes, he's doing a bit of upkeep on her before we get ready for the party tonight."

"Glad to hear you're coming," I said.

"We are, although we will be a little late. I hope that's okay. Todd has a conference call with some business partners that he simply can't avoid." Kelly tugged up the strap of the turquoise swimsuit she was wearing under a gauzy white beach cover-up.

"That's perfectly all right." I tried to catch Kelly's eye to offer her a smile, but her gaze was darting about the shop, looking at everything except Julie and me.

"Thought I might pick up a beach read. We'll be heading out on Sunday, and I particularly enjoy reading when we're sailing. Something about being on the water, you know." Kelly's gaze settled on Julie.

"You've been given permission to leave the area, then?" I asked, fighting to keep my tone casual.

"Yes, the authorities said we were free to go. As long as we leave contact info so they can stay in touch if they need to ask more questions, of course." Kelly finally cast me a glance. "What is that you have there? Something you'd recommend?"

I realized she was referencing the book I was holding. "This? It's a novel by Daphne Du Maurier. *My Cousin Rachel*. Have you read it?"

Kelly shook her head. "No. I've read *Rebecca*, which I liked, but not that one. Is it good?"

"Very," Julie said. "Although it's one of those dark and twisty stories where it's hard to tell who's good or bad."

"Sort of like life," I said without thinking.

Kelly cast me a sharp glance before turning back to Julie. "I do enjoy mysteries," she told Julie, "but maybe that's too heavy for me right now."

"I understand. We've all been through a lot of stress this week," Julie said, sharing a look with me. "Here's something that's popular right now." She plucked another book off the table and handed it to Kelly.

Flipping it over, Kelly held the book close to study the back-cover blurb, making me wonder if she typically used reading glasses. "Oh no," she said, thrusting it back toward Julie. "It has a missing-child theme. I can't read anything with that story line."

Julie, looking concerned, took the book and pressed it to her chest. "So sorry."

"It's okay, you couldn't know. It's just that my older brother went missing when I was a child. He was fifteen. There was ten years between us, so I don't remember much, only that it was traumatic. It cast such a dark shadow over our family . . ." Kelly used one hand to fan her face, even though she appeared pale, not flushed. "Anyway, I try to avoid anything with that theme."

"I can understand that," Julie said, her tone sympathetic. "He was never found?"

Kelly shook her head. "No. My poor parents, who were killed in a car accident about six years later, never got over it."

"I imagine not," I said, thinking of the magazine story I'd read about the Rowleys. According to that article, Kelly's older brother had inherited his parents' estate. Which was odd, if he'd gone missing at fifteen. Although I supposed that even if he'd returned years later, the trauma of his disappearance would linger in Kelly's mind. "That's terrible. You didn't have any other family?"

Kelly ducked her head until her long hair veiled my view of her profile. "Just my grandparents. They raised me after my parents died. But they passed away many years ago. Not long after . . ." She tightened her lips and snapped her head up, tossing her blonde hair out of her face. "Anyway, everyone deals with some sort of tragedy in their life, don't they?"

Her smile was as brittle as a sand dollar. Thinking of my own loss, I nodded and offered her a sympathetic smile in return. "I suppose they do."

Kelly glanced at her watch. "Look at the time! I should get back; Todd might need my help." She flashed Julie an apologetic smile. "I'm sorry I won't be able to buy any books right now, but if you come across a few light and fun reads, bring them to Chapters tonight, okay? I can pay you with a check. Will that work?"

"Yes, that's fine," Julie said. "I'll see what I can find that I think you might like."

"Thanks so much. See you later!" Kelly gave a quick wave before turning on her heel and heading out the shop door.

As the bells fell silent, Julie placed the book she'd been clutching back onto the display table. "That was a little weird."

"Yes," I said, but didn't tell her the strangest part—the discrepancy between Kelly's story and the magazine article's depiction of her past.

Julie walked over to a white-beadboard-paneled counter. Circling behind the counter, she stared down at the desktop computer that functioned as her register. "I'll try to find her something, even though it's difficult to choose books for someone you don't know well."

"That is tricky," I agreed.

"But I'll see what I can do. Poor thing." Julie shook her head. "Losing her entire family like that." She looked over at me. "I guess I'm lucky, really. I've never lost anyone significant. Not yet, anyway."

"I'd say that was fortunate."

"It's strange. You never really know about people, do you?" Julie straightened a stack of bookmarks stuck into a clear plastic brochure holder. "Lincoln lost his parents when he was fairly young, too. I kind of wondered if that was one reason he was so . . ."

"Selfish and arrogant?" I said, before I could check myself. "Sorry, I shouldn't speak ill of the dead. But honestly, I don't think any loss, no matter how tragic, is an excuse to behave the way he did."

"No, no, you're right." Julie pursed her lips and looked me over. "You must think I'm a fool, falling for a guy like that."

"We've all been fools at some time or another. Especially where love is concerned. Now, I guess I'd better be getting along as well. It's probably time to check on Alicia and Damian and finish any other prep for tonight's event."

"Okay, I'll see you there," Julie said, before wishing me a good day.

Outside, I walked to the end of the boardwalk before turning around and heading back toward Chapters. Pausing where I could see the gleaming *Celestial*, I watched as Kelly climbed onto the yacht.

She had money, good looks, health, and what seemed to be a perfect marriage. A lot of people would say she'd been blessed by life. But she'd also endured tragedies that few knew about. Like so many of us, Kelly Rowley had her own pain to overcome. After one last glance at the Rowleys' gorgeous yacht, I set off at a brisk pace, anxious to reach Chapters. I had a part to play tonight, an important task that could expose a murderer while clearing my friend and any other innocent parties.

I hoped I was up to the challenge.

# Chapter
# Twenty-Nine

I didn't have a chance to confer with Ellen before the start of the event. I phoned her, but she didn't answer. Assuming that Ellen was possibly being fitted for her wire by the police, I finally abandoned any attempts to reach her and focused on preparing for my role in the operation instead.

I'd strolled the block when I'd returned from my walk, noting a plain van parked around the corner. Not visible from Chapters, but hopefully close enough for officers to reach the house within minutes if Ellen or I sent the alarm.

Detective Johnson had asked us to use a code word, and Ellen had suggested *sand dollar*. She said it was innocuous enough to slip into conversation without raising eyebrows but not something people mentioned on a regular basis. Giving Ellen another one of her speculative looks, like she was sizing her up for future consulting possibilities, the detective had agreed.

A short time before the start of the discussion, I wandered into the kitchen. "That looks good," I told Damian as I checked over a tray of hors d'oeuvres.

Alicia sniffed. "This crowd will probably do more drinking than eating. Seems to be their way, if the past week is any indication."

"Well, you have to admit this has been a strange week," I said, before steeling myself to make a request. "Listen, I know it's not in your job descriptions, but could you help me out with the activity for this evening? I wondered if you would be willing to at least sit in on that part of the event." I pressed my palms together in front of my chest, as if in prayer. "It might help the atmosphere to have you in the room. Lessen the tension between the guests and all that."

"I'd say no, but since you've been kind enough to keep me employed, even after my meltdown last week, I guess I owe you that much," Damian said.

Alicia made a face. "All right, if you insist."

"Thank you. Now, we'd better get a move on. The guests should arrive any minute."

Scott was waiting in the library when we carried in the food and drinks. He helped Alicia and Damian adjust the seating while I hurried to answer the ringing doorbell.

The Sandberg sisters were the first to arrive. I had to stifle an urge to laugh when I saw they were both wearing deerstalker hats.

"How apropos," I said, after welcoming them inside.

"We thought it would be fun to get into the spirit of things," Ophelia said. "Although Bernie drew the line at wearing long coats."

"Too darn hot for that," Bernadette said, before turning to greet Pete and Sandy, and Julie, who'd all just appeared at the door.

Jennifer Delamont came down the stairs then, but paused on the bottom step when Julie stepped inside. She looked the younger woman up and down. "Surprised you have the gall to show up, Ms. Rivera."

"And hello to you too, Ms. Delamont," Julie said, not batting an eye. She strolled down the hall toward the library without waiting for a reply.

"I think everyone is here now, except for my neighbor, who'll be here any minute," I told Jennifer. "Oh yes, and the Rowleys, but they told me they'd be a little late. If you'd like to accompany me to the library . . ."

She made a derisive noise but followed me.

As we entered the library, I noticed that Julie had selected the seat next to Scott. Pete and Sandy had also chosen the wooden chairs, leaving the softer armchairs for the Sandberg sisters.

"Please, everyone, grab some snacks and drinks. I thought we could enjoy a little mixer before starting this evening's event," I said, motioning to the desk, which was once again serving as a table.

Of course, I was actually stalling for time, waiting for Ellen and the Rowleys before I dove into any leading questions that might help the authorities.

I surveyed the group, wondering what their own secrets might be. I wasn't a trained investigator, or even an experienced amateur detective. It was possible I'd made false assumptions about everyone.

As all the guests—except Jennifer, who remained slumped in her chair—mingled over the food and drinks, I headed for the kitchen to remind Alicia and Damian to join us.

But as I walked down the hall, Ellen appeared at the back door. I hurried to let her in. "Ready for this?"

"Born ready," Ellen said, giving my arm a pat. "Don't worry. All you're doing is asking questions and making comments. For anything beyond that"—she pointed to her chest—"we have backup."

I nodded and told Ellen to wait in the hall while I asked Alicia and Damian to join us so we could walk into the library together.

"All right, if everyone can take a seat, we'll get started," I said, grabbing my folder of notes from one of the library shelves. I slipped the folder under my arm and poured myself a glass of water before sitting in a chair near the door. Ellen sat down next to me, while Alicia and Damian slipped behind the desk and remained standing.

Jennifer shifted in her chair, her expression darkening. "I don't know about this. Discussing murder mysteries sounds too much like the misery I've already suffered through this week."

Ophelia whipped off her wool hat and used it to fan her face. "It's just a game."

"It *is* odd to be talking about fake murders when we have a real one that still needs to be solved," Julie said, fixing Jennifer with an intense stare.

Jennifer threw up her hands. "I know you all think I killed Lincoln, but I didn't. Honestly, I shouldn't have agreed to this. I don't appreciate being treated like a criminal when I've done nothing wrong."

I glanced over at Ellen. The evening was going in a direction I hadn't expected, but as we already seemed to be touching on some of the questions Detective Johnson wanted me to raise, I had no intention of guiding things back onto the rails.

"Now, now," Sandy said, in a soothing tone. "No one thinks that, Mrs. Delamont."

"Oh good heavens, of course we do," Bernadette snapped. "It's usually the spouse in these situations, isn't it? Not that I blame Mrs. Delamont in this case. In my opinion, that Lincoln fellow was enough of a jerk to deserve killing."

Ophelia waved her hat furiously. "Really, Bernie, the things you say."

"I'm not going to sit here and listen to this." Jennifer leapt to her feet, her chest heaving. "For your information, I can show that I didn't murder my husband. Yes, I argued with him right before he was killed, but when I left him, he was very much alive."

"And you can prove this?" Julie asked, as Scott leaned in and laid his hand on her arm.

"Easier than you can prove you didn't kill him, I imagine." Jennifer straightened her back and stared around the room. "I changed my clothes, except for my headscarf, and went for a walk right after I last saw Lincoln. Just strolled around the block, to clear my head. But apparently someone in a neighboring house saw me." Jennifer crossed her arms over her chest. "They confirmed it recently, after the police canvassed the neighborhood a second time. The neighbor clearly remembered seeing me. And they could confirm the time because they'd just glanced at their watch. So now the police know for certain that I wasn't anywhere near Lincoln when he was killed."

"Just like they know Tara wasn't there," I said, earning inquisitive glances from Scott and Julie. "That's why they allowed her to leave. They had proof of her being on the phone in her bedroom at Chapters. When they put together all the time factors, it appeared she was there during the time of the murder."

"Yes." The lines bracketing Jennifer's mouth softened. "Both of us are in the clear. The police asked us not to say anything, though. They didn't want to tip off the real killer to the fact that the list of suspects had been shortened."

"That the net was closing in, you mean," Scott said.

I studied him for a moment, looking for any signs of concern. Finding none, I decided to throw out my own nagging question. "Sandy and Pete told me about you lurking about the carriage house earlier than you originally claimed. How do you explain that?"

Scott exhaled a gusty sigh. "As I already told you, Charlotte, I was contemplating putting on some costume pieces so I could join the party that night. Stuff I'd stored in that garden bin."

"That's where that junk came from," Damian said. "Man, you should've spoken up about that sooner. Would've saved me some questioning."

"Sorry," Scott said. "I didn't even think of it at first. After falling over a dead body, I mean." He rubbed his temples with his fingers. "I decided to store my laptop inside the carriage house before I did anything else, and that's when I found Lincoln's body."

Julie turned to him, her eyes wide. "You didn't see anyone fleeing the carriage house?"

"No. They must've left before I got back."

Pete glanced around the room. "So, we have Jennifer arguing with Lincoln, then heading out for a walk."

"And Tara, who heard her dad talking with another woman before she saw Jennifer approach. Which made the girl run off to her room in the house."

Bernadette rubbed her chin with one hand. "Which means that the woman with Lincoln before his wife approached him must have hidden in the carriage house before Jennifer got there."

"I didn't see anyone," Jennifer said, as she sat back down. "You mean that woman was hiding in there the entire time we were arguing?"

"Sounds likely," Bernadette said, turning to look straight at Julie.

"Now, wait a minute," Julie said, holding up her hands in a defensive gesture. Her dark eyes darted about the room, finally landing on Pete. "Help me out here. You mixed me another drink right after that, remember? Even asked me why I was so upset."

"Yes, that's right," Pete said. "You came over to the bar while I was fixing myself something and told me you'd just had a foolish argument and needed a drink to wash away the bad taste in your mouth."

"Right." Julie gazed about the room triumphantly. "Which proves I wasn't the woman hiding in the carriage house. And"—she shot Pete a grateful look—"that Pete wasn't near the carriage house at that point either."

"Anyway, I don't think anyone could mistake my deep voice for a woman's," Pete said. "Although that's a moot point, since I don't know why anyone would suspect me of killing Delamont. I had no motive."

"Same on both counts," Damian said, stepping forward.

I opened my mouth but snapped it shut without saying anything. No sense in dragging Damian's rejection letter, or any possible connection to a scandal in Liza Nelson's past, into the mix now.

Ophelia scrunched her deerstalker hat in her hands. "That leaves—who? Surely you don't think Bernie or I had anything to do with a murder. I can't imagine Sandy being involved either. And I think it's been proven that Charlotte was at the store and didn't get back until after Scott found Lincoln's body." Her eyes widened as her gaze fell on Alicia.

"Now wait one darned minute," Alicia said, striding forward to stand beside Damian. "Don't you be going and accusing me of murder, Miss Ophelia Sandberg. Not when I know a few things about you—"

Bernadette jumped to her feet, taking a fighter's stance. "Don't attack my sister for a reasonable conclusion."

"Reasonable?" Alicia barked out a laugh. "Let me get this straight—I was supposed to dash outside with a knife, have a little chat with Delamont, then hide in the carriage house until I killed him? Without anyone seeing me? Are you kidding? The minute I stepped out of the kitchen, I would've had you lot swarming me, asking me to clean up this or that. Or to bring you a special snack or drink or something." She snorted. "Not like I can just swan around like a guest, free to wander without being accosted by people wanting something from me."

"So you didn't go outside," I murmured, recalling Kelly's assertion that she'd seen Alicia head for the carriage house. Which was apparently a lie.

*Why would Kelly lie about that?* I frowned. It didn't make sense.

"That may be true, Alicia. But you did have access to the carriage house key and the knife," Pete said. "You can't dispute that."

"Just like all of you. It's not like we locked up those things. I was in and out of the kitchen enough times earlier in the evening to allow anyone to grab both of them without my knowledge." Alicia tightened her lips and fixed her stare on the Sandberg sisters. "And if you recall, Ophelia, you saw me in the kitchen about the time that the murder supposedly happened."

"Oh, right. Sorry, how could I forget?" A blush suffused Ophelia's cheeks. "When Bernie and I were inside Chapters, looking for my glasses, I saw Alicia at the sink, rinsing out a stain on her apron."

"One of those sauces from the dinner party," Alicia said. "It dripped on my apron when I was clearing the dishes, I guess. I wanted to rinse it out before it set."

*That explains the missing apron.* "Which would make the timing difficult for you. To be the murderer, I mean." I spoke slowly as my mind raced, chasing thoughts of whom this left on the suspect list.

"Impossible, I'd say. Not that there was any reason to suspect me anyway," Alicia asserted, without looking at me.

There was one compelling motive, but I thought better of dragging my great-aunt's past into the discussion. Especially now that it looked like it had not been the reason for Lincoln Delamont's death.

*Although I believe something from the past must figure into it*, I thought, turning my head at the sound of footsteps in the hall.

"Hello, everyone. Sorry to be so late," Kelly said as she entered the library. She fluttered one hand in greeting. "Todd got caught on a phone call, but he'll be along in a few minutes."

As everyone focused on Kelly, I realized we were all probably thinking the same thing—she'd been the only other female at the costume party. The only one without an alibi. *Or at least*, I thought, *the only woman who hasn't shared one yet.*

Kelly, gripping her purple quilted purse close to her body, shifted from one Greek sandal-clad foot to the other. "I hope we didn't miss anything important."

"Just playing a little game of amateur detective," Julie said, her eyes narrowing. "Care to join?"

# Chapter Thirty

In her short, finely pleated, lilac cotton sundress, with her braided golden hair pulled back and twisted into an elegant bun, Kelly looked like some Grecian statue come to life. She lifted a well-toned, tanned arm and used one finger to delicately dash a bead of sweat from her upper lip.

"Of course. Isn't that the point of this evening?"

"Well, the original plan has devolved into something a little different," Scott said, rising to his feet to offer Kelly his chair.

"Really? And please, Mr. Kepler, sit down. There's an extra couple of chairs off to the side there, next to the lady I met the other evening." Kelly arched her golden brows. "Ms. Montgomery, I think it is?"

"Yes, Charlotte's next-door neighbor," Ellen said.

"That's right, we met at the Thursday night cocktail party. We didn't get a chance to really talk then, though," Kelly said. "What are we discussing—more thoughts on Tey's books?"

"No, our very own murder mystery," Ophelia said. "The death of the unfortunate Mr. Delamont."

"Really? That sounds a little macabre." Kelly shot me a questioning look as she sat down.

Bernadette jumped in before I could say anything. "Actually, we were comparing alibis just before you arrived. But we hadn't quite gotten around to our personal theories on who the murderer might be. Perhaps you'd like to start there, Ms. Rowley?"

"Oh, well, I don't know." Kelly crossed her bare legs, hiking her dress up higher on her thighs. "I'm not sure my thoughts would shed much light on the situation."

Julie stood, shaking out one foot as if it had gone to sleep. "I'm sure your theories are as reasonable as any others I've heard." She crossed over to one of the lower library shelves and picked up a stack of paperbacks. "I did find you some books, by the way. If you still want them."

"Yes, that would be lovely." As Kelly reached into her purse, something glinted. "Darn, it seems I forgot my checkbook, but I'm happy to send you a check before we leave Beaufort. I'm good for it, I promise," she added, with a bright smile.

Ellen stirred in her chair. "So, Mrs. Rowley, I'm curious, do you actually have any theories on who killed Lincoln Delamont?"

"Not really. At first, I thought it was probably some stranger. I mean, someone not part of our group. Someone who had a beef with Mr. Delamont and tracked him here." She shrugged. "Maybe they confronted and killed him during an argument, then fled the scene."

"But you don't think that now?" Scott, who hadn't reclaimed his seat, paced across one end of the library.

"No, because . . . Well, just some things I picked up when the police were questioning me made me think it might be someone else." Kelly bit her lower lip and looked at the other guests, her gaze darting from face to face. "Someone in this room."

"But everyone in this room has an alibi," Bernadette said, her voice hardening. "What's yours?"

"Do they? Well, I'm at a disadvantage, since I missed hearing all that, but of course I had nothing to do with Mr. Delamont's death. I barely knew the man, after all, whereas some of you seem to have much closer connections to him. And I don't just mean his wife and daughter." Kelly cast a swift glance at Jennifer.

"They both have been cleared by the police," Pete said. "Airtight alibis, apparently."

"But I believe Mr. Kepler knew Delamont before this week, as did Ms. Rivera and Mr. Carr. Isn't that right?" Kelly's golden lashes fluttered over her clear blue eyes.

"It is," I said, "but I'm not sure how you would know that, Kelly."

She lifted her hands in a dismissive gesture. "I did a little investigating of my own after this whole mess started. Just to make sure I wasn't associating with dangerous criminals."

"And you found out what?" Bernadette asked, her tone barbed as a fishhook.

"That Lincoln Delamont cheated Mr. Kepler's father out of a significant amount of money, for one thing." Kelly smiled sweetly. "Todd and I have some connections in the book world, and in case you were all unaware, Mr. Kepler's dad was Nathan Caine."

"Really?" Julie turned to stare at Scott. "That was your dad?"

Scott bobbed his head but kept his gaze focused on Kelly. "You asked around and found out about Delamont swindling my father? Okay, I admit it does give me motive, but what did you discover about the others you claim to suspect?" He pointed toward Julie and Damian. "I doubt they have famous parents who are known by your wealthy friends."

Jennifer chimed in before Kelly could reply. "Well, Julie Rivera was having an affair with my husband."

"Not an affair," Julie said. "Not really."

"You mean, not yet." Jennifer tossed her thick dark curls. "Found out the truth in time instead."

Kelly's gaze ranged from Julie to Jennifer and back again. "Yes, that one was obvious. Lincoln Delamont was leading Ms. Rivera on, and when she found out he was still quite married, perhaps she snapped and stabbed him."

"As if I would risk prison time on some guy," Julie said, sharing a glance with Scott. I was glad to see he looked unperturbed, which meant Julie must've already told him the truth about her relationship with Lincoln.

Hoping to get the discussion back on track, I stared down at my notes. *Lincoln Delamont was apparently something of a scammer*, one bulleted point said. *Ask about deception in relation to Tey's books, which often included that theme.* "Perhaps we should get back to talking about Tey," I said. "I wrote out a few discussion starters—"

"Such as how most of her books deal with murders?" Bernadette asked, arching her eyebrows. "I thought we were dealing with that topic already."

"Yes, but she also wrote a lot about deception. Many of her characters were engaged in scams of some kind," I said, allowing my gaze to sweep around the room. "There was the con man brother and the astrologist in *A Shilling for Candles*, for example. Betty in *The Franchise Affair*. And of course, deception lies at the heart of *Brat Farrar*."

"You know my opinion on that," Bernadette said, with a sniff. "Not a likely scenario, not by a long shot. Family would always know their own."

"I don't know. It might be different for family members, but I think everyone can be fooled, if the con artist is good enough." Scott spoke slowly, as if trying to untangle a knotted skein of thoughts. "My father, who was a very intelligent man, was conned." He met Julie's sympathetic gaze. "Charlotte knows this story, and I just told Julie the other night, so I guess there's no reason to keep it under wraps. As Ms. Rowley just revealed, my dad was scammed out of a considerable amount of money by Lincoln Delamont."

I glanced at Jennifer, whose expression was as frozen as a glacier.

"I don't believe that," she said coldly. "He may have been unfaithful, but Lincoln didn't need to cheat anyone for money. He had plenty of his own." She shrugged. "That was the one thing I could count on, at least. The money. Most of it was invested, and he used the interest to fund his business, not the principal, so it wasn't like he was going broke anytime soon."

"Really? And where did all this money come from?" Scott asked, ignoring the hand Julie had laid on his arm. "Maybe from other, earlier scams?"

"No." Jennifer met Scott's stare with a glare of her own. "If you must know, Lincoln's parents died in an automobile accident when he was around twenty-one. He inherited the money from them."

I bolted upright in my chair. *An automobile accident, an inheritance . . .* As I sneaked a surreptitious glance at the woman sitting next to me, an image of Lincoln Delamont flashed through my mind.

He'd been slender, blond, and blue-eyed, just like Kelly Rowley. In fact, they looked enough alike that Lincoln could've easily passed as her brother.

I swallowed a swear word and clasped my hands tightly on top of the notes in my lap as my mind processed a new, unexpected theory.

Kelly Rowley had lost her parents in an auto accident, just like Lincoln Delamont. Kelly when she was around eleven, Lincoln at age twenty-one. A ten-year age gap. Which was exactly the age difference between Kelly and the older brother she'd claimed had disappeared from her life. But he must have returned and, according to the magazine profile, inherited her parents' entire estate.

*Leaving her with nothing?* I gathered up my notes and carefully placed them on the floor beside my chair.

Bernadette stood, placed her hands on her hips, and surveyed the people in the room. "Why are we wasting time talking about Tey's books? I don't know about the rest of you, but personally, I still want to hear Ms. Rowley's alibi."

"I can't see that I need one. I never met Mr. Delamont until last Friday night," Kelly said.

I wondered if Kelly's tinkling laugh sounded as forced to everyone else as it did to me. "Because we think it was a woman, you see," I said. "Tara heard a woman talking with her dad before he was killed. A woman who must've hidden in the carriage house when Jennifer Delamont appeared on the scene."

Julie leaned in closer to Scott. "And all of the rest of us females have solid alibis, it seems."

"Is that why you all are staring at me with those suspicious expressions? Because you think I had something to do with Delamont's death?" Kelly covered her mouth with one well-manicured hand and giggled. "Honestly, that's the most ridiculous thing I've ever heard. I mean, I scarcely shared three words with the man before he was found stabbed to death."

Julie pulled away from Scott and crossed the room to stand in front of the desk. "That's curious, because I'm sure I saw you chatting with him for quite some time at the Friday night cocktail party."

"And you would've noticed, I suppose," Jennifer said, her tone etched with acid. But she nodded when Julie glanced at her. "Yes, I saw that too. Figured he was hitting on another pretty woman. He backed off pretty quick when Mr. Rowley came over, though. I guess he realized he couldn't compete with a man like that."

"I think you're mistaken. I don't remember spending much time talking to him at all," Kelly said.

A sidelong glance displayed a crack in Kelly's perfect composure. Sweat now dampened her brow and temples as well as her upper lip, and there was a twitch afflicting her right eye.

Here was my opening, if I was brave enough to take it. "Maybe you were talking about your shared tragedy?" I asked, keeping my tone as light as possible.

Ellen shot me a sharp look as a hysterical bubble of laughter escaped Kelly's lips. "What in heaven's name are you talking about?" Kelly asked, when she was able to speak.

"Didn't you both lose your parents in car accidents when you were young? Well, you were only eleven, if what I read in a magazine article is true. While Lincoln was around twenty-one when his parents died."

Ellen cast me a swift glance. Her expression told me she'd just come to the same conclusion I had.

"Yes, we both lost our parents. What of it? It's not like that made us instant soul mates or anything." Kelly's fingers tightened on the clasp of her purse.

Scott joined Julie at the desk, where Damian had poured out some wine. The three of them each grabbed a glass while I looked on, wishing I could join them.

Ellen stood and turned to face Kelly. "It's just an odd coincidence, don't you think? He was forty-six. You're thirty-six. He lost his parents to a car crash at age twenty-one, you at eleven. That's matching ten-year age gaps. I mean, they could've been the same parents, given the facts."

"That's absurd!" Still clutching her purse, Kelly leapt to her feet to face off with Ellen. "I don't know what you're suggesting, but whatever it is doesn't make any sense. Besides, like I told Ms. Reed and Ms. Rivera at the bookstore earlier today, my brother went missing when I was only five."

"Then how did he inherit the bulk of your parents' estate?" I asked, rising to stand beside Ellen. "That was another thing I read in the article profiling you and Todd. How you had to start your track career without a lot of help, financially and otherwise, because your older brother inherited your late parents' money and didn't bother to support you."

Kelly's face blanched white as paper. "You're mistaken," she said in a strangled voice.

"No, it was in that same article. So either the reporter made something up, or—"

"You did," Ellen said, finishing my sentence.

Kelly slung the gold chain handle of her purse over one bare shoulder. "I don't have to stand here and listen to this nonsense." She strode out of the room, tossing, "And you can keep your books, Ms. Rivera," over her shoulder.

"I don't understand," Ophelia said. "What's going on?"

"Not sure myself, but I think there's more to this little evening of fun and games than meets the eye," said her sister.

"Everyone, please stay here. Enjoy some more wine and snacks. I'll just go and see if Ms. Rowley is okay," I said, then dashed toward the hall.

"I'll come with you," Ellen said.

We didn't see Kelly but heard the back door slam.

"Time to call in the cavalry?" I asked.

Ellen, striding down the hall, waved me forward. "Yes, but let's also make sure we know where she's headed so we can clue them in," she said, before pronouncing "sand dollar" in a loud, clear voice.

Outside, I surveyed the patio but saw nothing. As I considered heading for the garden, Ellen grabbed my arm and motioned toward the holly hedge.

"Spied some movement there," she said, dropping my arm and making a beeline for the carriage house.

"Shouldn't we wait for the police?" I cast a final glance at the driveway before jogging after her. Ellen might have been trained as a spy years ago, but she was seventy-five now. Probably no match for a fit young woman.

A loud crash forced me into a run.

I rounded the hedge, reassuring myself that the police were on the way.

Besides, even if Kelly was the killer, and had somehow obtained another knife, she'd have to get pretty close to someone to use it. Surely Ellen, with all her training, was too smart to allow that to happen.

The door to the carriage house was kicked in, which explained the sound I'd heard. Just inside I made out the silhouettes of two people.

Kelly stepped out into the light, and I realized what she held in her hand.

Not a knife this time. A gun. Pointed, not at me, but at the temple of a woman standing beside her.

"If you want your friend to survive this, you'd better get in here now," she said.

I choked back my urge to scream. "The police are on their way."

"So your neighbor told me. Which is why I am taking you both as hostages. My bargaining chips." Kelly bared her white teeth in the semblance of a smile.

"This will not end well for you." Ellen winced as Kelly popped her temple with the gun.

"Get inside, Charlotte," Kelly commanded.

I could've made a break for it, but that would've left Ellen at the younger woman's mercy. Sensing Kelly's desperation, I wasn't convinced she could be trusted not to shoot my friend.

*You can do this*, I told myself, as an image of Brent throwing his body against a door to save a roomful of children flashed through my mind. He'd probably been terrified too, with winds roaring like a freight train bearing down on him. But he'd done the right thing.

I could too. I curled my fingers, as if clasping an unseen hand, and followed Kelly and Ellen into the darkness.

# Chapter Thirty-One

As my eyes adjusted to the dim light inside the carriage house, I noticed that Kelly's other hand—the one not holding a gun—was trembling.

*She isn't as calm and in control as she's trying to make us think.* I slid closer to Ellen. I wanted to ask her if we should try to tackle Kelly, gun or no gun, but the quarters were too tight. Kelly would hear anything we said, even a whisper.

"You can't believe you can get away with this," I said, before Ellen grabbed my hand and squeezed it so hard that my eyes watered.

"All I need is an opportunity to reach the *Celestial*," Kelly said. "Holding you two as hostages just might give me that chance."

I wondered whether Todd Rowley was a willing accomplice to Kelly's crimes. Perhaps he knew everything and would gladly ferry her away from facing the consequences of her actions. Although that would undoubtedly mean the collapse of his business empire.

"I'm sure you must have had an excellent reason to kill Lincoln Delamont," Ellen said, her voice infused with a sympathy that made me shoot her a questioning glance.

*Of course. She's just trying to get in Kelly's good graces. Establish a rapport that will humanize us, making Kelly less likely to shoot. Ellen knows what she's doing—she was trained for situations like this.*

I pressed my lips together to silence any further comments, realizing I should let the professional use her skills.

"I didn't plan to do it. I didn't set out to harm anyone." Kelly turned to me. "And I didn't want to hurt you the other night either. But I had to get away after I dropped off the knife."

"And I suppose you just wanted to scare me when you chased me around Fort Macon?"

"Yes. I knew you were snooping around. Asking too many questions of people who'd been at the party. I was afraid you'd find out that someone had seen me doing something odd, like shoving my balled-up cloak, with the knife stuffed in the pocket, into the lilac bush."

"Because they both had blood on them?" Ellen asked.

Kelly nodded. "I was able to collect the cloak, with the knife, before the police could find anything, and carry both off to the *Celestial.* That was one reason I begged Todd to move from Chapters to the yacht in such a rush. I knew I could weigh the cloak down and dump it in the ocean when we finally set sail. That way it would be gone for good. I didn't think anyone noticed me stashing or grabbing the cloak. But when Charlotte was making it her business to talk to people who were at the party, I worried that someone had seen me, thought it odd, and might say something that would allow her to put the pieces together."

"That wasn't what did it," I said.

"I realize that now, but at that point I just hoped maybe you'd back off if you were scared enough. I hoped dropping off the knife at the murder scene would send the message that the killer was still in town, and having someone chase you might make you think twice about continuing to snoop around."

"You obviously don't know Charlotte very well," Ellen said under her breath.

Kelly defiantly lifted her chin. "Anyway, I didn't mean to hurt Charlotte. Just like I never meant to physically harm Lincoln, much less kill him. It wasn't premeditated."

Ellen held up one hand in a placating gesture. "I'm sure it wasn't. Which does make a big difference, you know."

"I know. I'm not stupid." Kelly's aim wavered.

"Of course not. And if Lincoln was your brother, who basically stole your inheritance . . ."

"He wasn't my brother!" Kelly's voice rocketed up another octave on the last word.

"Okay, then who was he?" Ellen's voice remained perfectly calm, as if she was simply passing the time of day with a new acquaintance.

"An impostor," Kelly spat out. "A liar and a scoundrel."

Emboldened, I decided to speak up. "Lincoln wasn't the brother who went missing when you were a child?"

"No. Other people thought he was, but I knew better." Kelly used her free hand to wipe a bit of spittle from the corner of her mouth. "My brother's name was David. He disappeared when I was five. People told me I couldn't remember him well enough to know that Lincoln was an impostor, but I did. I swear I did."

"Of course," Ellen said in a soothing tone. "You were family. You would know."

"Exactly," Kelly said.

The ferocity of her reply reminded me of her comments about the family in Tey's *Brat Farrar* accepting the counterfeit nephew and brother, Brat, as one of their own. "Did Lincoln show up right after your parents' deaths?"

"No, he was too clever for that. He waited six months before appearing at my grandparents' house, claiming to be David."

"And they believed him?" Ellen asked gently.

"Yes, the fools." Kelly tapped one foot and rolled her shoulders. She appeared to be struggling to retain a hold on her violent emotions, which didn't make me feel good about her wielding a gun. "Of course, they wanted to believe. They'd just lost their daughter and son-in-law. They desperately desired the miracle that Lincoln Delamont offered them."

"That their missing grandson had returned? That's understandable." Ellen dropped my hand and took one step to the side.

"He was well informed." Kelly's blue eyes glazed over. "I guess he'd made a study of our family, planning the whole masquerade. I don't know how he did it, but he knew details about my parents, about our past experiences and activities, that convinced my grandparents he was actually David."

"But what did he say to explain his earlier disappearance?" Ellen asked.

"Oh, he had this whole story concocted. About how he'd run off when he was fifteen because he was feeling so pressured by my parents to succeed." Kelly frowned. "I guess that was true. Some of David's friends did confirm that he was experiencing those emotions when he left. But I assume Lincoln talked to them at some point to gather information."

"What do you think happened to the real David?" I asked, hoping to keep Kelly talking long enough for the police to set up their operations outside.

"Dead," she said, in a hollow voice. "I knew it, not long after he disappeared. There was just this void in my head, you know, when I tried to remember him."

"Lincoln may have somehow known David was dead as well," Ellen said thoughtfully.

"I'm sure he did." A single tear slid down Kelly's cheek.

"But why did he stay away so long?" I asked. When Kelly's frown turned into a glower, I quickly added, "I mean, what was Lincoln's contrived excuse for not returning to the family sooner?"

"Oh, he said he found a home with some family who were willing to take him in without too many questions. He claimed they believed his story about being abused, even though he wasn't, and so they didn't contact social services for fear he'd be returned to his terrible family." Kelly snorted. "As if my parents would've ever laid a hand on either of us."

"Lincoln concocted this story, and your grandparents swallowed it hook, line, and sinker?" Ellen asked.

"Yes. Like I said, they wanted to believe. And Lincoln knew enough background information and looked enough like our family to make it plausible. I wanted them to have his DNA tested, or something more official, but they were so dazzled by the idea that they had regained one of the three family members they'd lost that they refused. They said such testing wasn't necessary. They accepted his lies and were more than happy to sign over my parents' estate."

"Cutting you out?" I asked.

"Yes, but they didn't mean to hurt me. They honestly thought my *brother* would take care of me."

"But he didn't?"

"No, but that wasn't the worst part." Kelly audibly swallowed. "He had them put all the funds in accounts under the name he was using at the time. Which wasn't Lincoln Delamont, by the way. He used another identity when he swindled my grandparents." Kelly snorted. "He had a story all prepared—told them he'd legally established a new identity and wanted to keep it, rather than revert to his birth name. Due to business reasons or something. Of course, it was all part of his con, but my grandparents didn't care what name he used as long as they had their 'David' back."

"He got control of the inheritance in another name? Clever," I said.

"Yes, then left again as soon as he had the money. According to the private investigator I later hired, Lincoln then transferred everything to new accounts under his real name and fled town. My grandparents were devastated."

"I'm sure they were," Ellen said. "He never contacted them again?"

"No, he just vanished."

"But he was living under his real name, I mean, as Lincoln Delamont, at that point?" I asked.

"Yes, but I didn't know that for some time. Not until after . . ." Kelly choked on the last word. She cleared her throat before continuing. "After my grandparents died. They were so broken by the second loss of their grandson, who they still believed was the real deal, that their health declined rapidly. They died within months of each other, only a year after Lincoln absconded with the family fortune."

Ellen made a sympathetic noise. "Leaving you alone."

"Broke and alone." Kelly's knuckles whitened as her grip on the pistol tightened. "Some cousins took me in and raised me until I was eighteen. I handled everything on my own after that. College, my track career, everything."

"That just proves your strength," Ellen said.

Kelly's arm wavered. She lowered the gun slightly. "But it shouldn't have been that way. Lincoln Delamont stole my life. Not just my money, but my grandparents, and even the memory of my real brother. He desecrated that, with his selfish, criminal actions."

A voice, amplified by a bullhorn, rang out just outside the carriage house. "This is the police. Release the hostages safely, and we promise we can discuss your situation."

Kelly stiffened and pointed the gun back at Ellen. "How did they get here so fast?"

Ellen replied without hesitation. "I suppose they suspected someone from the party had committed the murder and were keeping surveillance on this week's events at Chapters."

I glanced over at her, amazed by her calm demeanor in the face of an unstable killer. But then again, perhaps she'd been caught in just such a situation—or worse—before.

"You said you didn't plan to kill Lincoln," I said, hoping to pull Kelly's focus off Ellen. "But I assume you did know he'd be here this week?"

"Of course. I'd been tracking him for some time. Ever since that private detective I hired discovered that Lincoln Delamont truly was the man who'd posed as my brother years ago. Anyway, when I found out that Lincoln intended to attend the Tey celebration at Chapters—I mean, the idiot put it on his Facebook page, so it was out there for everyone to see—I convinced Todd to register us as well." Kelly tossed her head, loosening one of the braids. It flapped down onto her shoulder like a whip. "I wasn't planning to hurt him, of course. I just wanted to confront him, once and for all. To let him know he'd never fooled me."

"What happened?" I asked, as the request from the police boomed out again.

Kelly's lips trembled. Widening her stance, she kept the gun raised. "He didn't recognize me at first. Not until I talked to him at that welcome night cocktail party. Then he realized who I was, I guess. Or at least had some suspicion, even though he hadn't seen me since I was a child. The next evening, after dinner, he said he wanted to talk to me in private." Tears welled in Kelly's eyes. "He demanded that I meet him. I was scared, to be honest. He seemed threatening. But I wanted to confront him, so I agreed to meet him at the carriage house during the party."

"But you took a knife for protection." Ellen did not frame this as a question.

Kelly bobbed her head. "I grabbed one from the kitchen and hid it in a pocket sewn inside my cloak. I guess Lincoln stole that key that went missing, because when I met him, the carriage house door was already unlocked and standing ajar."

The pieces fell in place in my mind. "You argued with him. That's what Tara Delamont overhead, before you both headed into the carriage house to continue your conversation. But then you stayed inside when he went out to talk with his wife."

"Yes. Lincoln waited until she was gone, then came back into the carriage house to continue talking with me."

"Did he attack you?" Ellen asked gently. "Because that would be a mitigating factor, you know. Self-defense."

"Not at first. But when I threatened to expose his sordid past, to strip him of his ill-gotten fortune, he lunged at me." Kelly lowered the gun. "I didn't mean to kill him, but we struggled, and he was trying to grab the knife, and I just . . ."

"Defended yourself," Ellen said firmly.

Kelly bowed her head and mutely nodded.

"But you should have just told the police all this right away," I blurted out.

"How could I?" Kelly lifted her head. Her face, ravaged by grief and guilt, appeared aged by at least twenty years. "I had to consider Todd's business interests. A scandal like that . . . well, I didn't know what it would do to him. And I was scared. How could I trust that anyone would believe me, when they hadn't believed me in the past? All those years ago, when I'd told them that Lincoln wasn't David, when I'd sworn he was an impostor, no one believed me. Not my friends, not my extended family. Not even my grandparents."

A voice blasted from the bullhorn again, but this was one that made Kelly back away with a sob.

"Kelly, please let Charlotte and Ms. Montgomery go and come out of there," said Todd Rowley. "We can work this out, Kelly. I'm here for you. I'll stand by you, I swear. Just come out."

The gun slipped from Kelly's fingers and clattered to the floor. Ellen dived down and scooped up the weapon using a silk handkerchief. *To shield it from her fingerprints*, I thought, marveling at how her training had automatically kicked in during such a traumatic moment. Sharing a look with me, Ellen pocketed the gun while Kelly covered her face with her hands and wept.

She didn't move as Ellen and I made our way outside, announcing ourselves and yelling, "Don't shoot," while raising our hands over our heads.

Detective Johnson grabbed me while another officer took hold of Ellen. They ushered us behind a line of officers, where I collapsed onto the strip of grass separating the driveway from the back door stoop.

Ellen remained on her feet. She handed Kelly's gun, still wrapped in the handkerchief, to one of the officers, then strolled over to speak with Detective Johnson.

Kelly, encouraged by Todd's continued requests, walked out of the carriage house a few minutes later. She was immediately swarmed by officers, who handcuffed her over Todd's protests.

Ellen helped me to my feet. "They're going to take her to the station to book her, I suppose," she said. "But I convinced Detective Johnson to let us give our preliminary statements here and wait until Monday to come in to the station." She brushed a bit of dirt from my sleeve. "I thought that would be better, since it would allow you to resolve things with your other guests."

"Yes, thank you," I said, my attention drawn to the forlorn figure of Todd Rowley, who was begging to be allowed in the police car set to follow the cruiser taking Kelly away. "Seems he had no idea about any of this."

Ellen gazed after the cruiser as it took off, lights flashing. "Poor man. It appears she loved him too much to confess and perhaps harm his businesses, but not quite enough to trust him with the truth."

"You heard her—she wasn't believed when she told the truth as a child. And honestly, it's not always easy to share our deepest pain, even with the ones we love." I thought of how I'd bottled up my agony over losing Brent. Oh, I'd displayed the acceptable amount of sorrow, of course. But no one, not even my parents or sisters, had ever seen the true depths of my despair. I had deliberately shielded them from that.

"We do want to protect them, don't we?" Ellen said, as if echoing my thoughts. "Even though that sometimes causes additional problems."

I studied her serious expression for a moment. "You were her handler, so I'm guessing that made you one of her few confidants. Which means I have to wonder—did Isabella ever share what she really felt with you? I mean, about Paul Peters, or living a double life, or being forced to go through life alone?"

"No," Ellen said shortly, and turned away. "Come on, Charlotte. We need to tell the others what's happened. The police kept them blocked inside, so they're probably frantic with curiosity and concern by now. And honestly, I, for one, could use a drink."

"Only one?" I asked, as I followed her into the house.

"One before we give our statements." Ellen cast me an amused glance as we headed for the library. "Several after. But I think we'd better move to the privacy of my house to enjoy those."

"Now that sounds like the kind of covert mission I can get behind," I said.

# Chapter
# Thirty-Two

A few weeks later, after numerous sessions with the police, and after I'd heard that Kelly had been released on an astronomically high bail but confined to her primary home in Annapolis, Maryland, until her trial, I faced some of my Tey week guests in the library again. Minus the Delamonts and Rowleys, of course.

This was a regular meeting of the book club we held at Chapters once a month. Although other guests staying at the bed-and-breakfast were always invited to join this activity, they usually declined. This Sunday was no exception—my paying guests had chosen to take an ecotour of some of the barrier islands near Beaufort. Which I really couldn't argue with. Visiting the shore without indulging in at least one boat trip always seemed like a missed opportunity to me.

"I guess they figured she was a flight risk," Bernadette said. "Which makes sense when your wealthy husband owns a yacht and a jet, not to mention property in other countries."

Julie stretched out her legs and wiggled her feet in her scarlet espadrilles. "I'm surprised she made bail at all."

"Oh, I don't know. It was basically self-defense, from what I've heard," Scott said. He'd told me earlier that he'd decided to join our discussion of John le Carré's latest espionage thriller because he needed to "take a break from his research."

Or so he'd said. I observed him eyeing Julie's shapely legs with a smile. It seemed Scott had a new reason to visit Beaufort, unrelated to the history of pirates. Which was, in my opinion, at least one good outcome from the Tey celebration week.

"Just imagine, though, stabbing someone and having to spend the rest of the week pretending everything was normal." Ophelia fiddled with her seashell necklace. "I couldn't have done it."

"She was living on the yacht, though," I said. "I think it would've been more difficult if she'd been forced to stay at Chapters."

Ellen nodded as she took a sip of her lemonade. "True. But she was clever, I'll give her that. Pretending to lose her cloak and then retrieving it and carting it off to the *Celestial* before anyone could check it for bloodstains. That was quick thinking."

"Apparently she ditched it in the back of the garden and was able to grab it and ball it up, inside out, before anyone thought to confiscate it," Scott said. "Of course, everything was so confused that night, I suppose one can't blame the police for missing that."

"And there was really no reason to suspect her at that point." I mouthed a silent *thank you* as Alicia brought in a tray of snacks.

"I have to say, she was a cool customer," Alicia said, turning to face everyone after placing the tray on the desk. "Reminded me of a few of Ms. Harrington's guests. All polish on the outside, but they showed a razor edge from time to time."

"Oooo, I remember a couple of those." Ophelia waved her copy of *A Legacy of Spies*. "Always wondered if they were secret agents or something."

I sputtered over a swallow of lemonade. Waving off the others' concern, I finally found my voice and choked out, "I'm fine. Just went down the wrong way."

"You've been reading too many thrillers, Ophelia." Ellen's tone was smooth as her bright-pink silk caftan. "Speaking of which, I hear le Carré has a new book coming out later this year. You might want to preorder it, if you like that sort of thing."

"Don't you like spy stories?" Pete asked. "I find them fascinating."

Sandy glanced over at her husband. "He likes the films too. So do I, although I draw the line at the James Bond–type stuff. Too far-out for me."

"They are a bit over-the-top," Ellen said. "And not just because of the gadgets." She pressed one palm over the cover of the hardback book balanced on her knees. "I find books like this more believable."

Scott cast her a questioning glance. "You mean the grittier stuff. Not all bon mots and martinis?"

"Exactly," she said. "I mean, think about it. Who would make a better spy? Some high-living dandy like Bond, or a nebbishy guy who looks like he works for a failing accounting firm?"

Scott grinned. "Because real spies would want to go unnoticed. Yeah, I've often thought the same thing. I even mentioned it to my dad in relation to some of his books, but he told me that readers expected their heroes to be dashing daredevils."

Ellen shrugged. "Fiction versus reality. Real life can be so boring, I suppose. Not something anyone wants to read about."

I side-eyed her as I took another sip of my drink. She'd called my great-aunt "reckless," but she seemed to possess a bit of that quality herself. All this dancing around the truth . . .

"Not always," I said. "I think our recent experiences have proven that real life can be just as exciting as books and movies. Of course, I'm not sure that's always a good thing," I added with a grimace.

"You have to admit it's ironic that a celebration of a murder-mystery author would result in a murder." Julie sat back in her chair and shared a smile with Scott. "I mean, you couldn't have planned that any better, Charlotte."

"Fortunately, I had nothing to do with it," I said dryly. "Even if some of you did suspect me early on."

Julie pointed a finger at me. "You suspected us too. Admit it."

"Hmmm . . . maybe," I said, burying my face in my glass.

Ellen laughed. "Oh, we had quite a list." She glanced around the room. "Although we did eliminate Sandy and the Sandberg sisters."

"So just me, Pete, and Julie? Thanks," Scott said, with a sarcastic grin.

"No, Ms. Simpson and Damian Carr were prime suspects too," Ellen said. "And the Delamont women, of course."

"But not Kelly Rowley," I said. "Not until much later, anyway. Which just goes to show that I should leave the detecting to the professionals."

"Oh, I don't know." Ellen shot me a conspiratorial look. "I'd say you have some skills in that area."

"Yeah, you must've suspected Kelly Rowley there at the end, the way you took out after her," Bernadette said. "Which was rather foolish, if you ask me."

A vision of Kelly pressing a gun to Ellen's head flashed through my mind. "Probably not my smartest move."

"But so brave." Ophelia widened her blue eyes. "Ellen, too. I don't know how either of you kept from falling apart, being held hostage like that."

"Shock, pure and simple," Ellen said. "And you didn't see me later, quaking on my bed so hard that I upset poor Shandy. He kept whimpering and licking my arm. Trying to make me feel better, I guess."

"Dogs are good for that," Pete said.

Sandy looked over at him, pouting. "So why won't you let me get one?"

"Dogs in a café?" Pete raised his eyebrows. "That doesn't sound like it would work."

"The dog could stay upstairs in our apartment," Sandy said.

"And bark all day?"

Sandy motioned to her husband as she looked at Ellen and me. "He's just looking for an excuse to say no."

"Keep at it," Ellen said, with a smile. "I bet you can eventually wear him down."

"Now, wait a minute. I feel outnumbered." Pete turned to Scott. "Back me up here."

"Not me," Scott said, throwing up his hands. "I'd love to have a dog, but I travel too much. If I was living in one place most of the time . . ."

I couldn't help but notice his swift, sidelong glance at Julie.

"Way to cop out, man," Pete said with a smile.

Julie, who'd obviously missed Scott's significant look, toyed with the end of her long braid. "Well, Charlotte, I imagine you won't be planning any more literary events celebrating murder-mystery authors anytime soon, will you?"

"I certainly haven't scheduled anything like that." I stood up and crossed to the desk to refill my glass. "Anyone else?" I asked, lifting the pitcher.

After serving the remaining lemonade to the rest of the party, I returned to the desk and grabbed my own glass before sitting down again.

"Actually, to answer Julie's question, I am focusing the rest of this year's events on classics, historical fiction, and a few local authors. Although I'm sure I'll do an event related to mysteries or thrillers again. Next year," I said firmly. "Along with something celebrating children's book authors and illustrators. That could be fun."

"Especially if you could get a few to visit during the week," Julie said. "I have some contacts, so just let me know."

"Will do." I looked at each of my guests in turn. "I do want to offer each of you a complimentary event of your choice. To make up for the Tey week going so wonky. I've offered that to the Delamonts too, although I'm not sure either Jennifer or Tara will ever want to return to Chapters."

"You don't have to do that," Sandy said. "We all understand it was something you couldn't control."

"Exactly." Bernadette drummed her fingers against the book in her lap. "It wasn't your fault that someone was murdered during one of your events. Just bad luck."

"Something that seems to follow me around, I'm afraid," I said.

Ellen turned in her chair and looked me up and down. "I don't think it's bad luck. I believe it's the universe drafting you into solving problems. Which you do quite well, by the way."

"Oh heavens, not sure I want to subscribe to that theory." I gave an exaggerated shudder. "Sounds terrifying."

"I think it would be exciting," Bernadette said.

I shook my head, but when I glanced back at Ellen, I noticed her lips twitch before she took a swallow of her lemonade.

*She really can read people*, I thought, before launching into a monologue covering my thoughts on the le Carré book.

Because Bernadette was right, and Ellen knew I knew it. The idea of sleuthing out clues and solving mysteries *was* exciting. And something, I realized, that I would welcome. Despite the potential danger.

I sat back in my chair, considering the possibility that I might have inherited more than Chapters from my brilliant, reckless, and free-spirited great-aunt. And mulling over the fact that her former handler—my neighbor the garden-club member, world traveler, and small-dog owner—had recognized those qualities in me long before I had.

Which made me wonder, as I sipped my lemonade and listened to my guests discuss their thoughts on *A Legacy of Spies*, whether I, like Isabella, had been recruited into something before I knew what was really happening. Maybe not espionage, but the possibility of future investigations and adventure.

I glanced over at Ellen, who raised her glass and gave me a wink. "To Isabella," she said, in a voice so soft only I could hear her.

I lifted my glass in response.

That was it, then. I was in the game.

# Acknowledgments

Sincere thanks and boatloads of gratitude to:

Paul D. Burdette, Jr., Chief of Police for the Town of Beaufort, North Carolina, who provided me with details on his department and also taught me that "CHAOS" actually means "Chief Has Arrived On Scene."

Paul Branch, Park Ranger, Fort Macon State Park, Atlantic Beach, North Carolina, who provided me with information needed to clarify an important scene.

My agent, Frances Black of Literary Counsel, who champions my work and helps me navigate the swirling waters of publishing.

My talented and supportive editor, Faith Black Ross. Also, thanks to the entire team at Crooked Lane Books, especially: Matt Martz, Jenny Chen, Melissa Rechter, Chelsey Emmelhainz, Rachel Keith, and Ashley Di Dio.

Richard Taylor Pearson and Lindsey Duga, my critique partners, who offer truly invaluable advice and encouragement.

Angela Hart of Books Are My Hart and Courtney of Courtagonist: booktubers who've graciously hosted me on their channels and have boosted the visibility of my books.

# Acknowledgments

Lori at Great Escapes Book Tours, who supports cozy mystery authors via her wonderful virtual blog tours and her website Escape With Dollycas Into a Great Book.

All of the bloggers and reviewers who have mentioned, reviewed, and boosted my books.

My husband Kevin, my son, Thomas, and the rest of my family, who support my work and tolerate, with good humor, my frequent disappearances into the "writing cave."

My friends, including the online writers' community.

My readers. Without you, these books could not exist.